MW00461646

JAMES HARPER

BAD TO THE BONES

This is a work of fiction. Names, characters, organizations, places, events and incidents are either products of the author's imagination or are used fictitiously. Any resemblance to actual persons, living or dead, or actual events is purely coincidental.

Copyright © 2017 James Harper.
All rights reserved

No part of this publication may be reproduced, or stored in a retrieval system, or transmitted, in any form or by any means, electronic, mechanical, photocopying, recording, or otherwise, without express written permission of the publisher.

www.jamesharperbooks.com

ISBN 10: 1978161948
ISBN 13: 978-1978161948

CHAPTER 1

'HEY, YOU! What the hell you think you're doing, you pervert?'

The indignant shout carried all the way across the quiet of the parking lot, cutting through the steady drizzle that had been coming down for the past hour. Evan turned towards it, saw a guy coming out of the motel lobby, starting towards him, something black in his hand.

I'm going to kick this door in, what does it look like?

But then the guy stopped, thinking better of it.

'I'm calling the police right now.' He turned back towards the office, paused again when Evan didn't move. 'You hear me?'

Evan heard him, he wasn't deaf. Wet and cold, feeling slimy, but not deaf. It was now or never.

He hated this.

He hated all of it, but this was the worst by far. It made him loathe himself. Made him want to poke his own eyes out. It brought home just how grubby and squalid it all was. How far into the stinking gutter of humanity he'd fallen. How warmly that gutter had embraced him. The guy was right. It had turned him into a degenerate and a pervert.

It was confrontational and dangerous with all the testosterone and adrenalin bouncing around the room. He could look after himself if it all kicked off, but you never knew how they'd react, what kind of drugs they might be on or if there was a gun on the nightstand. So he'd backed his car up as close as possible, left the door open with the motor running, the rain soaking into the driver's seat.

He'd followed the woman making the *oh, oh, oh* sounds on the other side of the door to this shabby, sad motel and watched her as she waited in her car, the windows misting with her hot, excited breath as the rain beaded on the glass. The guy he'd dubbed Mr Pneumatic had arrived, unfolded himself from his car and stood, his hand resting on the car door, surveying the place like he'd built it. Evan had taken a number of shots as they embraced quickly before dashing into the room together. That was the easy part squared away. Now he needed them naked, their faces clearly identifiable—what he thought of as the *money shot.*

But still he hesitated. You'd think he'd gotten used to it by now, but each time it got worse, not easier. He stood in front of the door, the sounds on the other side increasing in their intensity, took a deep breath and drove the heel of his boot into the cheap door just below the lock. The flimsy frame splintered with a sharp crack. The door flew open, revealing the cheating minx and her lover in all their sweaty, naked glory.

Perfect.

He stepped quickly into the room, breathed in the warm, salty aroma, the dirty, musky smell of sin. He shook his head to clear it as the earthy odor rose up from the bed and flowed zephyr-like across the room to welcome him.

'Hey! What the . . . you can't do that.'

Outside in the parking lot the manager changed direction again, broke into a run. A door opened a couple of rooms down. A guy in a striped bathrobe stepped out to see what all the commotion was, pressed himself into the wall when he saw the look on the manager's face as he charged past.

Evan got off a half-dozen fast shots as they gawked at him open-mouthed, too astonished to even cover up. He was back at his car before the guy's indignant shout was past his teeth. The manager was twenty yards away, coming on fast, his blackjack arm already raised, an unintelligible howl spewing from his mouth. Evan jumped in and stomped on the gas, slamming the door and spinning his wheels as the tires bit and he took off.

But the guy in the room was fast. Unbelievably fast. Either he'd had a lot of practice doing this or he was just naturally fast at pulling on his pants. He pushed himself off the woman. His elbow squashed her firm, tanned breasts, made her squeal like a stuck pig. He vaulted off the bed, pulled on his pants and was out of the room before Evan had gone ten yards.

He didn't get much further as two fast-moving bodies came together as one. He smacked bang into the manager, their heads colliding with a bone-jarring thump and the two of them bounced off each other. The manager went down on his ass and landed in a puddle, blood pouring from his nose. The guy from the room flew backwards into the door frame. He pushed himself off again, leapt over the manager's sprawling arms and legs and ran, holding up his pants with one hand as he chased after the car, screaming blue murder at it.

And, despite his remarkable bedroom performance, he still had a ton of energy left. His adrenalin-fuelled legs pumped up and down like well-oiled pistons, his bare feet pounding across the parking lot, impervious to the grit and the gravel and the broken glass that littered the ground.

Behind him, the nosy neighbour helped the manager to his feet. The manager gave him an irritated, ungrateful shove and started running again, yelling at the top of his voice. All around the parking lot lights went on and doors opened, curious faces peeked out.

Evan pulled out of the lot and slowed to a crawl. He looked in his mirror. The guy was almost touching the trunk, his mouth stretched into a rictus of fury, streaks of spittle spraying across his face. He'd never seen such wild eyes—not on anything that walked on two legs and didn't live in a cage.

He had to time it just right.

He stomped on the brakes. The guy slammed into the trunk, bounced off and landed hard on his ass in the gutter. Two yards behind him the manager tried to stop, to swerve. He was way too close. He slipped on the wet pavement, caught the guy in the side of the head with his knees, went down on his chin in a tangle of flailing legs.

Evan gave the horn a couple of toots as he slowly pulled away. The guy pushed and shoved at the manager lying dazed across him, scrambled up and tore after him again. Evan smiled to himself, one eye on the mirror the whole time.

It was working.

The guy had to think he had a chance of catching him and keep chasing after him. He needed to draw him as far away as possible before rational thinking overrode the rage and the testosterone and he turned around and went back for his car. The down side was that the guy was getting a good long look at his license plate.

It took the guy two blocks before he finally realized what was going on. Evan watched him in the rear-view mirror as he stopped and bent forward, his hands resting on his knees, chest heaving and his head hanging down as he stared at his feet, blood mingling with dirty rainwater on the wet asphalt. Then he raised his head. And even at the distance away he was, Evan felt the burning hatred in his eyes on the back of his neck.

This one would be a problem.

The slowing down trick had worked, but, even so, his heart was trying to kick its way out of his chest. He needed a drink to calm his nerves. He drove slowly back to his office. The guy wouldn't follow him now. Another day, yes, but not tonight. He had a lot of explaining to do tonight.

CHAPTER 2

HE PARKED IN THE shadows behind his office building and sat still for a long time, staring out into the empty darkness. The indefinable smell of sex lingered in his nostrils, taunting him, the guy's feral eyes still fresh in his mind. He picked up his camera and looked through the images he'd just taken.

Perfect.

The pair of them, buck naked in high definition. Two startled faces looking exactly like a pair of stupid goldfish with their mouths hanging open. He spent a moment admiring the woman's obvious attractions, then turned his attention to the guy. He had no idea who he was, but he clearly spent all his time in the gym when he wasn't screwing somebody else's wife.

Dropping the camera on the seat, he rested his head on the steering wheel. A rising tide of self-loathing and disgust overcame him, as it always did after the adrenalin had leached away. What on earth had happened to him? This wasn't how it was meant to be. Not exactly Philip Marlowe chasing down long-lost heiresses for aged billionaires in sunny California.

And the worst was still to come.

He went up to his office, made a pot of coffee and loaded the images onto his computer while he waited for his client to arrive. The client was already late—nobody shows up early for an appointment with the man who's about to bring their world crashing down around their ears.

The coffee was long since cold by the time the elevator pinged and he went to the door to greet his client. He felt like a cross between an undertaker and a priest about to administer the last rites. Stanton kept his eyes on his shoes as he entered. Evan was used to that, made sure his own were always presentable. He didn't mind but sometimes a grunt would have been nice.

It never got beyond an uncomfortable, stilted formality with any of his clients. He liked to keep a certain professional detachment. It made things easier when it was time to dismantle their lives. As for the clients, you don't rush to get on first name terms with the man who's just finished watching your wife being screwed by another man. And who's about to lay out the evidence in front of you on his grubby little desk. And who then expects you to pay him for humiliating you.

Kevin Stanton looked dull. A forgettable man in his early forties, medium height with a blue suit, no tie and brown suede shoes. Not fat or ugly, adequate personal hygiene—he just didn't look like he was much fun to be with. He wore rimless eyeglasses like an accountant, the impression reinforced by his battered leather briefcase. It wasn't surprising his wife looked elsewhere for her kicks. The man sitting in front of him was just plain dull. And now it was his job to add pain and unhappiness to his sad life.

Stanton had come to him a week earlier and poured out his heart. He was sure his wife was having an affair. He had no idea who the bastard might be. Often Evan was the first person they confided in, the first time they voiced their concerns. And so it all came gushing out. Then, once it was out, they felt embarrassed. They either clammed up entirely or resented Evan as if it was his fault or he was judging them.

When he spoke, Stanton's voice was like a chair scraping across a tiled floor.

'Well? Is she seeing someone else?'

His cheeks were flushed. He took off his glasses, inspected them and decided they were clean enough, put them back on. He still didn't look Evan in the eye. Evan was used to talking to the top of people's heads. With a lot of people, it was the best view.

Evan nodded.

'I followed them to a motel earlier this evening.'

Stanton stifled a low moan.

'You've got evidence? Photos?'

'They're on here.'

Evan tapped his computer, adjusted the screen so they could both see it. He was about to open the file when Stanton put his hand on top of his to stop him. The hand was warm and moist, his whole arm shaking.

'Is there any chance it's a mistake? A misunderstanding?'

He looked up into Evan's eyes for the first time. Evan forced himself to not look away from what he saw—the last vestige of hope. Hope that he was about to grind into the dirt.

He bit his lip, shook his head slowly.

'No.'

God, how he hated this.

'I'm sorry.'

Stanton dropped his eyes again.

'I don't know if I can do this.'

'It's your decision. I'm not here to make you do anything you don't want to. But, in my experience, if you don't see it for yourself, you'll end up convincing yourself it's not true.'

Stanton swallowed hard and nodded, told him to just get it over with.

Evan opened the first image. It showed Stanton's wife and Mr Pneumatic climbing out of their cars in front of the motel room. Stanton shot his hand out and clamped it over Evan's, a look of horror spreading across his face. Evan was surprised by the strength in his grip.

'Stop! Zoom in on that.'

Evan twisted his hand, pulled it out from under Stanton's. He zoomed in on his wife's face.

'Not her, you idiot. *Him!*'

He jabbed the screen so hard, the monitor rocked back on its stand. Evan panned across onto the man's face, now clearly identifiable. Stanton slumped back into his chair, all the color gone from his face.

'You bastard,' he hissed at the screen, his fingers digging into the leatherette arms of the visitor's chair, the tendons standing out on the backs of his hands. 'You cock-sucking bastard.'

It wasn't the time to point out he had that the wrong way around.

'You recognize him?'

'Recognize him?' he screamed, slamming his fist down onto the table. 'You could say that. I have to look at his oh-so-pretty face eight hours a day, every day of my life. That'—he jabbed his finger at the screen again—'is my bastard of a business partner. Hugh McIntyre.'

Evan didn't say anything, waited for him to go on. Stanton was lost in his thoughts.

'It all makes sense now. I can't believe I didn't see it.'

Evan had learned from bitter experience to stay silent and wait for Stanton. People lash out blindly when they're hurting. A badly chosen word, an inappropriate tone of voice or even the wrong emphasis could end up with the overwrought client turning on him.

'I suppose you've got more photos? That bastard and my wife. Every gory detail.'

Evan nodded, put his hand back on the mouse to move on.

'I don't want to see them.' The words came out in a jumbled rush as Stanton leaned back, holding up his hands as if he could simply push it all away. 'I know what you said. But I've seen enough. I don't need any more proof. It all fits together now.'

'No problem. I've copied them onto a thumb drive. In case you need them as evidence.'

Evan pushed the thumb drive across the desk. Stanton stared at it like he was being offered a radioactive dog turd. Evan couldn't stop the thought crossing his mind that he could have stopped after the first photo in the parking lot. No need to kick down the motel door. No need to get chased down the street by a guy who wanted to rip his head off. No need to give a guy who looked like an advertisement for steroids a reason to come looking for him with a baseball bat.

'What happened when you took the photos of them . . .'

Stanton couldn't finish the sentence. He coughed. Made some meaningless gesture with his hand. For a second Evan thought he was going to make a circle with his index finger and thumb and poke the other finger in and out.

'Why do you want to know?'

It wasn't a question he was expecting.

Stanton shrugged.

'I don't know. I thought I knew the bastard, but it seems I don't. Just curious what he did.'

'He pulled on his pants and chased me down the street, screaming and threatening to kill me.'

Stanton cocked his head and frowned.

'You were on foot?'

'No, I was in my car.'

The creases on Stanton's forehead got deeper.

'I kept slowing down to make him think he was going to get me. At one point I stomped on the brakes and he crashed into the car and ended up on his ass. He chased the car for half a mile like a rabid dog until it finally clicked or he ran out of steam. I'm not sure which.'

Stanton's mouth curled into a smile as he listened. It turned into a grin and then he burst out laughing. Evan couldn't help himself and laughed with him, the tensions of the evening riding out with it. Stanton leaned down and opened his briefcase, came back up with a bottle of scotch, a question on his face.

'I had a feeling I'd need this tonight. I was planning on taking it home, but here seems as good a place as any. If that's okay by you?'

Evan fetched a couple of glasses, put them on the desk.

'So long as you don't tell anyone. I'm supposed to be the one who keeps that in the bottom drawer. I'd get disbarred.'

Stanton poured them both a couple of fingers and pushed one across the table. Evan regarded it a lot more favorably than Stanton had viewed the toxic thumb drive. Stanton knocked his back in one, lined the glass up for a refill.

'I wish I'd been there. I'd have reversed back over the bastard.'

Evan pictured it, reversing at the exhausted McIntyre as he panted for breath, the look on his face changing from fury to disbelief to panic.

'I wish I had. He got a good look at my license plate.'

'Uh-oh. Rather you than me. He's got a very short fuse. And he's never heard of forgive and forget.'

Stanton finished his second drink and appeared to be in no hurry to get going. Not that he had much left to go home to. What the hell, Evan thought, nodding at the offer of a third drink, I haven't got anywhere to go either.

When Evan finally called him a taxi a couple of hours later, the bottle was empty and they'd moved on to Evan and Kevin. Suddenly their respective problems didn't seem nearly so bad after all. Even so, Evan made sure Kevin took the thumb drive with him. Things would be very different in the cold, unforgiving light of morning. A hangover would only make it worse. Then he dug out the sleeping bag he kept for emergencies and made himself as comfortable as he could on the floor.

CHAPTER 3

EVAN WAS DRAGGED FROM his fitful sleep by someone hammering on his office door. Inside his head a jackhammer was bouncing off the sides of his skull. Now some idiot was doing their best to break his door down. His first reaction was that the guy from the motel, Hugh McIntyre, had found him already, but that wasn't remotely possible.

He crawled out of his sleeping bag and slowly stood up, resting his hand on the desk to steady himself. His mouth tasted like the bottom of a bird's cage, his throat dry and scratchy. Kicking the sleeping bag into the corner, he crossed to the door.

'Who is it? What do you want?'

'Police. Open up.'

It wasn't the answer he was expecting. Perhaps the motel manager had reported the damage to his door and McIntyre had given them his license number. He unlocked the door and looked out at the two people waiting impatiently in the corridor.

A short, fat man was standing right in the doorway, a taller woman half hidden behind him. The one in front looked him up and down with ill-concealed distaste. Evan was acutely aware of his crumpled clothing and the stale smell of whisky and sweat that wafted out from the room. On cue, Fatso sniffed suspiciously at the air.

'Evan Buckley?'

'That's me. What can I do for you?'

'You can invite us in to start with. Unless you want everyone in the building to listen in.'

'Sorry. Of course. Come in.'

He stepped aside to let them squeeze past. He saw the empty whisky bottle and two glasses still on the desk at the same time they did. It wasn't a large office, so they couldn't miss his sleeping bag lying in the corner either, looking very much like someone had just crawled out of it.

The short one wrinkled his nose.

'Nice professional setup you've got here. Mind if I open the window, let in a bit of fresh air?' He didn't wait for an answer. 'Had a party in here last night, did you? Been sleeping it off?'

'Do you mind telling me what this is about, Officer . . .'

'*Detective* Ryder.' More like *Detective Donut*, Evan thought. 'We'd like to ask you some questions, Mr Buckley.'

'Sure, go ahead, why not.'

'Do you know Mr Kevin Stanton?'

That was the second surprise in less than five minutes. Faint alarm bells went off in the fuzzy recesses of Evan's head.

'Yes, why?'

'We'll get to that in a minute. Can you tell us what your relationship is with Mr Stanton?'

'He's a client.'

'A *client*.'

He made it sound like something to be ashamed of, flashed a cold smile at Evan.

'And what exactly do you do for your *client*, Mr Stanton?'

'Why do I get the impression you know all the answers before you ask the questions?'

'Just answer the question please.'

'Actually, that's between me and Mr Stanton.'

Ryder gave him a long-suffering look but didn't press it. Seeing as he knew the answer anyway, he didn't need to.

'Okay. Can you tell us when the last time you saw him was?'

'Last night. Here, in my office.' He pointed to the glasses on the desk. 'If you want to dust one of those glasses you keep staring at so disapprovingly, you'll find it's covered with his fingerprints.'

'You were having a party, were you? Do you do that with all your clients?'

'Not a party, just a few drinks. And Stanton brought the whisky with him.'

'I'm sure he did.' The detective made a show of sniffing the air. 'More than a few as well by the look—and smell—of things.'

Evan let out a long, weary breath at the relentless jibes. His head was pounding, his stomach churning. That was punishment enough. He didn't need any of this.

It was about to get a lot worse.

'Is this going anywhere, Detective?'

'Not for Mr Stanton it isn't. I'm sorry to have to tell you that Mr Stanton committed suicide last night.'

Evan took a step backwards as if he'd been slapped, dropped heavily into his chair. He was suddenly very cold, palms sweaty. He shook his head in disbelief. It couldn't be true. Stanton hadn't been suicidal when he went home. Something must have happened at home. Ryder was saying something else, his mouth turned down in disgust.

'Sorry, what was that?'

'I said, it appears Mr Stanton had spent the evening drinking heavily. We now know that at least some of that was done here. With you.' There was more than a hint of accusation in his voice. 'He then went home where he spent some time looking at pornographic images on his computer.'

Evan groaned inwardly. He didn't want to hear what was coming.

'Not just the everyday porn your average Joe can get off the internet, either. *Bespoke*, you could call it. Pictures of his own loving wife being screwed stupid by another man.' It was a full-blown accusation now. 'And when he'd had enough of that, the poor bastard went out to the garage and hanged himself from a rafter.'

He shouted the *hanged himself* in Evan's face, then paused to allow time for the full, dreadful implications of his words to sink in.

'Which is where his wife found him this morning. Luckily for us, she became hysterical and ran straight to the neighbors. She was so distressed, poor thing, she didn't think to go into his study and remove the evidence that pointed to her starring role in this sorry little tale.'

Evan sat there completely dumbfounded, unable to think clearly, although one thought was all too clear—he should never have given Stanton the thumb drive with the photos.

'It was also in his study that we found your business card,' Ryder continued. He made *business card* sound dirty too, as if it was one of the ones you saw pinned up in public phone booths back in the day. 'And seeing as we're detectives we sort of worked it out.'

He held up his hand and flicked out a not very clean little finger.

It looked like a short, fat sausage.

'One, here's a depressed man who just hanged himself after looking at pictures of his wife screwing around.' He flicked out a second, sausage-like finger. 'And two, what have we got here? Some low-rent P.I.'s business card. So, yes, Mr Buckley, we do already know the nature of the *work* that you did for Mr Stanton. Although how anyone can call what you do *work* is beyond me. I bet you even charge the poor saps for ruining their lives.'

Flecks of spittle showered Evan as he spoke. Ryder stood in front of him, looking down at him in his chair, daring him to contradict his words. The look of undisguised disgust on his face made Evan want to punch it. But he had to keep his temper under control. They would've liked nothing better than an excuse to work him over and toss him into the cells. Ryder wasn't finished yet.

'That's why we came down here to this shithole you call an office this morning. To get confirmation from the horse's mouth—more like the horse's ass if you ask me—and to see if you can provide any further information.'

'I can tell you who the man in the photos with his wife is.'

'We already know that,' Ryder snapped. 'You might be the lowest type of bottom feeder, but at least you know how to use a camera. We got his license plate from one of your pictures. We'll be talking to Mr McIntyre shortly.'

'I hope you give him as hard a time as you've given me.'

It was out before he could stop it. He could have bitten his own tongue off.

Ryder put his hands on his hips and snorted.

'Hard time? Who are you kidding? I've called you a few names, that's all. At least I don't go around ruining people's lives. Christ, haven't you got any self-respect?'

Evan wished he could have argued. But it sounded too much like the nagging head voices he lived with every day.

'Are you sure it was suicide? He didn't seem suicidal in the slightest when he left here.'

'How the hell would you know? You were as drunk as he was.' Ryder was shouting now, his face reddening. He cracked his knuckles loudly. 'But to answer your question, there is absolutely no evidence whatsoever of foul play. The man topped himself'—he emphasized the words—'because he couldn't face life after looking at your pictures. I know it would make you feel a whole lot better if he hadn't committed suicide, but he did.'

Evan thought he'd finished. He was wrong.

'And it's your fault'—he jabbed his finger into Evan's face—'so you better start learning to live with it.'

Evan tucked his hands under his legs to stop himself from grabbing the finger in his face and snapping it at the knuckle.

'Did he leave a note?'

'Yeah, he left a note. His tramp of a wife threw it in the trash but we dug it out. It was torn but it wasn't difficult to read seeing as it was only one word in nice big capital letters—BITC—we figured the rest out.'

Ryder and his partner, who hadn't said a word the whole time, turned to go. But Ryder just couldn't let it go. He hesitated at the door.

'I just can't understand why anyone would want to spend their lives doing this shit.' He made a sweeping arm gesture taking in the whole room. 'Helping people ruin their lives day in day out. Why don't you do something to help people for a change? Find missing kids or something worthwhile like that.'

Something important snapped inside Evan. A sudden surge of

heat flushed through his body, a roaring rush of blood to his head like it was about to explode. Ryder had touched the rawest of nerves. He couldn't stop himself. He leapt from the chair. Lunged at Ryder, screamed into his face.

'You sanctimonious bastard. You have no idea what you're talking about. You know absolutely nothing about me.'

Ryder's partner stepped quickly between them, put her hand flat on Evan's chest. It was a strong hand. And she was an athletic woman, broad in the shoulders, narrow in the waist. Her eyes held Evan's.

'That's enough. Calm down now.'

'Calm down! I've had to listen to this holier-than-thou, fat prick insult me from the moment he walked in and now he tells me I should spend my life doing something useful. He wouldn't know what useful was if it bit him in the ass.'

'I don't know what you're getting so riled up about,' Ryder spat from behind his partner. 'You do what you do, you gotta expect people to hate you.'

'Do either of you two idiots know the first thing about me? My name doesn't ring any bells? Come on, you're the great detectives.'

'I don't know what you're talking about,' Ryder said again. 'Why the hell would we know anything about a lowlife like you? Unless this isn't the first time you pushed a guy over the edge.'

Evan lunged again. Ryder's partner pushed him back.

'Five years ago. Sarah Buckley. My wife. Disappeared off the face of the planet. Ring any bells yet?'

Ryder looked at him like he was making up words. There was a faint glimmer of recognition in his partner's eyes.

'I remember something about that. Didn't you cause a big scene down at the precinct? Punched the Captain. Got arrested?'

Evan ignored her, thinking it wouldn't take much for him to do it again.

'Allow me to refresh your memories. One day, out of the blue, she went to work and didn't come home. Disappeared without a trace. I reported her missing. You lot were about as much use as a one-legged man in an ass kicking contest. What was worse was you didn't give a damn either. Back then I was a journalist, I had a good job. But I couldn't stand just sitting around waiting for lazy idiots like him'—he jabbed a finger at Ryder—'with their heads up their asses doing sweet F.A.'

'You better watch your mouth, Buckley.'

Evan was too far gone to stop now.

'Or what, you fat bastard? Or what?' He was screaming now, a red mist engulfing him, fists clenched at his sides. 'I packed in my real job so that I could start doing yours. And no, I didn't find her. But at least I tried which is more than you did. And I'm still trying, and I'll keep on trying.'

He paused to gulp air into his heaving lungs, chest shaking against the other detective's hand.

'So, when some useless tub of lard comes in here and spends ten minutes being abusive before he tells me to do something useful with my life, I get a little uptight.' He spat the last word into Ryder's face over his partner's shoulder, pushed harder into the hand on his chest.

'On top of all that I still have to pay the bills. And that means I have to do whatever my *clients* pay me to do, however distasteful the sainted Detective Ryder might find it. It's called the real world, and you should go there some time. See how you get on without a badge to hide behind.'

He sagged visibly, the outburst leaving him drained of strength or caring. Ryder's partner saw the fury had gone. She dropped her hand from Evan's chest.

'Okay, we're leaving now. If you can think of anything that might be useful, or you just want to talk, give me a call. The name's Guillory.' She gave Evan her card and they left.

AFTER THEY'D GONE Evan sat down at his desk, rested his head in his hands. It was like a terrible nightmare, one he wouldn't be waking from any time soon. This was his life now. He didn't like the things Ryder had said but he couldn't fault the logic. Sure, it was Stanton's wife and McIntyre who were the root cause of it all, but it was his photographs that pushed the man over the edge.

He should never have given him the thumb drive.

Until he got home, Stanton had only seen the first picture of the two of them standing outside the motel. There was still room for an innocent explanation. He'd asked Evan about the others but he hadn't wanted to see them. But then, sitting at home, full of whisky and with the thumb drive burning a hole in his pocket, he hadn't been able to stop himself from looking. Evan imagined him getting it out of his pocket and turning it over in his hand. Maybe he threw it in the trash only to go back and dig it out again, knowing all the while that in the end he would have to *know*, just like Evan had said.

And what he'd seen had robbed him of the will to live. Ryder was right. It was his fault and he was going to have to learn to live with it for the rest of his life. But if he thought the worst was over, he was wrong. Fate had one last nasty surprise for him.

And it had kept the best to last.

He fired up his computer to check his email, saw something

that took his breath away. Stanton had sent him an email in the small hours of the morning. His first, gut reaction was to delete it immediately. There couldn't be anything in it that he needed to read, needed to know.

But now fate had him where it wanted him, twisting in the wind. Just like Stanton the previous night. To look or not to look? And just like Stanton, he didn't have any choice. He clicked it.

Hey, Evan. I know this is a bad idea and it's probably the whisky, but I just wanted to say—please don't blame yourself. I'm sure it won't help, but I wanted to say it.

Evan stared at the words, swallowed thickly. Thought about head-butting the screen. Stanton's words pulsed in front of his eyes, trying to jump off the screen. He hit delete, smashed his finger into the keyboard so hard it split his nail when it asked him if he was sure.

Just get it out of my sight.

It didn't make any difference. The message was saved where it was beyond deleting, in some dark corner of his mind, ready and waiting to be recalled at a moment's notice to torment him. It didn't rob him of the will to live. But it made him want to live any place other than inside his own head.

CHAPTER 4

THERE WAS ANOTHER, SOFTER knock on the still open door. Evan looked up and saw Tom Jacobson filling the doorway. Filling was the right word. Jacobson was a huge man with a grizzled beard who'd played college football before he tore the ligaments in his knee badly enough to end his career. His teeth were crooked and uneven which always surprised Evan since he carried on a dental practice in the office downstairs. Evan often imagined he heard the drill and the patients screaming. He also owned the building, making him Evan's landlord.

'Tom, come on in. Some root canal work would just about round off my morning. Got any novocaine on you?'

Jacobson smiled and looked at his watch—it was still only eight thirty in the morning. He dropped into the visitor's chair.

'Not a good day so far? I heard shouting, thought I'd come and see if everything's okay. I passed a couple of people on my way up. They looked like cops.'

Evan could see it didn't look good. If he was a landlord, he wouldn't want a tenant like him. The whisky bottle and glasses were sitting on the desk not more than six inches from Jacobson's left elbow. The sleeping bag was still crumpled on the floor, the air in the room stale despite the open window. Cops were involved and there'd been a lot of shouting. All it needed was for someone to get shot in his building now.

'You're right, they were cops—'

Jacobson held up a large hand to stop him. The fingers looked like they could pull teeth without needing pliers.

'I can see something's been going on, Evan, but I've got a patient at nine. You look like you could do with getting it off your chest. Why don't we get some lunch together and you can tell me all about it then?'

'Yeah, that'd be good.'

Jacobson was right. He did need to talk to someone, especially after Ryder had touched a raw nerve and set him off about Sarah. His income and ability to pay the rent were also about to take a nosedive.

Jacobson got up to go, gave him a lopsided grin.

'I'll give you a call about twelve thirty. And if you still want a root canal afterwards, we'll see what we can do about that too.'

THEY WENT TO A nice place around the corner from the office, called the French Washroom or something like that. The sort of place frequented by successful dentists, rather than struggling P.I.'s, where they won't let you have ketchup. The prices made Evan's eyes water but Jacobson had insisted up front that it was on him.

The maître d' looked at Evan as if the last time he'd seen him was when he'd caught him taking a shit in the alley outside the kitchen door. He didn't want to let him in, despite being *Monsieur*

Jacobson's guest. It got better when they got to their table. The waitresses all wore short skirts and frilly white blouses that had shrunk in the wash. Evan's silent prayer was answered when a young and pretty waitress came over to serve them. She brought them their drinks and a couple of bread rolls that looked like they were made from whole vegetarians. He felt healthier just looking at them.

There was a small plate of olives on the table. He took one and ate it, fished the pit out of his mouth. He never knew what to do with them, certainly not in a place like this. If it hadn't been for Jacobson, he'd have flicked it at the maître d'.

'You know that song *Novocaine for the Soul*,' he said, once he'd taken a swallow of his drink, 'well I feel like I need a large dose of that, right now.'

'I don't know it, but I guess this is a whole lot more serious than a couple of cops giving you a hard time.'

'Uh-huh. You know I'm a private investigator, a private eye or whatever you want to call it.'

Jacobson nodded, didn't say anything. He took a sip of his mineral water and waited for Evan to continue.

'It probably doesn't come as any surprise to hear that it's not quite as glamorous or exciting as it's made out to be in the movies.' Evan took a large swallow of his Margarita and licked the salt round the edge of the glass. 'Do you know what I spend most of my life doing?'

'I would guess it's divorce work.'

'Exactly. What one of those cops called *snapping dirty pictures* of some guy or other screwing my clients' wives. Or vice versa. It doesn't make you feel very good about yourself.' He slumped back into his chair and ran a hand through his hair.

'I don't suppose it does.'

'But you get over it. This helps.' He held up his almost empty glass. 'It's uncomfortable and embarrassing when you give them the photos or whatever else you've dug up. Some of them cry, mainly the men. Some of them get angry and shout at you like it's your fault. But then they all get up and go back to what's left of their lives and you never see or hear from them again.'

'But not this time?'

'No, not this time.'

He drained his glass, looked round for the waitress before he remembered Jacobson was picking up the tab. Jacobson waved a hand and told him to go ahead, it sounded like he needed it. Then Evan told him all about Stanton and how they'd sat drinking together and how Stanton had gone home seeming as good as could be expected in the circumstances. And how the next thing he knew, Stanton was swinging from a rafter in his garage.

'And you blame yourself because you made him take the thumb drive home?'

'Wouldn't you? That's what tipped him over the edge.'

'I don't know, it's impossible to say. But I do understand how it would make you feel that way.'

'And that's not all. He sent me an email, told me not to blame myself. Can you believe it?'

'He was in a bad place, Evan. Don't obsess on it.'

The waitress brought their food. She really was very pretty. Evan was sure she was smiling at him more than the other diners. He dug right into his steak. It was excellent. So were the fries. He wouldn't have put ketchup on them even if they'd allowed it. At least he hadn't lost his appetite.

'I can see why you want that novocaine,' Jacobson continued, 'but I'm afraid time is the only thing that's going to make you feel any better.'

They ate in silence for a while before Evan spoke again, a decision made.

'You're right, but there is one thing I can do.'

Jacobson heard the change in his voice, waited for him to go on.

'I'm not doing any more divorce work. I've always hated it, and now this happens. So that's it. Finito.' He chopped the air emphatically with his hand, almost knocked his glass over.

'Sounds good. Where does that leave you?'

Evan didn't need to spend much time thinking that one through.

'Realistically? Sitting on my butt in my office with rent to pay and no clients.'

'Well you can forget about the rent to start with. That's not a problem,' Jacobson said through a mouthful of seafood risotto. 'I'm happy to wait until you get yourself back on your feet.' He grinned. 'Maybe you can check out my wife for free . . .' The grin slipped off his face. 'Sorry, that was a really crass thing to say.'

Evan looked down at the table for a moment, looking hurt. Then he looked up and grinned right back at him.

'That's okay, I've already got those photos . . .'

Jacobson did a double take. He realized he'd been had and punched him on the arm. With someone Jacobson's size, it hurt.

'I'm about ready to do that root canal you were asking about. Did I mention I'm all out of anesthetic?'

After they'd finished eating, Jacobson had one last question that was on his mind. Evan told him to fire away.

'What was all the shouting about? I would have thought it

would've been quite a somber visit.'

'So would I. But the fat one was riding me really hard. Letting me know what a worthless sack of shit he thought I was.'

Jacobson looked like he was weighing up the answer in his mind. It obviously came up short.

'That's it?'

Evan looked at him, wondering how much to tell him. He really didn't want to get into it now, but a couple of Margaritas had loosened him up a bit. The guy had been pretty good to him—so what the hell.

'No, that's not all. He touched a very raw nerve and I completely lost it.'

Then Evan told him all about Sarah and how she'd disappeared five years ago, how he'd tried to find her and that was why he'd ended up doing what he did now.

Jacobson shook his head slowly, took an embarrassed sip of his water.

'Jesus Christ, Evan, I had no idea.'

'Not many people do. I don't talk about it much. Besides, people just want to forget about things like that and get on with their own lives. Nobody really *gives* a shit. Just another sad story that had everyone's attention for about five seconds. Before they got distracted by something more important, like a great new breakfast cereal flavor.'

Jacobson nodded, that's the way it goes.

'I know what you mean. Most people have the attention span of a goldfish. What about the police?'

'They went through the motions, but they weren't interested. They decided early on there wasn't any foul play involved, so they dropped it. Not officially of course, but that's what happened.

People disappear of their own free will every day.'

'Do you have any idea what might have happened?'

Evan didn't say anything for a long moment. He didn't know what had actually happened, but there were plenty of ideas that had passed through his mind over the years. Most of them unwelcome. And nothing he wanted to voice now.

'Nope. She just disappeared without a trace.'

CHAPTER 5

BACK IN HIS OFFICE Evan was as good as his word—he sat around on his butt wondering what on earth he was going to do to drum up some business. Business that didn't involve sneaking around motel parking lots in the middle of the night. Business that didn't make people's lives worse than before. If he didn't manage to come up with anything it wouldn't just be himself he was letting down now, he'd be letting Jacobson down too. It would have been easier if Jacobson has given him an ultimatum on his rent arrears instead of being so damn understanding.

Not only that, but an idle mind is the devil's workshop, as the old saying goes. It was certainly true in Evan's idle mind today. The empty whisky bottle sat in the waste paper basket, an unwelcome, accusing reminder of the previous night and the irreparable damage that he'd caused. He'd be beating himself up for a long time to come. He desperately wished there was something he could do to make the situation better but there was no way he could make amends. Stanton was dead and he was probably the only one who cared.

Then there was Sarah. It wasn't that he'd forgotten. Anybody meeting him would never guess at what went on under the surface. There wasn't a day went by when he didn't think about her—although time had softened the edges of his pain. The bitter argument with Ryder that morning had changed all that, taken him straight back to when she first disappeared, the rawness of his grief, his impotent frustration and anger at the police.

The drinks at lunch hadn't helped either. He rarely had a drink at lunchtime, sticking with coffee to keep him sharp. But today hadn't been a normal day, so he'd cut himself a little slack. Problem was, it had made him lethargic. He made himself a pot of extra strong coffee to keep sleep and his demons at bay, then slumped down in his easy chair to watch the news on the TV.

HE WASN'T SURE WHEN or even how he'd fallen asleep—the coffee should've kept him awake for a week—or for how long. It was dark in the office, quiet outside. Something had woken him. There it was again, a tentative knock at his door. Who the hell was coming around at this time of night? Had Hugh McIntyre tracked him down? But would he even care now? He'd got Stanton's wife and Stanton's half of the business for himself now. Besides, he wasn't the type to knock politely on the door and wait to be invited in. He'd kick it down like Evan had done to him. Or wait for him in some dark alley.

'Come on in,' Evan called, 'it's not locked.'

But instead of opening the door, whoever it was turned and retreated back down the corridor. He heard the fast click of a woman's heels. That surprised him, but then an awful thought crossed his mind. What if it was Stanton's wife? He was in two minds whether to follow her or not. He couldn't hide from it but was today the right time?

In the semi-darkness he jumped up from his chair too quickly and sent the still half-full coffee pot flying. He made a desperate attempt to catch it but only managed to lose his balance and crash into the filing cabinet behind the desk. Ignoring the pot as it emptied the last of its contents into Tom Jacobson's carpet, he leapt to the window to see if he could catch sight of his visitor.

He saw her as she ran across the parking lot towards an old Toyota Corolla that had seen better days. She was parked in the corner furthest from the street lights. All he was able to make out was a blond woman in her mid-forties. He'd never seen her before—it wasn't Stanton's wife—and he had no idea what she wanted. Or why she changed her mind and ran.

There was still time to catch her.

Forgetting everything else, he grabbed his car keys, bolted out the door and ran for the stairs. He took them three at a time, the adrenalin and caffeine supercharging his system. She was turning left out of the parking lot as he crashed through the main doors and sprinted for his car. He leapt into the driver's seat, slammed it into gear , then fish-tailed it out of the lot and into the traffic behind her, horns blaring as he shot in front of the oncoming traffic. He spotted her three cars in front, settled down to a more reasonable speed. Traffic was just right. Enough to cover him, light enough to easily keep her in sight. Whatever turmoil was going on in her head worked in his favor too.

He followed her for a couple of miles into a quiet residential neighborhood. Like her car, it had seen better days. Dropping back further as the traffic thinned to almost nothing, he lost sight of her. He made a left where he guessed she'd just turned, then pulled sharply into the curb, stopping in the shade of a tree. She was turning into a driveway fifty yards farther on. He waited for five minutes until he was sure she would be inside, then drove slowly down the street, made a note of the house address and license plate number as he drove by. A hundred yards down the road, he pulled over and stopped.

Should he approach her or not? If she was a potential client, he didn't want to waste any time—he needed to lose himself in something other than guilt over Stanton as soon as possible. And she might not come back. On the other hand, having him knock on her door in the middle of the night, his pants smelling of spilled coffee and his breath of lunchtime's booze might freak her out.

He had to do it, hope she wasn't too spooked. He got out of the car, walked back to the house. The lights were still on. He put his ear to the door. A faint TV sound came from inside. He rang the bell. The TV sounds immediately got louder, then muted again as an internal door closed. That told him all he needed to know.

Despite that, he'd give it a couple more minutes, having come this far. He strained his ear towards the door. A dog suddenly barked behind him. He jumped and spun around. An old guy with a yappy little dog and a cigarette stuck to his lip stood ten feet away, staring at him while the dog lunged on its leash.

Evan nodded, put a pleasant smile on his face. 'Evening.'

The guy grunted back. Took a long drag on his cigarette, dropped it on the sidewalk.

'She won't answer, not at this time of night.'

He spat noisily into the gutter which set the dog off barking again.

'How do you know?'

'Because she's barely come out that door in ten years.'

Evan shrugged. 'It was worth a try.' He turned back to the door, called over his shoulder, 'Have a good night.'

The old man stared at his back a few beats, then nodded and set off again, dragging the still-straining dog behind him. Evan waited until they'd turned the corner, the dog's yaps faded to nothing, then rang the bell again. Nothing. Then, in the distance, the sound of a police siren. Was it coincidence? Or had the dog walker called it in? He couldn't risk it. He wasn't going to get anywhere that night anyway. And he didn't want to have to explain himself to the police, not smelling like he did. He left a business card in her mailbox and jogged briskly back to his car.

Halfway to the corner a police cruiser swung wide into the street ahead of him, slowed and straightened up, its red and blue lights dazzling him. The two cops gave him a hard stare as they rolled slowly past. He smiled back at them, breathed easy. They were looking for a dangerous intruder on foot after all, not a man in a car. Lucky the nosy old man hadn't seen him get in it.

It was just after nine p.m. when he got back to the office. He made himself some more coffee, then settled comfortably into his chair, legs stretched out, ankles crossed. He decided against turning on the TV. With his fingers laced over his stomach and his eyes closed, he tried to clear his mind of Sarah and Kevin Stanton and his mystery visitor. And anything else for that matter.

The next thing he knew, it was almost midnight. He was still in his chair with a stiff neck and an aching back. The coffee on the table next to him was cold and untouched. He was shocked he'd dozed for so long. He massaged the back of his neck, tried to ease the kinks out of it, then took a sip of cold coffee before pouring the rest of it down the sink. He'd have to check to make sure he hadn't accidentally bought decaf.

CHAPTER 6

EARLY NEXT MORNING JACOBSON came by to see him again. Since his last visit, Evan had thrown out Stanton's whisky bottle, washed and stacked the glasses. His sleeping bag was neatly rolled up out of sight behind the armchair. It was a beautiful spring day and the window was open, early morning sunlight slanting across his desk. Sitting at it, Evan looked for all the world like a conscientious, hardworking P.I. getting right into his heavy caseload. He was just about to look up his nocturnal visitor.

'You're looking a lot better than last time I came up,' Jacobson said, dropping into the visitor's chair.

Evan wished he wouldn't keep sitting there. It made him think of Stanton.

'Yeah, I think I'm over the worst of it,' he lied.

He'd actually been feeling pretty good until Jacobson sat there and reminded him again.

'I hope I'm not going to be the one to spoil that, but there's something you should know about.'

'That sounds ominous.'

'It's probably nothing. I was at a seminar yesterday and came back here around ten p.m. to sort a few things out, get ready for today.'

Evan hoped the surprise he felt didn't show on his face. Jacobson must have come back while he was asleep and he hadn't even woken up. He hadn't realized he'd been out so completely. He'd have sworn he was only dozing.

'I was just about to leave when I heard somebody outside in the corridor. I thought it must be you. I know you've been keeping pretty late hours. They were headed up here.'

Something about the way he said it told Evan that Jacobson was aware he was virtually living in his office. But there was no edge or accusation in his voice. Maybe it was just his guilty conscience.

'I locked up and then, on a whim, I thought I'd come up, see if you wanted to go for a quick beer.'

Evan waited for him to go on, even if he already had a good idea of what was coming next. Because it hadn't been him in the corridor outside Jacobson's office.

'When I got up here there was a man outside your door, trying to look through the glass. I asked him what the hell he thought he was doing. He turned around and walked towards me, started to say something or the other. Then suddenly he shoved me out of the way, ran back down the stairs and out of the building. I ran down after him but he was fast and my knee isn't so great. He was already across the parking lot by the time I got outside, so I gave it up. It would have been different in the old days.'

Evan shifted uncomfortably in his chair, a cold triangle of sweat sticking his shirt to his back. He'd slept through the whole thing. The intruder—it had to be Hugh McIntyre—had found him and gotten into the building, had been only seconds away from breaking into his office. On top of that, there'd been a scuffle in the corridor right outside his door. And he'd slept through it all.

But what did McIntyre want? The lights had been off in his office. He'd been quietly asleep in his chair. The office would have looked empty. Unless McIntyre had followed him to the office hours earlier and waited outside all that time, he'd have believed he was breaking into an empty office. He must think Evan had something in his files, something he wanted to get rid of.

'What did he look like? Actually, don't bother trying to answer that. Let me show you a picture.'

He opened up Stanton's file, clicked on an image of McIntyre and Stanton's wife outside the motel.

'Is that him?'

'That's him. No doubt about it. I assume that's the guy who was fooling around with your client's wife. And that's the wife.'

'You got it. Hugh McIntyre.'

'What's all this about, Evan?'

'I have no idea. I thought the guy just wanted to break a few bones, that sort of thing. But it looks like he's after something else.'

'The photos?'

'Can't be, it's too late. The police already have Stanton's copies.'

They both sat thinking it over, the traffic noise coming through the window the only sound. Evan was positive he didn't have anything else of interest to McIntyre.

'Beats me,' Jacobson said, 'but you need to be careful. This guy obviously means business. Whatever it is, he wants it badly.'

He got up to go. Evan stopped him.

'There's something I want to ask—or tell—you, Tom. McIntyre isn't the only strange visitor I've had recently.'

Jacobson gave him a look that suggested he might already be

regretting his understanding attitude. He lowered himself carefully back down.

'Do I really want to hear this?'

'No, it's not connected. At least I don't think it is.'

Then Evan told him all about his elusive visitor and how he had no idea who it could be or what she wanted.

'The thing is, Tom, you've been really understanding and generally great about this whole situation I'm in. It crossed my mind you might have steered some work my way. Someone you know who needs my sort of services.'

Jacobson shook his head.

'No, it's nothing to do with me. If I could help out that way, then I wouldn't hesitate to recommend you. I've got my rent to think about after all. But I'm afraid I can't lay claim to this one, Evan. It looks like you've got two mysteries on your hands.'

CHAPTER 7

WITH HER ADDRESS AND license plate number it didn't take Evan long to find out that the woman's name was Linda Clayton. The name didn't mean anything to him, but he knew a good place to start his digging. Around five thirty he went downstairs to see Jacobson again. Jacobson had lived in the area forever and would be a good source of local information. He found him getting ready to go home, suggested they go for the beer they hadn't had the previous night. Jacobson was more than happy to join him when Evan told him he'd identified the mystery woman.

They walked to a bar called Arnold's just down the street, a beautiful old place with original woodwork and what looked like some of the original customers too. Evan liked it because it was a no-bullshit local bar. Not a *lounge* which is what everywhere seemed to be called these days. You wait for a plane in a lounge, not drink beer.

They got settled up at the bar, and the bartender served them a couple of cold ones. Evan told Jacobson that although he'd found out who his mysterious nocturnal visitor was, he still had no idea what she wanted.

'Her name's Linda Clayton. Since you've lived around here for about a hundred years, I wondered if you maybe knew her. Perhaps she's been the lucky recipient of some of that famous root canal work.'

Jacobson smiled. 'Well if she had, I wouldn't be able to discuss her personal information with you. Luckily for you, she's not a patient. But I know exactly who she is.'

He drained his beer, put the glass down on the counter. Sat back in his stool without saying anything more. Evan, perceptive as always, called the bartender over and ordered another round.

'I'm treating this as rent-in-kind you know.'

'I also know why she came to see you. She's well known around here. Not exactly a celebrity, but everyone knows who she is. And her story.'

He took another long pull of his beer, then sat lost in his thoughts, as if Evan wasn't there. Evan waved his hand in front of his face.

Jacobson flinched slightly.

'Sorry, I was just thinking back to when it all happened. It's like it was only yesterday, but it must be ten years ago at least. Everything in Linda Clayton's life was rosy. Nothing out of the ordinary, just a normal family. Happily married to a good man, Robbie, with a great kid. Daniel.'

He swallowed thickly, cleared his throat. He wasn't a sentimental man and Evan knew not to expect any kind of a happy ending to the story.

'Then in the space of a month her husband and the boy both disappeared. She's never recovered.'

A shiver rippled across the back of Evan's neck as if someone had walked over his grave. He didn't know what to say. He understood more than most what it was like to lose someone you loved too early. But your husband and your child in such a short space of time was unthinkable.

'So what happened?'

Jacobson cleared his throat again, his eyes fixed on the beer glass in his hand.

'Actually, I've got that the wrong way around. The boy disappeared first. And then the husband.'

'Were they connected?'

'Who knows? They must have been, too much of a coincidence otherwise. They both just disappeared off the face of the earth.' He looked directly into Evan's eyes. 'I'm sorry, Evan, this must be terrible for you.'

He was right. But he would never understand quite how terrible. For the second time in seventy-two hours Evan had been transported back in time to a place that he didn't know if he wanted to forget or live in for the rest of his life.

'I think it's obvious what she wants,' Jacobson said. 'But why you and why now, I have no idea.'

Evan felt something rising up inside him. A festering, deep-seated resentment that he'd lived with for the past five years.

'Did the police do anything? I mean, a missing kid's important, right. Something to be taken *seriously*'—it came out as a sibilant hiss—'a totally different kettle of fish to a missing adult. Someone who probably *chose* to run away.'

He knew he sounded bitter, couldn't help it. He didn't much care anyway. Not after three or four or was it ten beers. Fleetwood Mac's 'Gypsy' was playing on the jukebox. Thank God it wasn't 'Sarah'.

Jacobson put a massive hand on his shoulder and squeezed, then let it rest there. Evan took a deep breath, rubbed his face.

'Page one of the manual states, and I quote, 'Do not form an emotional attachment with the client'. How do you think I'd do on that score if I take her on, Tom?'

'I think you'd give it your best shot. That's all that matters. And I think it would be good for you. Catharsis.'

'Did they get anywhere at all with the kid? What about the father?'

'They pulled out all the stops on the kid as you'd expect. But they didn't get anywhere. They took a hard look at the parents as they always do. Then when the father disappeared too, they pretty much assumed that he'd done the kid in and then cut and run. But they didn't find him either.'

Evan shook his head as he tried to comprehend what Linda Clayton must have gone through.

'So Linda Clayton had to live with the loss of her husband and son, and, as if that wasn't enough, listen to all the whispered gossip that her husband had probably killed the boy. Jesus wept.'

'That about sums it up. I'm sure you're aware how unkind people can be. End result is, she's pretty much become a recluse. You never see her out in the daytime. That's why she came to your office at night.'

'I still don't understand why me. I'm not what you'd call a famous detective. My reputation doesn't exactly precede me everywhere I go.'

Jacobson was kind enough not to point out the simplest explanation—that she'd tried everybody else already.

'You'll have to ask her that when you meet her.'

He was right. There was no way on earth he was going to let

this drop now. Even if Linda Clayton didn't want to talk to him, he wouldn't be able to walk away. Patterns he didn't want to see wormed their way into his mind. He didn't want to think too hard about the possibility of a connection between a young boy and a grown man disappearing ten years ago and Sarah's disappearance five years later. Unfortunately, you don't have much control over the things your subconscious decides to push to the forefront of your mind. You just have to deal with them once they're there.

There was a loud crack as Evan's glass exploded in his hand. He'd been gripping it so tightly, it had shattered. The remains of his beer mingled with his blood from where a shard of broken glass had cut him on the palm. He sucked the blood and beer out of it as the barman picked up all the pieces, didn't say a word about the mess. Not to a man with a look like that on his face.

Then he ordered two more of the only answer he could think of at the moment. They weren't the last two either.

HE COULDN'T GET TO sleep that night, lying awake in his sleeping bag, thinking about the Claytons, and what might have happened to them. That segued far too easily into morbid thoughts about Sarah and what might have happened to her. His mind played horrible tricks on him at times like these.

Had she deliberately left him? He would get vague memories suddenly spring into his mind of a terrible argument they'd had the night before she disappeared. The worst part was, he could never swear for sure that it hadn't actually happened. He had a recurring nightmare that he'd killed her, buried her in their yard. Then he'd sold the house and forgotten all about it until now, when the new owners had dug up her body and he was about to be caught.

But whatever strange tricks his mind played on him, there was always a common thread running through it all—it was *his fault* she was gone.

THE GLASS PANEL IN the door exploded inwards, showering Evan with tiny shards of glass. A hand reached through the hole and unlatched the door. Evan struggled to sit up in his sleeping bag. He couldn't move his arms. He'd tossed and turned so much, they were trapped in the twisted folds of the bag.

The door swung open and Hugh McIntyre stepped into the room. He was dressed exactly as when Evan had last seen him, wearing just his pants and without any shoes. His chest was broad and muscular, his stomach flat and rippled. A prominent bulge strained at the front of his pants. Sweating heavily, the salty, almost chlorine, smell of sex came off him in waves.

He smiled contemptuously, his eyes still wild, as he watched Evan's pathetic attempts to free himself.

'You should have reversed back over me when you had the chance, you pervert,' he said in a voice that sounded a lot like Stanton's. 'That's a mistake you're going to live with for the rest of your life.'

Evan tried to speak but nothing came out, his mouth opening and closing uselessly like a goldfish. He watched helplessly as McIntyre walked slowly across the room, oblivious to the shards of glass as they crunched and lacerated his feet. He twisted frantically from side to side trying to get himself free. But the more he struggled, the more caught up he became.

With a shock he noticed McIntyre was carrying a coil of thick rope—the sort Stanton must have used. Where the hell had that come from? He hadn't been carrying that a minute ago.

Everything was moving in slow motion. McIntyre walked over to the desk. He saw the bottle of scotch. The smile grew wider.

'Even better.'

He dropped the rope on top of Evan. Picked up the bottle and slowly unscrewed the cap. He threw back his head, took a long pull on the drink. Mesmerized, Evan watched his Adam's apple bob up and down as he poured the whisky down his throat. Then he stopped, stretched his arm out over Evan, up-ended the bottle.

Evan tried to cry out but again nothing came. He watched the amber liquid as it fell slowly through the air before splashing onto his face and hair, the stinging liquid running into his eyes and throat, making him cough and splutter. He threw his head from side to side, just made it go up his nose. He was choking. He couldn't free himself. The bottle was never ending. The whisky ran off his skin and soaked into the sleeping bag and the carpet until he was lying in a pool of it.

McIntyre whooped and threw the bottle at the window, smashing the glass and letting the chill night air in. He pulled a box of matches from his pocket. He struck one, casually let it drop. Horrified, Evan watched it as it tumbled through the air, slowly turning over and over. McIntyre struck another one, then another.

'Toot! Toot!' he laughed, mimicking the sound of Evan's car horn. 'Remember that, do you?'

The first match landed in the pool of whisky on the floor and sputtered out. The second one landed in Evan's hair. So did the third. The scotch ignited with a roar. Evan felt a searing heat crawl over his scalp. He screamed and jerked himself into a sitting position. Looked around him, the scream dying on his lips.

McIntyre was gone. The door was closed, the glass intact. The window wasn't broken. His hair and his body were slick and sticky but only with sweat. The sleeping bag was damp with sweat too. There wasn't a rope or any whisky. It was just a dream. He ran his hand through his hair and flopped backwards, lay staring up at the ceiling waiting for his heart and his breathing to slow.

CHAPTER 8

THERE WASN'T ANY MORE sleep for him that night so he was up early the next day. He got to work researching the case, but soon realized he wasn't going to find out much more than Tom Jacobson had told him the night before. The newspaper archives told a familiar story with the media's rapidly dwindling interest mirroring the lack of any palpable progress by the police. The only piece of information of any use that he could find was the name of the chief of police ten years ago—Matt Faulkner.

His personal experience predisposed him to seeing the faults in anything the police did. Even so, he couldn't help but feel they'd been far too quick to pin the blame for the boy's disappearance on the father, once he too disappeared. He made up his mind to go to see Faulkner, try to get more information out of him before doing any more digging himself. If Faulkner talked to him, he'd save himself a lot of unnecessary legwork.

He would have liked to talk to Linda Clayton first. So far, she'd made no further attempts to contact him. It didn't cross his mind that he wasn't actually working for her. Somewhere between the beer and the nightmare and the cold light of day it had turned into a personal crusade.

His best bet was to drive out and talk to Faulkner immediately. He'd retired some years ago and was now living in a trailer park on the outskirts of town. Evan didn't bother ringing ahead. He wasn't sure Faulkner would agree to talk to him. The case wasn't what anyone would call his finest hour.

The man locking the trailer door as Evan walked up certainly didn't look like Evan expected him to. The trailer park wasn't the greatest place he'd ever been, but if he thought Faulkner was going to be sitting around his trailer all day in a wife beater and grubby old pants, drinking beer and smoking, he couldn't have been further from the truth.

Faulkner was mid-sixties with short, steel-gray hair above a flat, square face. Tall and slim, he looked like an advertisement for healthy living. He looked like he was on his way to the gym when he saw Evan approaching.

'I'm on my way to the gym. I don't want to buy whatever it is you're selling.'

'I'm not selling anything, Mr Faulkner. I'd like to ask you a few questions.'

'Sorry, I don't do surveys. I'm in a hurry. Can you come back another time? Maybe four or five years.'

'It's about one of your past cases.'

Faulkner clearly wasn't expecting that reply. He looked at Evan suspiciously.

'What, you want to write my memoirs?'

'No, it's just one case I'm interested in.'

Faulkner's eyes narrowed. Evan had the impression he'd guessed which one it was going to be.

'And which one might that be?'

'Daniel Clayton.'

Faulkner stiffened momentarily when he heard the name. It was so fast it would have been easy to miss.

'As I said, I'm in a hurry.'

He started walking towards his car.

'Linda Clayton hired me to look into the case,' Evan blurted out.

He didn't know what made him say it. But it sure got Faulkner's attention. He stopped and looked at Evan, raised his eyebrows.

'You sure about that?'

'Of course I'm sure. Why else would I be here?'

'You tell me, son. It's just that as far as I know, Linda Clayton gave up on that boy years ago. Gone soft in the head too, if you ask me.'

'Losing a son and a husband in the space of a few weeks can do that to a person.'

Faulkner nodded, a tight expression on his face. Evan had the distinct impression he was being assessed, the eyes weighing him up. Or maybe he was embarrassed by what he'd just said about Linda Clayton.

'Okay, I'll give you five minutes. For all the good it'll do you.'

He walked back to the trailer and unlocked the door.

'Come on in. I don't want to talk about it out here.'

Evan was surprised for the second time that morning as he entered the immaculately kept trailer. Faulkner saw it on his face.

'What did you expect? Empty beer cans and overflowing ashtrays all over the place? Isn't that how trailer trash live?'

'Do you live here alone?' Evan asked, inadvertently digging himself further into the hole.

'Yeah, but the maid comes in every morning and tidies up after me.'

Evan felt a flush creep up his face, his ears impossibly hot. He wasn't sure what to say.

'Don't worry about it, son. Let's just hope for Mrs Clayton's sake—and your career's—that you don't bring your ill-informed preconceptions to the rest of your life.'

He gestured for Evan to sit, a wry smile curling the corners of his mouth.

'Want a beer?'

'Why not? I'm Evan Buckley by the way.'

Evan smiled with him as Faulkner handed him a cold beer.

'Pleased to meet you Mr. Buckley. Here's hoping you get further than the rest of us did. What do you want to know?'

'Well, all of it really. If you could talk me through it from the beginning.'

Faulkner raised his eyebrows.

'Is that all? Okay, here we go. One day, about ten years ago, on his way home from school, Daniel Clayton disappeared off the face of the earth. He left the classroom same as usual and started to walk home. He never took the school bus. His mother thought the exercise was good for him. Plus, he wasn't a very popular kid and the other kids picked on him a lot. He never made it home and he's never been seen since.'

Faulkner leaned back in his chair and rubbed the back of his neck. He didn't say anything more. Took a careful sip of his beer.

'That's it?'

Evan couldn't decide whether Faulkner was being deliberately obstructive or he just wanted to make him work for it.

'That's all the facts. The school bus driver said that he normally saw Daniel walk past the bus on his way home, but not that day. So, if you believe the bus driver, Daniel disappeared somewhere on the campus. That's if the bus driver wasn't picking his nose at the time and missed the boy as he passed. Or that he hung around and left the campus a bit later than normal. Or that any one of a million other things happened.'

'What did you concentrate on? You must have had some suspicions.'

'You need to realize there were two very distinct time periods here. Before the father disappeared and after. After he disappeared, we pretty much came to the conclusion that he was responsible for the boy disappearing, and he decided to disappear himself before we could prove anything against him.'

'I thought you said the boy never made it home.'

'Sorry, you're right.' He took another pull on his beer, looked at Evan over the top of the bottle. 'I should have said the boy wasn't home when the mother got home from work. So he could have come home like normal and something happened to him there. The father was out of work at the time, so he could have been home when the kid got back.'

'What do you mean, could have?'

'He said he was in a bar and didn't get home until after the mother. But nobody remembered seeing him in the bar he claimed to be in. And everybody knows everybody else in that bar. They're probably all related, it's that sort of place. None of them remembered him—or anyone—who wasn't part of the usual crowd.'

'And on that basis, you assumed it was him. He's either in the bar drinking or he's killing his son. No other options.'

Faulkner ignored the comment.

'It wasn't just that, but then he disappeared himself. Given the complete lack of any other evidence pointing elsewhere, we reckoned it was the most likely explanation.'

The more he talked to Faulkner, the more it seemed to Evan that they hadn't looked very hard for an alternative explanation.

'Convenient.'

Faulkner glared at him.

'Convenient my ass. Suddenly we've got two missing bodies and a new prime suspect who happens to be one of those missing bodies. We'd have preferred it if it was the local pervert.'

'That can't have gone down very well with Linda Clayton.'

'You can say that again. I think it's fair to say she was adamant there was no way on God's green earth that her dear husband could have been involved in their son's disappearance. It rather soured relationships between us.'

'I can see that it would. No doubt made worse by the fact that you promptly gave up on any other avenues you might have been pursuing.'

'You've got a nerve. If you put on a wig and a dress, I'd swear you were her come to give me a hard time.'

Evan held up his hands. 'Sorry, I didn't mean it to sound like I'm judging you.'

Faulkner didn't look particularly appeased. He mumbled something under his breath, went and got himself another beer. Evan declined the offer. Faulkner's eyes crinkled as he took a pull.

'This is more like it, eh? Living up to stereotypes. Sorry, sad old cop drinking beer in his trailer, haunted by unsolved cases. But as I remember the story, the next thing you know, the sad old cop gets the bit between his teeth again and gets back out there and solves it.' He shook his head. 'I'm sorry, but it's not going to happen this time, son.'

Evan stared at him. Just because Faulkner had made up his mind, it didn't mean he had to agree with him. Linda Clayton didn't.

'What about before the father disappeared?'

'What about it? A load of dead ends and time wasters. A whole bunch of people saw a 'suspicious-looking' pickup truck'—he did the quotes thing with his fingers—'some other people saw a suspicious-looking camper van and half the town saw a suspicious-looking dark sedan cruising around that afternoon.' He gave a short, humorless laugh. 'They're always *dark* sedans. Like a white sedan is always driven by the good guys. And what the hell is a suspicious-looking vehicle for Christ's sake? One with some legs sticking out the window? I think at least one 'witness' saw Elvis that afternoon.'

Evan laughed. 'I suppose it brings all the cranks out of the woodwork.'

'You have no idea, and it's not just the cranks. People have an argument with their neighbor and call us up and say they saw body parts in their trash just to get them back.' It appeared Evan had set Faulkner off on a favorite diatribe. 'Some of the guys in the bar who didn't remember seeing Robbie Clayton were helpful enough to remember seeing all manner of other people. Suspicious-looking people of course. People with shifty eyes, that sort of thing. The barroom wisdom was really running high that day. In fact, I think that's where Elvis was spotted, having a beer with Hank Williams.'

Evan smiled and waited for him to go on. Seemed he'd run out of steam.

'And . . .' he prompted.

'And nothing. Absolutely zip. Nada.'

'Who else did you look at? What about the bus driver?'

Faulkner gave him a long-suffering look. A *God-give-me-strength* look. He shook his head wearily.

'If you find me a ten-year-old phone directory, I guarantee we talked to most of the people in it. Even though—'

Evan started to interrupt but Faulkner held up a hand to stop him.

'*Even though* we didn't have the benefit of you guiding us along, showing us how to do our jobs. Oh, and the benefit of ten years' worth of hindsight, of course.'

Evan ignored Faulkner's sarcasm. He was surprised Faulkner didn't ask him to leave. It wouldn't be long. He needed to keep pressing him.

'You must have had a prime suspect.'

'We did. Based on Carl Hendricks' statement—'

'Who's Carl Hendricks?'

'The bus driver. Based on his statement which we believed to be accurate, it appeared that Daniel disappeared on the campus.'

Evan was struck by the inconsistency of what Faulkner was saying. He was about to say something when Faulkner held up his hand to stop him.

'Don't worry, it hasn't escaped me that if we believed the father was responsible, then Hendricks' statement must be inaccurate. He really was picking his nose and didn't see the boy walk past. But at the time, and remember, no hindsight allowed'—he wagged his finger in mock admonishment—'we had no reason to think it wasn't true. So we concentrated on looking inside the campus. The most likely candidate seemed to be his teacher, Ray Clements. Like I said before, Daniel wasn't the most popular kid in his class, but he got on well with Clements. It turns out the kid would hang around sometimes and Clements would give him a ride home. He'd drop him off a couple of blocks away so his mother wouldn't find out. Which also meant nobody else really knew it was going on.'

'Did he have an alibi?'

'Nothing we were able to check. He said he went for a drive that afternoon because it was such a beautiful day. He showed us a receipt for gas, but there's nothing to say you can't fill up with a kid hogtied in the trunk.'

'But nothing came of it?'

'No. We leaned on him pretty hard. Especially after he admitted giving the kid a ride in his car. We pulled the car apart and searched his house, but there wasn't anything. His wife was furious. You should have seen her. I bet he really caught it in the neck after we'd gone.' Faulkner smiled to himself at the memory. 'We also took away his computer and found a load of porn on it.'

'Kiddie porn?'

'No, just the normal stuff. And you don't have to worry that we missed some secret internet portal. We do have some bright people who know what they're doing.'

'It doesn't exactly single him out as public enemy number one.'

'No.' He smiled again. 'Mind you, if you were married to his wife, you'd look at a lot of porn.'

'Not what you'd call a looker?'

'Maybe if you're a male Hippo. Anyway, I feel pretty confident we didn't miss anything there.'

'What about the bus driver? Did he have an alibi?'

'What, apart from driving a busload of screaming brats home?'

'What about afterwards?'

Faulkner laughed. There was genuine amusement in it this time.

'What?'

'He went to a strip joint. Different strokes for different folks, eh? The teacher goes for a drive in the summer sunshine, and the bus driver goes to some dingy basement to gawp at saggy tits. It takes all sorts.'

'They remembered him?'

'Apparently he was one of their best perv . . . I mean customers. It must have been payday that day, because he paid for a number of private dances with the same girl. I use the word loosely—she was old enough to be my mother.'

'Could he have paid her to say he was with her?'

'Of course he could. And the FBI killed JFK.'

'It's possible,' Evan said defensively.

'Probable impossibilities are to be preferred to improbable possibilities. Do you know who said that?'

'No.' It sounded more like a tongue twister than a quotation.

'Look it up on the internet when you get bored with the porn. Now, are we done here? Or do you have any more *How the hell did I miss that* questions for me?'

They weren't likely to get any further forward. Evan could see why they'd been happy to pin it on the boy's father in absentia. It didn't make his task any easier. He got up to go, stopped to look at the wall of framed photographs and commendations. Lots of them showed Faulkner with a good-looking, dark-haired woman.

'That's me and the wife, God rest her soul.'

Faulkner had joined him, pointing to one of a younger version of himself and the woman, smiling brightly on vacation somewhere. It looked like Switzerland or Austria. He pointed to another one of an even younger version of the same woman standing with an older couple in front of an old, red barn.

'That's her and her folks before we got married.' He stared silently at the photograph as he must have done a thousand times before. 'She died last year. A blessing really, she'd been ill for a long time.'

Evan smiled softly as he reflected on the idyllic scene, thinking how every good thing must come to an end. And sometimes a lot sooner than it should.

'I'm sorry. I know what it's like to lose someone you love.'

CHAPTER 9

EVAN DIDN'T HAVE ANY choice now but to speak to Linda Clayton. He wasn't comfortable with the fact that he'd spoken with Faulkner under false pretences. More than that, it was obvious that Faulkner wouldn't have given him the time of day if he hadn't told the lie. Other people he wanted to talk to would be the same way. Besides, he wanted to meet her and help her. He certainly wasn't expecting her to pay him. He didn't have anything else to do with his time after all.

He drove straight to her house after leaving Faulkner. There wasn't going to be any fooling around this time. He parked directly outside the house, walked up the path and knocked on the door. Her car was in the driveway. Tom Jacobson had told him she didn't like to go out in the daytime, so he was confident she was at home. That didn't mean she was going to answer the door. He knocked a couple more times, then peered through the window. He couldn't see anyone moving around inside.

He didn't want to draw too much attention to himself after what happened last time, but it looked like he would have to talk to her through the door, try to persuade her to let him in. He looked up and down the street. There wasn't anyone around.

He cupped his hands around his mouth, put them to the door.

'Mrs Clayton, my name is Evan Buckley. I'm a private detective. I believe you came to my office the other night. I would very much like to talk to you. Please let me in. I'm not going away until I've talked to you.'

The door remained firmly shut. He tried again.

'I've just spoken to Matt Faulkner—'

The door was pulled open so fast he almost fell on top of her. She'd been standing right on the other side of it. Clearly, there was some kind of reciprocal arrangement with her and Faulkner's names. All you had to do was find the right button to push. He managed to keep his balance and stood upright.

'Mrs Clayton—'

'Yes, yes, I heard all that garbage through the door. What are doing talking to that old bastard Faulkner?'

Faulkner hadn't been exaggerating about soured relationships. And most of the sourness seemed to be going in one direction, but that was understandable.

Evan got his first good look at her. She was about five foot nine, slim and shapely. Her ash blond hair was pulled into a loose ponytail at the nape of her neck, the first streaks of gray visible. She had what you'd call a strong nose and her eyes would have been clear blue and sparkling if it wasn't for something behind them that stole the light from them. He wouldn't have called her beautiful, but she was definitely striking. The mention of Faulkner had brought a flush to her cheeks which suited her.

'I had to start somewhere. I tried you first, but you were a little reluctant to talk.'

'You didn't have to start with that horse's ass. You might as well come in, now you're here.' It wasn't said with what he'd call good grace, but at least he was in.

She led him down the hallway to a small lounge at the back of the house, waved her hand at an armchair for him to sit. She didn't offer him a beer. He sat down, looked around the room. From the number of photographs of her son and husband everywhere, it was clear that she didn't hold her husband responsible for her son's disappearance. She perched on the arm of the chair opposite Evan, hands clasped loosely in her lap.

'You're right, I wanted to talk to you. I came to your office but I got so nervous I couldn't do it.'

Evan put on his best *you-can-trust-me* face.

'There's no reason to be nervous about talking to me,'

'There is if you've been through what I have. If you've talked to Faulkner, you've already guessed that I wanted to talk to you about Daniel. I'm sure that evil old bastard has told you all his wicked lies about my poor Robbie. But I never believed a word of it.' She waved an arm, taking in the whole of the small room. 'I ask you, would I have all these photographs of him if I thought he could do anything to our boy?'

He was getting the feeling that now he'd gotten her started he might not be able to stop her talking.

'I never believed it and I told them so. And I told them they should keep looking for the monster who really took my boy and not blame my Robbie when he wasn't there to defend himself. But they'd made up their nasty minds. They didn't want to hear it. So they ignored me. If I collared one of them and they couldn't manage to squirm out of talking to me, they treated me like I was an idiot. Like I'd gone soft in the head. Even if I was soft in the head, I'd have more brains than that lot put together.'

She stopped for a moment, paused for breath.

'Trouble was, because their version was the official version, the gospel according to Saint Matthew, everyone else around here believed it. So they all started to treat me like I was crazy, too. You could see it in their eyes. You could see the pity too. As if any of them ever gave a shit.'

She paused again to stare into his eyes, searching for any sign of the offending emotions. She seemed satisfied that they weren't hiding in there.

'That's why I couldn't bring myself to talk to you. I couldn't stand the thought of you treating me the same way. Writing me off as some lunatic old woman, wasting your time.'

He couldn't vouch for the lunatic part at this early stage—it was still a definite possibility—but he certainly wouldn't have classed her as *some old woman*. She wasn't more than mid-forties. And she was still attractive, despite all the anguish she'd been through. Life had beaten her down and he could have forgiven her for looking a lot more haggard than she did.

'Well I'm glad we're talking now,' he said, 'and I promise you I won't treat you like an idiot just because you won't believe what the police tell you. I might treat you like an idiot for some other reason, but not that.' She put her hand up to her mouth to smother a girlish giggle. He liked her even more. 'I'm interested to know why you've taken this up again now and why me? I'm not what you'd call famous.'

'As far as taking it up now goes, I've never dropped it, but getting anyone to listen hasn't been easy. As for you, you were recommended.'

He assumed it must be Jacobson as he thought originally, even though he'd denied it. He was wrong.

'I'm good friends with Kate Guillory. She suggested I should talk to you.'

He recognized the name but couldn't place it. Linda saw his confusion.

'She's a police detective.'

Now he remembered. Guillory had been one of the cops who'd come to see him about Stanton's death. The woman, the reasonable one who hadn't said much. He was dumbstruck.

'I won't repeat what she said about you. She wasn't very complimentary.' She couldn't stop herself from smiling as she remembered it. 'But she said it would be killing two birds with one stone, helping me and giving you something *worthwhile* to do. That was the exact word she used.'

She paused to give him a chance to explain how it was that he needed to do something worthwhile. When it became obvious he wasn't about to volunteer anything, to bare his soul on their first meeting, she carried on.

'She also said that you would understand and have some sympathy for me'—sympathy was okay, it seemed, but not pity—'and you'd work your butt off, as she put it, as a result.'

He found it hard to believe what she was saying. But it made some kind of sense. Even though they'd told him he should be doing something worthwhile instead of snooping, he'd never have expected this. Linda was still talking. He supposed it happened like that when you were a recluse—when you did get to meet someone, it all came pouring out, not to mention that some of your social graces might have slipped. Like knowing when to stop.

'She didn't say anything more than that, but it doesn't take a rocket scientist to figure out that you've lost someone too.'

Once again, his emotional world was turned upside down. He was here to help this woman with her problems, not the other way around. And it had to be kept strictly business-like, he couldn't afford to get emotionally involved.

'Yes, I have. But then so have a lot of people,' he said a little too quickly. 'I think what Guillory was getting at was that I expressed my own dissatisfaction with the police's efforts fairly forcefully. In fact, I would have hit the other one, Ryder, if Guillory hadn't stopped me. From what you've just told me, she probably thought we'd get on like a house on fire.'

She smiled at him, and he thought again how attractive she must have been before a double dose of tragedy invited itself into her life.

'I think she's right. And it's okay if you don't want to talk about what happened to you. It's not why you're here.'

'Yes, but—'

'It's okay, really.' She leaned forward, put a hand on his knee. 'I'm sure you'll tell me some other time.'

He coughed nervously and met her gaze. Guillory was right. He would work his butt off for this woman. The problem was going to be how to avoid getting too involved, especially now that she'd guessed some of his past.

She jumped up and asked him if he wanted coffee, breaking the tension before it became awkward. He followed her into the kitchen.

'I don't know how much you know already,' she said over her shoulder, 'but let me tell it to you from my point of view.'

She ran through the same story that Evan had heard from Faulkner up to the point concerning her husband.

'Faulkner wants me to believe that Robbie was here at home

when Daniel got back from school. That he killed our son for some unexplained reason and got rid of the body somehow. Then the cold-hearted son-of-a-bitch stayed right here, living with me for a couple more weeks before making a run for it himself.'

The soft flush in her cheeks had turned a deeper red.

'Like I wouldn't notice if something was wrong, if he was hiding something. I knew my Robbie. And I know he couldn't have hurt Daniel if his life depended on it. He couldn't have fooled me either.'

She gave him a defiant look, challenging him to contradict her.

'I'm sure he couldn't. But the police say that Robbie's alibi didn't stand up. Nobody remembered him in the bar where he said he was.'

'Alibis are for the police to worry about. They're the ones who get all antsy if they can't check all the boxes and square everything away. I mean, it is just a paper exercise after all, isn't it?' She snorted contemptuously. 'But I knew my husband and I know he couldn't have done it.'

She looked down and was quiet for a moment, fiddling with the wedding ring she still wore on her finger. Evan thought she was deciding whether to tell him more. All she'd told him so far was that her Robbie couldn't have done it because she said so.

'Do you have a theory about his alibi?' he prompted.

She looked up and he saw tears welling in her eyes, saw what was coming too.

'It's the oldest story in the world. I've never mentioned this to anyone else . . . but I'm certain he was seeing somebody else. That's where I think he was. In some woman's bed, not in a bar. And he didn't want to tell that to the police.'

She swallowed thickly. He felt like a heel for pushing her. His voice came out hoarse when he asked his next question.

'Did you say anything to him about it?'

'You bet I did.'

The tears were gone as quickly as they'd appeared. He got the feeling it wouldn't have been a conversation her husband enjoyed. At the same time, with her face flushed and the wetness still in her eyes, he couldn't see why any man would want to look further.

'What did I care if all the old gossips around here laughed at me behind my back? If it meant the police would believe him and keep looking for the bastard who really did it, then it would've been worth it.'

'What did he say?'

'He denied it all, of course. Stuck to his story, said he'd been in the bar the whole time and it wasn't his fault if they all had a collective dose of amnesia. Said they were all too drunk to remember their own names, let alone his.'

'But you didn't believe him.'

'Like I said, I knew my husband. I know he didn't hurt our son and I'm also pretty certain he was seeing someone else. Men think they're so clever, that they can hide things like that. But they can't.'

She caught him looking through the doorway into the lounge where the walls were covered with photographs of her errant husband.

'So why are all those still on the wall?' she said. 'That's what you're thinking, isn't it?'

'It crossed my mind. Then again, one lapse doesn't mean a whole marriage is bad, does it?'

'That's the way I look at it. He's a man, he can't help himself.'

She laughed then but without any warmth or real humor. He laughed with her, despite being a man himself. He supposed it was quite funny, but only if you were sitting in the comfort of not being the injured party.

'Why didn't you say anything to the police?'

She gave a soft shrug.

'What would've been the point? Robbie would have denied it and that would have been the end of it.' She turned towards the kitchen countertop so that he couldn't see her eyes. 'He was obviously prepared to be considered a murder suspect in order to keep *her* name out of it. She must have been some woman.'

He felt an almost irresistible urge to put his hand on her shoulder, to comfort her. But it was inappropriate. He'd only met her five minutes ago. Somehow his hand didn't seem to know that, rising inexorably towards her back.

He felt the bitterness overlying the layers of hurt radiating off her like a heat haze in the desert. He wanted to ask her if Robbie had stopped seeing the other woman, or whether there was the possibility he had run off with her, but he couldn't bring himself to do it. She must have asked herself the same things a million times. An idea he didn't want to even think about suddenly came to him. He tried to push it away without success—what if Daniel had seen or caught the two of them together and they'd killed him in an attempt to keep him quiet? Had Linda thought the same thing over the years? It was a question he prayed he would never need to ask.

'You know what the worst of it is?'

She suddenly turned back to face him, caught him with his hand in mid-air. He ran it quickly through his hair, hoping she didn't think he'd been glancing at his watch. Anger had replaced the hurt in her eyes.

'It looks like it all came out anyway. Kate Guillory told me she'd heard rumors around town. Rumors which Faulkner must have heard too and which gave Robbie an alibi. But that was years later, just before he retired. Obviously, he couldn't be bothered to get up off his lazy butt and open it all up again.' Her eyes challenged Evan to come to Faulkner's defence. He could have told her it wasn't a cause he was about to take up. 'What did he care if I still felt like it was only yesterday? Guillory told me they had more than enough on their plates, what with budget cuts and all, to re-open an old case like that. It was only rumors after all, probably just old women's idle tongues wagging.'

He imagined how she must have tortured herself over the years. It was bad enough that a crucial fact was buried for all the wrong reasons at the time, but for it to come out anyway later on must have been almost too much to bear. And to know that the police knew it too and were too busy or indifferent to take it up again—he was surprised she hadn't gone crazy. He was even more surprised by what she said next.

'There are some wicked people in the world, you know. Not just the monsters who abduct and kill children, but ordinary, everyday folk who like nothing better than to cut a person to shreds with their dirty tongues, to spice up their sorry, sad lives.'

She threw her head back and ran her hand through her hair, as if mimicking his gesture. He thought what a nice neck she had, the skin still smooth and firm like a woman half her age.

'I'm told it's been said that my Robbie might have run off with his whore because Daniel saw them together, so they killed him to keep it secret and then ran away together.' The first tear was on her cheek now, making its way slowly down the side of her nose. 'Will you tell me what kind of a sick person makes up something like that?'

He didn't have an answer. He couldn't bear to look her in the eye. Whoever had told her—Guillory presumably—didn't have as much respect for her feelings as he did. No wonder she chose not to mix with people around town. Chose instead to hide herself away, refusing to listen to the rumormongers.

But he knew only too well you can't hide from yourself. In the small hours of the morning all your doubts and fears come to haunt you, standing silently at the bottom of your bed, before the gray dawn light seeps through the gap in the curtains, bathing the room in a creeping pale radiance that sends them back into the dark recesses of your mind for another day.

Linda sniffed loudly, wiped her nose on her sleeve.

'I'm sorry, it's been building a long time. I don't suppose you expected this when you knocked on the door.'

She gave him a small smile.

'I'm not sure now what I expected. But this is probably more than I bargained for. Certainly more raw emotion anyway, and that's fine.'

He smiled back at her, letting her know that he was Mr Emotional Sponge, the man with the inexhaustible capacity to absorb other people's problems. But he needed to get it back on track.

'Do you have any ideas about what might have happened?'

'Plenty of things might have happened. As far as what actually did happen, I haven't got the first idea. And there's not a day gone by when I haven't thought about it.'

'Faulkner mentioned the teacher, Ray Clements.'

Somehow, he managed to get Faulkner's name out without starting her off again.

'Ray Clements is a good man. As far as I'm concerned, he could no more have hurt Daniel than Robbie could. I know Faulkner

hounded him before he ha
never thought that was rig

It seemed to him
everyone—except Faul
they finally got arour
suspect—and he wa
going to come po
Faulkner. She certainly ha

'He didn't tell them he'd given
have looked like he had something to hide.

'If you'd seen what Faulkner was like back then, y
have been volunteering any information.' She snorted again.
seems such a nice guy now and everyone feels so sorry for him
because of his wife dying. But if he got you in his sights back then,
you'd have had a very different opinion. Ask poor Ray Clements.
He ruined his life.'

'What makes you so sure Clements was innocent?

'I can't say. But just because I can't prove why he didn't do it,
doesn't mean he did. I thought we had a presumption of innocence
in this country. Nobody seems to have told Faulkner.'

He agreed, but was getting the feeling that her reasoning was a
little light on facts and biased more towards whether she liked you
or not. It seemed you were just meant to accept what she told you.

'The only reason Faulkner concentrated on him was because
that low life Hendricks convinced him Daniel never left the campus.
And Ray Clements was an easy target. Faulkner likes easy.'

He wondered if they'd finally got around to the point where she
was going to let rip.

'I get the feeling you don't like Hendricks. You think he had
something to do with it?'

vas about to snort again, but she held it in this

kidding I don't like him. He's a really nasty piece of
t part of that man ran down the inside of his mother's

vitriol in her voice surprised him more than her language.
ut just because I don't like him, doesn't mean I think he had
hing to do with it. How could he have? He was driving a bus
ll of kids around at the time.'

She went suddenly quiet, twisted her wedding ring again. It didn't take a genius to work out what she was thinking. If only she'd allowed Daniel to take the bus like all the other kids, none of this would have happened.

Sometimes it takes a while to get there, but in the end, we all end up blaming ourselves.

'Hendricks might not have done it,' she went on, 'but I think it's fair to say he enjoyed watching what happened to Ray Clements after he convinced Faulkner that Daniel never left the campus on foot.'

'Did he have some reason for not liking Clements?'

'I don't think so. He's just one of life's truly horrible people. There are plenty of people like him. They call it schadenfreude.'

'How the hell did he get a job driving the school bus?'

'That I can't tell you.'

His exasperation must have shown on his face. He was going to have to work on keeping it under control.

'You must be wondering why you bothered speaking to me at all. It must seem like I just deny everything I don't want to hear and can't offer anything helpful—despite having thought about nothing else for the past ten years.'

Evan did a better job of controlling his face, but, privately, he thought that was a pretty succinct assessment.

'Of course not. It's been very useful.'

He didn't think that came out too well. His sincere voice needed some work too. Luckily she didn't ask him exactly *how* it had been useful.

'So what are you going to do next?'

'I think I need to talk to Ray Clements. And then perhaps Carl Hendricks.'

She was the first to offer her hand on the way out. He took it, a strangely formal gesture after so much raw emotion. She squeezed gently, rather than shaking.

'Thank you for persevering. I'm not sure I would have.'

He squeezed back.

'Thank you for being so honest. I'm not sure I would have.'

They stared at each other a few beats and then laughed together. He turned and almost ran down the path before things got out of hand.

CHAPTER 10

HE DIDN'T KNOW WHAT to think as he drove away. She was adamant her husband didn't do it, that he didn't run off with another woman either. He didn't know if he agreed with her or not. In the world he'd worked in until a few days ago, people lied and cheated on their partners and ran off with each other every day of the week. Did she really know him? She was probably right about the affair—in his experience most people had an inkling about what was going on or else why would they come to him.

But just because she got that part right didn't mean she was right about everything else as well. He couldn't just accept her word for it. He would need to look into it further, try to find out if any women went missing at about the same time. Even if he found out that he had run off with some other woman, it didn't mean he'd killed the boy. He had to agree with Linda on that score. It would take a special kind of monster to kill his own son in order to cover up something as run-of-the-mill as a bit on the side.

He still had Guillory's card. That would be the easiest way to find out. She might be able to give him the official take on the gossip and rumors Linda had told him about. He had more chance of developing a relationship with her. Faulkner was likely to be on the defense all the time.

He called her on his cell phone.

'Well, well, if it isn't Mr Peeper himself,' Guillory said after Evan identified himself.

'Mr *Ex*-Peeper.'

'Ex-Peeper, eh? Glad to hear it. Got any clients?'

'Ha ha.'

He felt her smile coming down the phone line. It didn't feel as if it was a cop on the other end.

'You liked that one, eh? So, you're working for Linda Clayton now are you?'

'That's right. And thanks for the introduction.'

'My pleasure.'

It wasn't just the routine reply. She sounded genuinely pleased that she was able to help.

'Pro bono, is it?'

'We haven't even talked about money.'

'That's good, because she hasn't got any. She might not believe her husband cut and ran and thinks he's dead, but the insurance company don't agree. No body, no life assurance payout. She's poorer than a church mouse.'

'It's not a problem.'

He meant it too.

'I know it's not. That's why I gave her your name. You're a man searching for your salvation. I don't think you'd charge her even if she was a Patty Hearst.'

He wondered how she'd managed to make such a good assessment in such a short time, supposed that was all part of her job.

'Okay, you made your point. I'm a sucker for a sob story. But I need some help.'

'And here I was thinking you just called me up to say thank you.'

'Thank you.'

'You're welcome . . . didn't we just do this? Anyway, what do you want to know?'

He told her about the rumors Linda had heard, and how she completely dismissed them.

'You're right, she won't have a bad word said about her husband. But anything like that should have been investigated at the time. All I remember is that one day he just wasn't around anymore. I don't recall anything about another woman.'

'I know it won't prove anything but it must be worth looking into. Besides, if he ran off with a single woman she probably wouldn't be listed as missing anyway.'

'No shit Sherlock, I'd never have worked that out.'

'Always happy to help.'

'Leave it with me, smartass. I'll see what I can dig up.'

He debated whether to ask the more delicate question that was on his mind. He didn't know her at all but she seemed pretty straight. What the hell.

'Can I ask you one more thing?' he said, immediately regretting it.

'Uh-oh. When somebody asks you if they can ask you something, instead of just coming straight out and asking it, you just know it's something they know they shouldn't be asking.'

She was right about that. He'd been about to ask her what she thought of Faulkner and his abilities. Now he decided not to. It could wait.

'You're right, no tongues on a first date. Let me know what you find out.'

He went to end the call when she interrupted him.

'For what it's worth, I think you're doing the right thing here. You reap what you sow. I bet you sleep better at night too.'

CHAPTER 11

EVAN DECIDED HE'D TALK to Ray Clements while he was waiting for Guillory to get back to him. He didn't think Clements would have a problem talking to him if he mentioned Linda's name. He no doubt thought of her as highly as she did him. Despite that he still decided not to call ahead and drove round to Clements' house, not far from where Linda lived. The house and yard were small but tidy and well looked after. They looked every bit like Evan expected a retired school teacher's house would look like.

As he pulled up, a large woman wearing too much makeup and heels totally inappropriate for her age came out the front door. Faulkner hadn't lied, she'd been hit repeatedly with the ugly stick. Her hair was scraped back so tightly, it stretched her skin taut over her face. He hated to think what happened when all that tension was released at bedtime.

'Mrs Clements—'

'You must be the private eye.' She looked him up and down in a way that made him feel that he didn't quite pass muster. 'Linda Clayton rang Ray, told him she'd hired someone to find out what happened to her husband and boy. You've got that grubby sort of look about you.'

He wasn't sure what she meant by that, didn't suppose she was being complimentary. Luckily, she was on her way out. His brief encounter with her gave him the impression she would have dominated any conversation he tried to have with her husband. He hadn't met the man, and already he was feeling sorry for him.

'Ray's inside. You go on in. I've got to go out.'

She left the door open, squeezed into her car and drove away. He knocked on the still open door, called inside.

Clements appeared from somewhere at the back of the house. He was tall and painfully thin with the beginnings of a stoop. He was the complete opposite of his wife. Evan was vaguely disappointed that he didn't have a neat row of pens tucked into his shirt pocket or leather patches on his elbows. At least he had a full head of mad scientist style silver hair.

'You must be Evan.' He stuck out a surprisingly large hand and shook energetically.

Evan was surprised by the firmness of his grip. He supposed he'd been expecting someone old and broken from the allegations made against him.

'Come on in. And call me Ray.'

'Word spreads fast.'

'You can't blame Linda. You're the first person to take her seriously for years. She told me you wanted to talk to me.'

Evan smiled to himself. He'd been right that Linda was busy lining up teams.

Clements led him through the house and out into the back yard. A couple of uncomfortable looking metal garden chairs sat on a deck at the back of the house. They sat down and Evan's suspicions were confirmed. They were as uncomfortable as they looked. It was a yard for working in, not relaxing, and it showed. Another immaculate lawn was surrounded by perfectly manicured shrubs and trees. There was a pond with a waterfall and Evan was disappointed again to see that there were no garden gnomes fishing in it.

'I hope you don't mind talking to me. I'm sure it'll resurrect some unpleasant memories.'

Clements shook his head, opened his arms wide.

'I've got nothing to hide. Unlike some people.'

He leant forward towards Evan in a conspiratorial way as he said it. It made Evan think of a large vulture inspecting the carcase of a dead elephant, deciding where to start.

'Besides, if there's any chance of finding out what happened, I'm more than happy to help.'

The guy seemed a bit too good to be true. And what was the *unlike some people* crack about? Perhaps Clements would turn out to be a better source of information. Evan leaned back to enjoy the warm afternoon sun on his face, then asked him to give his version of things.

'As far as I'm concerned there are two known facts and that's all. One, Daniel left my classroom same as usual, without a scratch on him and two, he was never seen again. Unfortunately, as far as some people were concerned, that made me the last person to see him alive. And, as we all know, two plus two equals five, or is it five hundred?'

'You're talking about Faulkner.'

'Who else? When you add the *testimony*'—he made a show of coughing into his hand—'of Carl Hendricks into the equation, supposedly proving that Daniel never left the campus, that was just about all Faulkner needed.' He raised his finger in the air in a eureka-style gesture. 'Except some evidence of course. The small matter of some *proof.* Or is that an unreasonable demand from a man whose life is on the line?'

Evan wondered if he'd taught drama at school.

'Faulkner said you didn't have an alibi.'

'Well, I must be guilty then. Just take me away.'

He jumped up and held out his wrists as if Evan was going to cuff them. Evan took the opportunity to get out of the uncomfortable chair himself.

'Or was I just unlucky to be the one person out of a hundred million other innocent people who don't go around with a verifiable alibi covering every minute of their day, who was asked for one.'

'He said you went for a drive.'

Clements let out a short, humorless laugh.

'That's right, while that scumbag Hendricks went to a strip club. They probably took the dried stains in his underwear as evidence he was really there. That, and the word of the tired old whore who'd been busy waving her syphilitic twat in his face all afternoon.'

A speck of saliva flew from his mouth and landed on Evan's chin. Evan tried to ignore it and not be obvious about wiping it away.

'At least he wasn't up to something really disgusting like *driving his car.*'

Evan was taken aback by the outburst. His mental image of what retired school teachers were like had been completely blown out of the water. Clements was clenching his jaw so hard by the time he finished, Evan was surprised he didn't crack a tooth.

'Faulkner also thought he'd caught me out in some huge, incriminating lie and cover up.'

'Giving Daniel a ride home a few times?'

'Yes. As you can see, we only live a few blocks away from each other.'

He took a deep breath, made a visible effort to relax his bunched shoulders. Then he set off towards the pond. Evan followed. Clements picked up a tub of fish food and started feeding the fish that had swarmed to the edge.

'It helps calm me down. Linda could be a bit strange at times. She had this thing about Daniel walking home. She was brought up on a farm, thought everyone should get lots of fresh air and exercise, that sort of thing. But you can take it too far.'

He cleared his throat and ran his bony hand through his hair, leaving little bits of fish food in it.

'So I used to drop him off now and then.' He cleared his throat noisily again. 'But there's no such thing as an innocent act of kindness, is there? There has to be something sinister going on. Some payment is required for the ride, a quid pro quo. And since young boys don't have much money, they have to pay in other ways. Q.E.fucking D.'

'And you didn't volunteer the information because you knew Faulkner would do exactly what he did do with it.'

'Exactly. People like Faulkner always like the easy answer. They get sent on a half-day profiling seminar in East Bumfuck, and suddenly they're Professor of Psychology at Harvard. Then they look at my wife and they look at me and you see their eyes narrow. You can actually see the wheels turning, see them thinking, 'Will you look at the size of her. And look at him, the skinny runt. I bet she makes his life hell at home. I bet he goes out and abuses little boys to make himself feel better. I bet he's got a *really* small pecker.' It's pathetic. It makes me sick.'

Evan felt a twinge of guilt for thinking the same thing—not the part about abusing little boys, just that his wife dominated him. It was too early to comment on his pecker.

Clements put the tub of fish food back down and stared absently into the dark water.

'Of course, it then looked much worse when it did come out.'

'How did it come out?'

Clements looked up and beamed at him.

'Guess.'

Evan thought about the whole situation. There was only really one explanation that he could be expected to guess.

'Hendricks?'

'Give the man a cigar!' Clements shouted, clapping his hands. 'First of all, he convinced Faulkner that Daniel didn't walk off campus, and then he tells him *I know someone who likes to give little boys a ride in his car*. You'd think he was trying to set me up.'

'What do you think about Hendricks' statement?'

'Carl Hendricks was and probably still is a disgusting, useless sack of shit. If we were talking about whether a naked woman walked past his bus unnoticed, that's a different matter.' His mouth curled into a sneer. 'She'd have tripped over his drooling tongue hanging down to the sidewalk. The way he looks at women in the street, I'm surprised he hasn't been arrested for jerking off in public. But one kid out of all the hundreds milling around? He didn't have a clue who passed his bus that, or any other, day.'

'Which became obvious when Faulkner switched his focus to the father.'

'Exactly. But it was far too late for me by then. Faulkner had me firmly in his sights. And it had been in all the papers. People start out standing by you, but then the doubts creep in, there's no smoke without fire. You can see it in their eyes.'

He looked down despondently. Evan understood exactly what it was like when people you thought were friends started to avoid you.

'There are also a lot of people who have so much faith in the police they think it must be true or why else would they be looking at you. A presumption of guilt, you could call it. Then there's all that unwelcome publicity for the school, of course. We need to punish the man who brought all this shit down on us.'

Clements had been picking at his fingernails the whole time. He stopped and stuffed his hands into his pockets.

'End result was, I lost my job. The next thing you know Faulkner has changed his mind and it's the father, not me. Sorry about your career, sorry about your life, you're free to go. Except you're not. Not in people's minds.'

There wasn't anything Evan could say to make him feel less bitter about the almost casual way his life had been destroyed as part and parcel of the investigation. Clements headed back up towards the house, then made a sharp right towards a plant that obviously required his immediate attention. Evan trailed behind him.

'What do you think about the theory that the father did it?'

Clements stopped and turned to face him.

'I think it's a crock of shit. I knew Robbie Clayton and I can guarantee he couldn't have hurt that boy. He wasn't perfect by a long stretch, but he adored that boy. He'd have done anything for him.'

'You say he wasn't perfect . . .'

'I'm sure you must have heard about the rumors that went around.'

Evan nodded, told him to go on.

'I know for a fact that Robbie sometimes had trouble keeping it in his pants. But that doesn't mean he killed his son because he caught him with another woman and then they ran off together. That would take a monster.'

'Why was Faulkner so convinced?'

Clements gave a small shrug, beats me.

'I can't say for sure. Most people like easy answers and half-baked solutions.'

The way he said it made Evan wonder if he was being put in the *most people* category. He got the impression that Clements thought he was back in school in front of an unusually dim class. He had that impatient, waiting-to-be-disappointed look on his face.

'And Faulkner likes it nice and easy, that's for sure. An expert in half-baked. More than that, it's no longer an embarrassing, unsolved double murder on his patch just before he retires. Now it's a nationwide manhunt and somebody else's problem. Much better all round. Not his fault when they come up with Jack Shit.'

'You really don't like him do you.'

'Can you blame me? He ruined my life. And his laziness ruined Linda's too.'

'Do you think Hendricks had anything to do with it?'

'Not really. He was a disgusting creep but it was the women he was after. You ask any of the women teachers who worked there back then. They couldn't stand him.'

'How did he manage to keep his job?'

'Beats me. Maybe he had friends in high places, or he had some kind of hold over someone.'

'So you don't think he was trying to point the finger at you to take the heat off him.'

'The heat was never on him, but no, I don't think that was it. I'm sure he thought he was just doing his civic duty, fine upstanding citizen that he is. What's sick is the obvious pleasure he got from watching what it did to me.'

Linda had said the exact same thing. The Clements-Clayton team were solid in their opinion of Hendricks. Evan found it ironic that the two people who had suffered most as a result of Hendricks' statement, also agreed that he wasn't responsible.

'Okay, forgetting Hendricks, what do you think happened?'

'I really don't know. I don't think anything happened to Daniel on campus. I think he walked out the gate like normal while Hendricks had his nose stuck in some stroke mag or something and didn't see him go past. I don't think he made it home. Something happened to him on the way and it had nothing to do with his father. A random attack by someone passing through most likely.'

'That doesn't give me a lot to go on, does it?'

Clements shook his head. 'I'm afraid it doesn't, but it's only my opinion. I could be wrong.' He shrugged as if to say *it has been known to happen*.

Evan was about to leave it at that when he remembered what Clements had first said.

'You implied earlier you thought *some people* had something to hide. What did you mean?'

Clements considered him carefully. Evan got the feeling he was being assessed for his level of trustworthiness. He put on his best open and approachable face. It worked, he passed the test.

Clements leaned in conspiratorially again. Dropped his voice to a whisper. He didn't actually put his hand up to his mouth, but Evan was sure he wanted to. He looked around to see who might be listening in, hiding in the bushes, but there was no-one.

'This didn't come from me, but I think Faulkner was hiding something. Maybe he still is.' He leaned back and held up his hands. 'I'm not saying he had anything to do with Daniel's disappearance, but I always felt he was hiding something, some guilty secret. In fact, I got the feeling long before any of this happened. That's not just me talking out of spite, because of what he did to my life, either.'

'I don't suppose you've got any idea what it might be?'

'No. It was just a feeling.'

'Did you ever say anything to anyone?'

Clements looked at him like he really was an idiot.

'Are you serious? Who would I talk to? Besides, who's going to listen to a man accused of abducting a child? A de facto pervert.'

Evan thanked him for his time and left him to his plants and fish and seething resentment. No doubt his wife would bear the brunt of his anger and frustration when she returned, but she looked like she was more than able to take care of herself.

CHAPTER 12

EVAN CAME AWAY WITH something very different to what he expected when he went in. He'd been hoping Clements would have some ideas about what might have happened, but he'd gotten nothing new that he hadn't heard before, just a different slant. One thing that he was picking up loud and clear was how much everyone involved hated each other. And then the unexpected revelation that Clements thought Faulkner was hiding something. He didn't know what to make of that. Was there something that Clements had picked up on? Or was he just being vindictive, despite what he'd said?

Admittedly, Faulkner hadn't wanted to talk to him at first. But the case hadn't been his finest hour so why would he? What kind of a secret could he have that might have any bearing on the case? Besides, if Clements' intuition was right, it pre-dated the disappearances anyway. Evan certainly didn't think Faulkner could have committed the crime, but was he involved in some way beyond his police duties?

His thoughts were interrupted by his cell phone. It was

Guillory.

'That was quick'

He felt her smiling into the phone.

'Well, we've got these new-fangled computer things here now, so I asked one of the grown-ups to show me how to use them—'

'Grown-ups in the police department? Whatever next?'

'Who knows, we might even offer you a job.'

'Okay, okay. I'm assuming you found something.'

He heard her tapping away two-finger style in the background.

'Okay, here we go. Don't jump to any conclusions, but there was a woman called Barbara Schneider who went missing about the same time Robbie Clayton disappeared. Reported missing by her husband, Max, and never heard of again. Right sort of age for Clayton to be fooling around with too.'

'So what happened?'

'Nothing happened. People go missing every day of the week. If it's an adult and there's nothing to suggest any foul play, then what do we care if some woman gets sick of her husband and runs off with some guy with a bigger johnson.'

'Nobody made any connections?'

'That's just it, isn't it? You'd be *making* connections that weren't there. Fabricating them yourself.'

'You know what I meant. Did anybody consider the possibility that these disappearances were connected?'

'What, like Robbie Clayton ran off with Mrs Schneider and his little boy and they're all playing happy families in California or wherever. And none of them ever showed up on the radar again.'

'It's possible. Was it even considered at the time?'

'You'd have to ask Matt Faulkner. There's nothing on the files to suggest it.'

'Do you think he'd tell me?'

'Depends if you ask nicely. That's not something you're very good at, is it?'

'I don't know what you mean. You've got to admit it's hard to ask anything without it looking like I'm judging him with the benefit of hindsight.'

'I can't help you there. And before you ask, no, I'm not going to ask for you. You're a big boy now. Besides, he'd know it came from you anyway.'

Evan wondered if there was anything else he could get out of her.

'Do you know if the husband still lives around here?'

'No idea. Anything else? Do you want me to pick up your groceries for you as well? I mean, it's not like I've got anything else to do.'

'What about the address where he used to live?'

'Yeah, I can give you that, seeing as it's in the phone book. Just don't go in heavy handed, okay.'

'Like Ryder you mean.'

'Do you want the address or not?'

He took down the address. She promised to let him know if she found out anything else and ended the call. At least it felt like she was on his side. She was responsible for setting it all in motion after all. He felt that gave him some leeway in what he could ask her. Whether he'd ever get to the point of being able to sound her out about Faulkner was another matter.

CHAPTER 13

HE WAS BUILDING QUITE a list of people he wanted to talk to and none of them were going to be easy conversations. Max Schneider was likely to be the easiest. He was only going to be digging up painful memories with him. Hendricks and his next conversation with Faulkner were going to be a lot more difficult.

He'd also like to eliminate the Clayton-Schneider liaison line of enquiry. He didn't want to have to take that back to Linda Clayton. It would completely destroy what she had left of her life. He didn't need any more of that kind of thing on his conscience. This new direction was supposed to give him a chance to do some good and help people.

Max Schneider lived in a small farmhouse a couple of miles out of town. At one time it must have owned all the land surrounding it. That had all been sold off long ago. There was an old pickup rusting in the yard and the whole place had a run-down feel to it. Evan could understand any woman wanting to run off with another man to get away. Or she might just be buried under all the junk in the back yard.

A man in his late fifties or early sixties answered the door. He was short and wiry with a completely bald head that shone as if it had just been polished. He had the large, bulbous nose of a heavy drinker, and peered up at Evan from under some of the bushiest eyebrows Evan had ever seen. If this was Schneider, he had clearly been a lot older than his wife who would only now be early forties if she was still alive. Did that make it any more likely that she ran off with a younger man? If only you could rely on all those preconceived ideas, life would be so easy.

'Max Schneider?'

'Yes, that's me.'

He had a faint German accent. He hadn't been born anywhere around here, that was for sure. It was only Evan's good manners that stopped him from stepping backwards as a strong smell of garlic on Schneider's breath caught him full in the face.

That would make anyone run away.

Schneider looked pleased to see him.

'Come in, come in. This way please.'

He led Evan down the narrow hallway to the kitchen, which had that peculiar smell of over-cooked cabbage that old people's houses have. Evan was surprised at Schneider's welcome. Linda hadn't phoned him and told him to expect a visit, but the man was obviously expecting him. Schneider pointed at the washing machine.

'There it is. Piece of Japanese crap. I knew I should have bought German.'

He looked around at Evan, his eyes narrowing.

'Where are your tools?'

Evan almost laughed out loud.

'I'm sorry Mr Schneider, there's been a misunderstanding. I'm not here to fix your washing machine.'

'No? Then why are you here?'

'I'd like to ask you a few questions.'

Schneider looked crestfallen although Evan couldn't really see why. From the look and faintly sour smell of his clothes, he didn't look like a man who did his laundry on a daily basis. Maybe the machine had been out of service for a month or two.

'Are you sure you can't fix this?' he asked plaintively.

Evan ignored his plea.

'I'm working for Linda Clayton, looking into the disappearance of her son and husband.'

Evan watched Schneider carefully for any signs of recognition. The name meant nothing to him, that much was clear. Either that or he was a lot better than Evan at concealing his emotions.

'Linda Claxton? Never heard of her. Why would I be able to help you?'

Either he hadn't heard any of the rumors or he was being deliberately obtuse. His mood had taken a marked turn for the worse.

'It's Clayton, not Claxton. They disappeared at the same time your wife did.'

Schneider looked at him as if he was crazy.

'My wife? What wife? I've never been married in my life. What are you talking about, you stupid boy?'

The way that he peered up through his eyebrows was disconcerting. Evan reckoned there was a very real possibility that the cantankerous old man was just plain nuts. The other alternative was that he had blocked the tragedy from his mind.

'Ten years ago, you reported your wife missing to the police.'

'Pah! How could I do that when I never had a wife?' he yelled, giving Evan another generous dose of second-hand garlic.

'So you never reported anyone missing?'

Schneider's eyes positively bulged as if someone was throttling him.

'Did I say that? Did I? I said I never reported my wife missing. Don't you listen to anything?'

Evan decided to try a different tack.

'Have you ever reported *anyone* missing to the police?'

'Ja, of course. My sister. Barbara. Who do you think? Are you here to find my sister?'

'That's right Mr Schneider. I'm here to investigate Barbara's disappearance.'

There was every chance the old fool would think he'd only reported it last week. If Evan didn't mention Linda Clayton's name again he doubted Schneider would remember it.

'Good. About time too.'

He nodded vigorously, happy that he was finally about to get some answers, even if he wasn't going to get his washing machine fixed. If he was given the choice, Evan reckoned Schneider would opt to have his washing machine fixed.

'Can you tell me what happened?'

'It started to make this funny noise.' He made a strange sound in his throat. 'No, more like this.' He made another noise that he was equally unhappy with. 'No, that's not it either—'

'I meant what happened to your sister.'

'She disappeared.'

He made another attempt at the noise. He was determined to get it right.

Evan waited but that seemed to be all Schneider had to say about his sister. He thought about calling Tom Jacobson—he had a lot of experience pulling teeth.

'Do you have any ideas about what might have happened to her?'

Schneider's eyes bulged again.

'Why would I call you if I knew that? I don't know what is wrong with you young people these days.'

Evan knew exactly what was wrong with this old person. He was having serious doubts about the reliability of anything he might say. He decided to ask what should be a fairly straightforward question.

'Do you have a photograph? Of Barbara,' he added quickly, to avoid Schneider running off to fetch a photograph of his washing machine, or maybe the Führer, or whatever else was dear to his heart.

Schneider nodded. He walked over and picked up a framed photograph sitting on the shelf, thrust it at Evan. A good-looking blond smiled back at him as he took it. The police report was obviously wrong—there was no way on earth this woman could have been married to the lunatic currently standing in front of him, looking up at him expectantly, as if he was about to pull Barbara out of his pocket, now that Schneider had performed his side of the bargain and supplied a photograph.

'She was so beautiful,' Schneider said. 'Such nice'—he cupped his hands and squeezed the air as if fondling a pair of breasts—'too.'

Evan looked down at the photograph again but it was only a head and shoulders shot. Looking at the photograph had a profound effect on Schneider. It was as if he'd been drunk and now he was suddenly stone cold sober. He'd regained control of his faculties for the moment. Evan wondered how long it would last.

'She knew it too. I had to beat the men off with a stick.'

He swiped the air with an imaginary switch, made Evan wonder if it was only the men who'd been beaten.

'But she wasn't too picky. Our parents were very strict with her. When they died she just let loose. Out every night. So many different men. She could have settled down with any of them. But she was having too much fun playing the field. And then she disappeared. Bitch.'

The last word was said so quietly Evan wasn't sure he heard it properly.

Had he just called her a bitch?

'Do you think she ran off with one of them?'

Schneider looked at him sadly and shook his head.

'That's what I want to believe, but it's not true. I was a lot older than her but we still got on too well for her to run off like that and never make any kind of contact. I know I tried to keep her under control, but we never had a fight over it or anything like that.'

He sat back down at the kitchen table and rested his head in his hands. Evan looked down at the shining bald dome and wondered what it must be like to be bald. There were a number of strange sticky patches that looked like glue dotted around his head. He choked back a laugh as he realized Schneider normally had a toupée glued to his head. Presumably he didn't wear it in the house so that he felt the benefit of it when he went out. Perhaps that was what he wanted to wash so desperately.

'I didn't make a habit of rummaging through her underwear drawer or anything like that'—he looked up sharply to make sure that Evan wasn't smirking—'but it didn't look to me like any of her clothes were missing.'

The comment made Evan think of his own situation. When Sarah had disappeared, he'd done the same thing. Anyone would.

And he'd realized that he couldn't say for sure if any of her clothes were missing or not. The discovery had shocked and dismayed him. What else had he been oblivious to? Had the reason for her disappearance been under his nose the whole time? He didn't know if it made him stupid or insensitive. Probably both.

'Are you listening to me?'

Schneider jumped out of his seat, his voice an angry bark, like a dog on a chain snapping at Evan, driving away his morose thoughts.

'Yes, I'm listening,' Evan said equally curtly, fed up with Schneider's rudeness. 'So you think something must have happened to her.'

'It's got to be one or the other. Either she hated my guts and I never knew it, or she's dead.'

After only ten minutes in his company, the first option seemed the odds-on favorite. But it was the second one that made Evan stop and think. The word hung in the air. It was the first time in the whole case that anyone had come out and said it. Up until then everyone had simply *disappeared*. Now it was out in the open, it brought it home to him that there was very little chance of a happy ending. The best he could hope to provide was the relief that comes from finally *knowing*.

'It's not too difficult to imagine, is it?' Schneider said. 'Some married man gets her in the family way . . .'

He stretched out his hands and gripped an imaginary pair of hips. Pulled them towards him, thrusting his pelvis back and forward, grunting with an obscene leer on his face.

It was all Evan could do to keep a straight face. The guy should be in an asylum.

'Was there anyone in particular that she was seeing?'

Schneider stopped his gyrations, thought for a moment. He nodded to himself.

'Actually, I think there was, just before she disappeared. I don't know who it was.'

'Did you tell this to the police back then?'

At first Evan thought he hadn't heard. He was staring absently at the table top. Then he gave a small shrug, sat back down again.

'I can't remember. I'd have told them if they asked. Why wouldn't I?' He grunted as if someone had kicked him. 'Not that it would have made any difference. Useless imbeciles.'

Evan hoped he didn't sound too much like Schneider when he talked about Sarah's disappearance. Schneider was still picking through the dregs of his memory.

'I think perhaps I talked to someone called Fukner.'

Evan coughed into his hand to hide a laugh. He couldn't take much more of this nutty old man. He wasn't sure whether it was his accent, or whether Schneider was just being offensive.

'You mean Faulkner?'

'That's what I said, wasn't it? Are you deaf too?'

Schneider was lapsing back into his quarrelsome self. Time was running out. He wasn't going to get much more out of him.

'What did he say?'

'He said he couldn't waste his time chasing after some low-rent whore.'

Evan was glad that he didn't chew gum because he would surely have choked on it.

'He actually said that?'

'Well, no. Not exactly,' Schneider admitted, 'but that's what he was thinking.'

'How do you know that?'

Schneider looked at him like he was dealing with a retard.

'I could see it in his eyes. He looked at me like I was some stupid old man making it all up.'

Evan was still holding the framed photograph. He set it down carefully on the table. Schneider scowled at it. Suddenly he back-handed it violently, smashing the glass with the force of the blow, sent it flying across the room. A small trickle of blood appeared on the back of his hand. He lifted his hand to his mouth, sucked noisily on the cut. Evan went over to where the picture lay to pick up the pieces. Schneider hissed at him like a bad-tempered snake.

'Leave it there. Where it belongs.'

He slammed his fist down onto the table, a misogynistic curse muttered under his breath. It sounded to Evan a lot like *filthy whore.*

The sudden outburst of violence and the venom in Schneider's voice surprised him. He felt guilty for invading Schneider's privacy, for digging up memories that were capable of producing such rage. But it also made him wonder if Schneider had been completely truthful about the happy home life he'd lived with his sister.

It was clear there'd been some sexual interest on his part. Hopefully it hadn't been reciprocated. You never knew in these rural areas. And it was obvious that it was him who thought she was a whore. Maybe he'd inherited his parents' strictness. Or perhaps he was just jealous because he wasn't getting what the other guys were. She might be locked in the basement as they spoke, desperately trying to get Evan's attention. Or buried in the back yard for refusing to play Doctors and Nurses.

One thing was for sure, he wasn't about to get anything useful out of Schneider now. Not that he'd gotten anything useful so far, apart from prima facie evidence that anyone living with Max Schneider would run off at the first opportunity.

Evan left him alone with his twisted memories and his dreams of a working washing machine.

CHAPTER 14

IT WAS GOOD TO get back outside into the fresh air and sunlight. Schneider's house had been oppressive and it smelled like the drains were backed up. That was probably the problem with his washing machine.

Evan got in his car, opened all the windows to let the wind blow through. Leaning back, he closed his eyes, wondered what to do next. His phone rang. He thought it would be Guillory but he didn't recognize the number when he looked at the screen.

'I've been doing a bit of research into you,' Faulkner's voice said down the line. 'Not exactly a career to be proud of. Let's hope Linda Clayton doesn't end up like your last client.'

Evan groaned. He could have done without any of this. Okay, he wanted to talk to Faulkner again, but not now, and not on Faulkner's terms. And even though Faulkner was just trying to rile him, the dig about Stanton still hurt.

'We've all got to make a living,' he said lamely.

'Yes, and when you couldn't make one doing a proper job, you decided to stick your zoom lens up—'

Faulkner sounded drunk.

'At least I'm not drunk in the middle of the afternoon.'

'Up yours, sonny.'

The front door to Schneider's house suddenly opened. Schneider's bald head poked out. He saw Evan's car, headed towards it, his hand in the air. Evan groaned to himself. He couldn't deal with fractious Faulkner on the phone and nutty Schneider at the same time. He put the car into gear, pulled away slowly. Behind him Schneider broke into a run, shouting excitedly. He'd remembered how the noise sounded.

'What was that?' Faulkner said.

'Nothing. Anyway, now we've got the pleasantries out the way, why don't we see if we can have a normal conversation?'

'Conversation? Let me look that up in my dictionary. Here we go. Conversation, as in some interfering individual, let's call him Mr Evan P-for-Peeper Buckley, bugs the hell out of some other person and asks him a whole bunch of questions that he's not entitled to have the answers to.'

Evan looked in his mirror, saw that Schneider had given up and gone back inside. He pulled onto the shoulder and stopped.

'Sounds like we've got the exact same edition. There's just one thing. I'm not bugging you, you called me.'

Faulkner laughed.

'You know, I can't help myself, but I actually like you.'

'Is that why you're calling me up? To tell me how much you like me? Or just to give me your considered opinion on my choice of career? Sounds to me like you've been discussing me with Detective Donut.'

'Who? Oh, Ryder.' He laughed again. 'No, I called to find out why you didn't come back to me if you needed more answers.'

Gotcha.

Obviously, he'd gotten under Faulkner's skin more than he'd realized. He grinned down the phone.

'So that's it. You can't keep the green-eyed monster in its cage.'

'I don't know what you're talking about,' Faulkner said defensively. 'But you should have come to me instead of Guillory.'

'Why? Guillory started me on this. And she's still on the force so she's got access to more resources than you.'

'That's what you think. Besides, she wasn't even there at the time. You need to get it from the horse's mouth.'

'The horse's what?'

'Do you want me to help you or not?'

Evan didn't think for a minute that Faulkner had suddenly decided to be über-helpful. More like he wanted to control the information Evan had access to.

'Is this an invitation to come over and have you fill in all the gaps for me?'

'Why not? Tell you what, let's reinforce all those preconceived notions you've got in your thick head and I'll tell you all about it over a beer. I'm not drunk, but it sounds like a plan to me.'

'Okay, where do you want to go?'

'Well, I'm afraid that's where the old clichés end. We're not going to some dive of a bar to drink cheap beer. I like up-market cocktail lounges. Especially when you're paying. And since I'm going to be doing most of the drinking, why don't you come by and pick me up.'

Evan was happy to go along with that. There was a chance Faulkner would loosen up once he had a few drinks and he'd be in a sensible condition to take it all in. He would have liked a bit more time, so he suggested picking Faulkner up about seven the following day. But Faulkner wasn't having any of it and Evan reluctantly agreed to pick him up that evening.

AFTER HE FINISHED ON the phone with Faulkner, he called Guillory to give her an update on Schneider.

'So what have you found out, Mr P?'

It looked like Guillory wasn't going to let the peeper moniker drop. At least there wasn't any malice in her tone.

'First off, Max Schneider is a certifiable fruitcake.'

'Okay, that's useful. I'll be sure to make a note of that. Anything else we can actually use?'

'It seems Barbara Schneider was Max Schneider's sister, not his wife.'

'What makes you say that?'

'That's what Schneider told me.'

'That would be Schneider the fruitcake? I'm sure that's not right. Let me check.'

He heard her tapping away in her two-finger style at her keyboard. They ought to send her on a typing course. The tapping stopped.

'No, she was definitely his wife. That's what it says right here in the report.'

'He gave me some story about her running wild after their parents died. Living it up, lots of different men.'

'Uh-huh. That doesn't mean she wasn't married to him.'

He could have kicked himself. He felt stupid for not thinking about the possibility himself, especially given what he'd spent the last five years doing. She didn't miss it either, her amusement oozing down the phone line.

'I would have thought your career before you became Mr *Ex*-Peeper would have alerted you to that possibility.'

'Sorry, that life's been expunged from my memory.'

'It sounds like he's invented some story to make himself feel better, soothe his injured pride. Tell yourself something for long enough and you come to believe it.'

'That's possible. As I said, he's not firing on all cylinders.'

'It could also explain her disappearance if there was another man. Either that or she's buried in the back yard.'

'He got quite angry at the end. Called her a filthy whore, smashed a picture of her.'

'Really? I might just take a look into that.'

But not Daniel Clayton?

He wondered why not as he ended the call. Did that mean she thought it was a dead duck and she'd just put him onto it to give him something to do? On the other hand, things were getting more complicated, the more he dug into them. He'd been hoping to be able to eliminate the running-off-with-another-woman line of enquiry but now it was growing legs.

CHAPTER 15

THE TIME HAD COME to talk to Hendricks. Evan realized he'd been putting the moment off, but when he thought about it he wasn't sure why. He'd picked up all the animosity towards him coming from Ray Clements and Linda. Subconsciously he was siding with them because Hendricks sounded like such a degenerate. More preconceived ideas. He couldn't argue with Faulkner about that.

He wanted to talk to Hendricks before he talked to Faulkner again, so he didn't have much choice but to drive straight out there. Hendricks' place surprised the hell out of him. All he knew about him was that he'd been the school bus driver. If he'd been asked, he would have said that Hendricks probably lived in a trailer park like Faulkner.

What he actually lived in was a beautiful old farmhouse surrounded by three or four acres of land with a couple of well-kept barns standing off to the side. There was a hand-painted sign that read *Beau Terre* and an old-fashioned farmhouse porch which wrapped expansively around the house. It was about as different to

Schneider's farmhouse as you could imagine. Either he'd made a ton of money selling drugs to the kids on the bus, or he'd inherited it.

Hendricks himself was sitting in a rocker on the porch enjoying the late afternoon sun, looking like God was in his heaven and all was right with the world. He had a pinched, bony face with a scar across the bridge of his nose, which had been badly set at some time in the past. He had a mass of black and gray hair that made Evan think there must have been a sale of wire wool at the dollar store. The sybaritic smile plastered on his thin lips made Evan want to slap him before he'd even said a word.

'You must be Buckley,' he said, as Evan climbed the steps up to the porch. 'Have a seat. Can I get you anything?' There was a pitcher of iced tea on the table beside him and two glasses. He waved towards them.

Evan declined the offer.

'How do you know who I am?'

'Matt Faulkner called me. Said you were working for that crazy woman Clayton, digging all that shit up again and would probably want to talk to me.'

His lazy, drawling way of speaking just reinforced the air of smug contentment, made Evan want to wipe it off with the back of his hand.

'He's right. I'm just surprised he called to—'

'Warn me? Is that what you were about to say?' He rolled forward in his rocker, spread his arms, palms towards Evan, in a universal gesture of openness. 'We haven't got anything to hide.'

A large white cat with a black patch on its head trotted up the steps, then jumped onto Hendricks' lap. He stroked it as it started to clean, rubbing its ears.

'Have we, Armstrong?'

It purred contentedly. Although he wasn't a cat person, Evan had to admit it was a good-looking cat. He wasn't sure which one of them was the most self-satisfied.

'I'm sure you haven't.'

He wasn't sure of that at all, didn't know how to take Faulkner calling ahead, either. *Warn* was exactly the right word to use. He asked Hendricks to give him his view of the events.

'Personally, I think it was Clements.'

It made a refreshing change for someone to say something other than they didn't have a clue.

'That doesn't surprise me. Clements doesn't have a good word for you either.'

'I'm sure he doesn't. But Ray Clements is a bitter old man and he's lucky he's not in jail if you ask me.'

'You seem pretty sure about it. What do you think happened?'

'Like I said at the time, the boy never left the campus. I don't care what anybody says about me not paying attention and letting him slip past. It didn't happen. That boy never left the campus except in Clements' car.'

He jabbed the table with his middle finger as if that clinched it.

'What about the fact that Faulkner ended up believing Daniel made it past you without being seen and it was the father who did it?'

'Just because Matt Faulkner called me up to *warn* me, doesn't mean we're so tight I can't disagree with him. The boy did *not* walk past my bus without me seeing him.'

'And that automatically makes it Clements, does it?'

'He tried to hide the fact that he'd given him a ride before. Why would a man with nothing to hide do that?'

'And it was you who told Faulkner about it.'

He nodded emphatically.

'You got that right. I think most people would agree it was the appropriate thing to do in the circumstances.'

The self-righteous look on his face made Evan want to punch it.

'He lost his job as a result. Over an accusation that was never proven.'

'No, he didn't. He lost his job because they wanted to get rid of him. This gave them the excuse they needed to do it.'

'Why do you say that?'

Hendricks poured himself another glass of iced tea. This time Evan accepted the offer of a drink. He wanted to see if the other glass had been used. He asked Hendricks again why he thought the school had wanted to get rid of Clements.

'Because he was a pervert, a pederast.'

'You mean a pedophile.'

'No, a pederast—there's a difference. He only liked boys. Why else would you give young boys a ride in your car?'

'Because he was a nice guy and the kid lived a block away?'

Hendricks gave him a scathing look.

'Doesn't happen if you ask me. You can see he's a pervert just looking at him.'

It wasn't even worth asking him what he meant, what particular facial or bodily characteristics marked you out as a pervert. In fact, Clements and Hendricks looked quite similar, particularly the hair.

'Were there other boys apart from Daniel?'

'Probably.'

'Did you ever see any of them?'

'No. Doesn't mean it didn't happen.'

Evan had heard enough of Hendricks' prejudices, put a harder edge on his voice.

'Was there any proof? Did anyone make an accusation? Or were they just as prejudiced as you?'

'I'm not prejudiced. I'm just saying what everyone knew.'

'According to you.'

'Whatever.'

It was obvious Evan wasn't going to get anything remotely objective out of Hendricks. That didn't surprise him. The trouble was, Hendricks' smug confidence in his own bigotry was really grating on him. It was time to wipe the smile off his face.

'Why did you take a job as a school bus driver?'

It worked. Hendricks jerked upright in his chair and glowered at Evan. Evan saw him wince as the cat leapt from his lap digging its claws into his leg as it went.

That's more like it.

'You better not be suggesting it's because I like little kids.'

Evan gave him a supercilious look.

'Why not? I like kids, just not in the way you're thinking. Why is it people like you automatically assume if you like children, you want to have sex with them?'

'I don't think that.'

Most of the smugness was gone now. The irritating smile had been replaced by an unpleasant curl of the lip.

'Yes you do. That's exactly what you think about Ray Clements.'

'Yeah, well he's different. I just needed a job.'

The comment had an unfortunate ring of familiarity about it. Evan had said pretty much the same thing to Faulkner to justify what he'd been doing.

'Do you know why Linda Clayton made Daniel walk home?'

The question threw Hendricks as Evan had hoped. His eyes narrowed as he leaned back in the rocker and contemplated him. He could see something coming, something he wasn't going to like, but he didn't know what it was. His voice was heavy with sarcasm when he answered.

'Because exercise is good for you?'

'No. Because she didn't like the look of you. She didn't want Daniel on your bus.'

He had no idea what made him say it. Linda hadn't said any such thing. He wanted to try to rattle Hendricks to see what happened.

'Bullshit.'

'If you say so.'

There was no dismissive *whatever* this time. All trace of smugness had been scrubbed from his face.

'You're making that up.'

'I would say, ask her yourself. Apart from the fact that she wouldn't talk to you if her life depended on it.'

He would have liked to carry on antagonizing Hendricks all night but he had to get away to meet Faulkner.

'You don't work there any more, do you?'

Hendricks relaxed slightly at the change of topic.

'No, I retired just after the kid went missing. It was a stressful time all round. Lots of bad feeling. I had this place and didn't really need the job so I quit.'

'I thought you just said you needed a job.'

There was a flash of anger in Hendricks' eyes. He was annoyed that he'd slipped up, but it didn't last long.

'What I meant was I wanted a job to give me something

worthwhile to do. Keep me out of trouble.'

He smirked at his own poor joke. He didn't say how it was that he came to own such a large property or that he didn't need to work. He could only have been in his late forties at the time it happened. Probably thought it wasn't any of Evan's business.

Evan made a show of looking around, nodded appreciatively.

'I can see you're doing okay. It's a nice place you've got here.'

'Sure is. Come on, I'll give you a look around. You can check the barns for bodies if you like,' he snickered.

Evan couldn't decide if he was jumping at the opportunity to change the subject completely, or he was simply a proud home owner. He had to admit he was just a bit jumpy as Hendricks showed him around. It was stupid but he had visions of Hendricks hitting him over the head with an axe handle and locking him in one of the barns. He didn't relax until he was back in his car and driving away.

Once again, he had the feeling that the more he talked to people, the more complicated it all became. All he had learned from his visit was that Hendricks owned a very nice house and he blamed Clements. Everybody was pointing the finger at everybody else. Hendricks might have been blaming Clements because the alternative—an innocent Clements—made him look stupid for sending the police barking up the wrong tree. Or he might have been using Clements to take the heat off himself.

Evan also had the feeling that there had been someone else with Hendricks just before he arrived. He was pretty sure the glass he'd drunk from had already been used. Unless Hendricks had OCD issues that made him use a fresh glass every time he refreshed his drink, he'd had a visitor who hadn't wanted to be seen there.

CHAPTER 16

EVAN GOT TO FAULKNER'S trailer just before seven. Faulkner wasn't ready so he had to wait around while he pulled on a pair of expensive-looking cowboy boots.

'I take it we're going to some shitkicker bar after all,' Evan said, nodding at the boots.

'Shitkicker my ass. These are alligator Luccheses, number five toe with a walking heel. Best boots you can buy.'

'According to Roy Rogers.'

Faulkner tossed an empty beer bottle to him.

'Why don't you do something useful and put that in the trash,'

Evan took it through to the kitchen, dropped it in the trash can. One wall of the kitchen was covered with more photographs, most of them of Faulkner's wife. A lot of them were duplicates of the ones in the living room—the two of them together on vacation and the ones of her with her parents.

'That's her with her folks,' Faulkner said joining him. 'I thought it seemed appropriate putting those up in here, a woman's place being in the kitchen and all.'

He seemed to have completely forgotten that he'd told Evan the exact same thing the previous day.

THEY WENT TO A noisy cocktail bar called Minge or Minx or something like that. It wasn't Evan's kind of place at all. He was surprised Faulkner chose it. They sat up at the bar and he ordered an over-priced beer. Faulkner started with a Margarita. The place was heaving and the music was way too loud, but Faulkner seemed to be enjoying it. Further down the bar a young woman in a pretty, pale pink dress was having a very public argument with her boyfriend. The guy said something and laughed. The girl stood up and slapped his face hard before storming out. Evan heard the slap above the music. It made his eyes water just listening to it.

'Ouch,' Faulkner said, watching the girl all the way to the door. 'I felt that.'

'I went out to see Carl Hendricks today. You called him and told him I was coming,'

Faulkner stopped rubbernecking, turned to face him.

'Is that a problem?'

'No. I'd just like to know why you did it. You didn't call Ray Clements.'

'True, but I knew the minute you'd finished with Linda Clayton, she'd give him a call. I thought it was only fair to give Jason the same advance warning.'

Evan leaned towards him, straining to hear.

'Who?'

'Carl Hendricks. Isn't that who we're talking about?'

'You said Jason.'

'No, I said Carl. You must have misheard. The music's way too loud in here. I don't know why you chose it.'

'Whatever.' Despite the noise, he was positive he hadn't misheard. 'You called him up so he could get his story ready.'

He caught Faulkner staring steadily at him in the mirror behind the counter. The dim—sorry, mood—lighting made it difficult to read his eyes. Was that all part of the plan? Picking this place so that Evan couldn't see or hear him properly.

'He doesn't need to. His story hasn't changed in ten years as you probably found out.'

Faulkner finished his drink and ordered another. Evan hoped he got something useful out of him because it was going to cost him an arm and a leg.

'Let me take a stab at what you found out from Clements and Hendricks,' Faulkner said. 'Clements hates Hendricks and Hendricks hates him back. How'd I do?'

'You could have told me that earlier and saved me two journeys.'

'You wouldn't have believed me. You're dead set on re-inventing the wheel. Who am I to stand in your way?'

'Why do they hate each other?'

'The original reason? Who knows, but I don't think it's got anything to do with the case. Just one of those things.'

'Hendricks said the school wanted to get rid of Clements before all this happened. That he was a pedophile, sorry, a pederast.'

'That's just Hendricks trying to cause trouble. Nothing new there. Besides, how would the school bus driver know what the school was planning anyhow?'

'True, but why would he want to cause trouble for Clements. He already helped lose him his job.'

'Because Clements helped him lose his.'

'He said he quit.'

'He would, wouldn't he? Clements didn't take all this lying down. He kicked up a real shitstorm, started spreading rumors about Hendricks to discredit his story. It all got very acrimonious. The school got sick of it all and kicked them both out.'

'Why didn't you investigate Hendricks?'

'We talked to him along with everyone else.'

'But you didn't give him the treatment Clements got.'

'There was no reason to. He didn't give the kid rides home in his car and keep it secret. Besides, Clements was badmouthing him, but all he was really saying was he had his head up his ass. Nobody was accusing him of anything, apart from being a totally useless piece of shit.'

'Still—'

Faulkner swiveled on his stool to face Evan. He studied him with hard, gray-blue eyes. With his steel gray hair and well-preserved physique, Evan reckoned he did pretty well with the women in here. He was a bit too old for the cougars but he probably did okay.

'How old are you son?'

'Thirty-two. Why?'

'Because when all this happened, I already had more years on the force than you've graced this planet with your existence. And my gut told me he wasn't a threat.'

'Your gut could've been wrong.'

Faulkner nodded in agreement.

'Maybe it could, at that. And when you're old enough to wear long pants, maybe we'll have that discussion. Luckily you're old enough to buy a drink.'

He pushed his empty glass towards Evan.

Evan wasn't happy with Faulkner's answer but he was going to have to leave it for the time being. If he pushed Faulkner too hard, especially after a few drinks, he'd either get angry or clam up.

After he'd ordered the next round, he changed the subject to a less confrontational topic before bringing up Schneider.

'How come Hendricks can afford such a big place?'

Faulkner stiffened almost imperceptibly but Evan caught it.

What the hell was that about?

'No idea. Maybe he won the lottery.'

'Has he always lived there?'

'I don't think so. I think he moved into town a couple of years before all this happened.'

Evan wanted to push it further but he was getting the feeling all Faulkner's answers were going to be negative. He suddenly remembered what Clements had said about Faulkner hiding something. Could this be what he meant?

'There's something else I wanted to ask about.'

Faulkner opened his eyes wide in mock amazement.

'No kidding?'

'Do you remember anything about a woman called Barbara Schneider? She went missing around the same time?'

'Not particularly. Should I?'

'There were rumors going around that Robbie Clayton ran off with another woman. Some of them even say that they killed the boy because he found them out.'

Faulkner was paying more attention now. Evan carried on.

'You thought Clayton took off, this woman disappeared at the same time. According to her husband she was playing around with other men. It all fits.'

'Most things do if you force them hard enough. You talked to the husband?'

'Yeah. He says he talked to someone at the time called Fukner. Was there anyone by that name in the department?'

'Don't be a smart ass. I don't remember him.'

Evan laughed. 'You wouldn't forget him. He's nutty as a fruit cake.' He made a circling motion with his finger at the side of his head. 'There's a good chance he made it all up.'

'Even so, I can't believe we didn't look into it.'

'Apparently the rumors didn't start until later so it wouldn't have been so obvious.'

'Rumors or not, we should have put it together.'

'I think Kate Guillory might be looking into it now.'

'Guillory's okay.'

Evan thought he was about to say more but he'd drifted off into the past. He was genuinely shocked that he might have missed something important.

'You know, I kind of lost focus at the end,' he said suddenly.

He looked down and twisted his wedding ring. Evan realized he'd not noticed that he still wore it. Maybe he didn't come here to pick up women after all.

'The wife was so ill. She wasn't sleeping, I wasn't sleeping, and it was affecting me at work. It was one of the reasons I retired. I could have carried on if I'd wanted to. You might not believe it, but they didn't want me to go.'

He gave Evan a wry smile.

Evan didn't say anything. It was quite an admission and he didn't really know what to say. Suddenly Faulkner didn't seem quite the hardass that Linda Clayton and Ray Clements made him out to be. In fact, it looked like he was about to get all maudlin.

'Don't worry about giving me a ride home,' Faulkner said. 'I'm going to have a few more and then I'll get a taxi home. You run along now.'

He patted Evan patronizingly on the arm. Despite that, for the first time that evening Evan was glad the place was so noisy and busy. If they'd been in a nice, comfortable bar with some good music instead of the shit they were playing here, he'd have been tempted to leave the car and get drunk with Faulkner. He thought that would have been a very bad idea indeed. But he was wrong. He'd have been much better off staying.

CHAPTER 17

EVAN DIDN'T SEE THE guy standing at the end of the bar as he walked out. And he didn't see him hastily down his drink and follow him outside. The parking lot was dark, a couple of lights out, pleasantly quiet after the noise inside, with a gentle breeze to blow away the cocktail of cheap perfume and pheromones that clung to his hair and clothes. He was almost at his car when he heard footsteps coming up fast behind him. He turned quickly. Just not quickly enough. A man with a baseball bat jabbed it hard into his gut. It punched the air out of his body, ripped a strangled grunt from his throat. His legs crumpled, body caving in on itself as he doubled over, heaving, gasping for air.

His attacker dropped the bat. Placed his palms lightly, almost gently, on Evan's head to steady it. Then he brought his knee up sharply into Evan's face. A blinding flash of pain erupted behind his eyes as his nose broke. The guy pushed him onto his face on the ground, dropped heavily on one knee onto his back. What little air was left in his lungs spewed violently out of him, spraying blood and spittle. The guy grabbed the bat, hooked it under his chin, pulled it back hard, crushing his windpipe. Evan couldn't breathe, no air going in or out. He tried to struggle. The guy was too heavy, his knee pinning him to the ground. It took everything he had just to suck air into his screaming lungs.

The guy jerked harder on the bat, pulled Evan's head further back, his throat stretched and exposed. But it wasn't the sharp, biting sting of a blade Evan had to fear. The man on his back leaned down. Put his mouth right above Evan's ear. Evan felt his hot breath on his cheek, smelled his aftershave. Then, without warning, he bit down onto Evan's ear, tore a vicious chunk out of it. Evan screamed, an excruciating howl cutting through the quiet of the parking lot. His tormentor rode him as he bucked and writhed on the ground, then spat a bloody piece of his ear high into the air. He leaned in again, hissed into his ear.

'That's what my ear feels like, the amount of grief I'm getting because of you. I wish someone would bite mine off.'

He jerked the bat again. Evan was close to passing out. Blood streamed down the side of his face, down his neck. Soaked into his shirt, dripped onto the ground. His lungs were on fire, the relentless pressure on his windpipe steadily choking the life out of him.

'You've got something I want.'

The pressure on Evan's neck suddenly eased. His body sucked in oxygen with a wet, whistling through his mouth and smashed nose, a spontaneous atavistic reaction. The guy dropped the bat, fished in his pocket, brought out some heavy-duty cable ties. He pulled Evan's arms roughly behind him, knelt on them until Evan felt his shoulders slip in their sockets. He looped a tie around Evan's wrists and pulled it tight. Then two more over the first one. Yanked them until the hard plastic cut into his flesh. Standing up, he rolled Evan onto his side with his foot, kicked him hard in the balls.

There was a searing stab of pain, stomach muscles contracting violently as he jack-knifed on the ground. Another kick like that and he'd pass out. His insides were caught in an industrial compactor, twisted and crushed. He wanted to vomit, soil himself at the same time.

The guy towered over him, the bat in his hands again. Like he was only just getting started.

'You ought to learn how to look after yourself. Get yourself in better shape.'

Evan forced his body to straighten, rolled onto his back. He heaved huge mouthfuls of beautiful air deep into his body, looked up into Hugh McIntyre's gloating face. McIntyre was breathing hard from his exertions. The last time Evan had seen him looking like that he was disappearing into the distance in his rear-view mirror.

'You blindsided me.'

McIntyre let out a sardonic laugh.

'Really? It wouldn't have made any difference, you pussy.' He prodded Evan with his boot. 'Get up shithead, we're going for a ride.'

Evan didn't think he'd ever stand up straight again. He rolled onto his front. Levered himself onto his knees. The effort filled every part of his body with pain. He couldn't concentrate on anything apart from the screaming ache spreading out from his groin. He let his head drop, tried to pull himself together. Blood dripped from his ear onto the ground.

'Hey, lazybones,' McIntyre called out in a sing-song voice, then swung the bat languidly at his head.

Evan looked up, raised his shoulder, twisted away quickly to protect himself. It caught him a glancing blow on the back of the head, knocked him flat onto his face. He struggled to get up. McIntyre pushed him over again with his foot.

'I said, get up. Didn't you hear me? Something wrong with your ears?'

He laughed, couldn't remember the last time he'd enjoyed himself so much.

'Hey! What the hell's going on over there?'

Faulkner's shout cut through the still night air. McIntyre's head shot up, the smile slipping off his face like birdshit off a windshield as Faulkner strode out across the parking lot towards them. He aimed another vicious kick. Through the hazy blur of his pain, Evan twisted into it, took it on the outside of his thigh, protected his balls.

'This isn't over, Buckley,' McIntyre spat.

Then he was gone, running across the parking lot with the easy, loping stride of a man with youth and fitness on his side until the darkness swallowed him up.

EVAN LAY IN AN ocean of pain. His ear, nose, stomach and balls all competed for his attention while Faulkner jogged across to him. Faulkner squatted down, got out his pocket knife and sliced through the cable ties. Evan sat up gingerly. He crossed his arms, massaged some life into them. Faulkner rested a hand on his shoulder.

'What was that all about?'

'That was the guy who's screwing my late client's wife.'

He was seized by a fit of coughing, the convulsions amplifying the pain that had claimed every corner of his body.

'He wasn't too happy about me, to use your delightful phrase, sticking my telephoto lens up—'

'Can't say I blame the guy.'

'Thanks a lot.'

'Maybe he got carried away a little bit.' Faulkner studied him for a moment before asking, 'Are you sure that's all there is to it? Seems a bit extreme.'

'Stanton told me he's got a very short fuse.'

He brought his knees up and hugged them to try to ease the dreadful ache coming from his groin. Resting his head on his arms, he closed his eyes, tried to find a quiet place beyond the reach of the pain.

'He says I've got something he wants. But the only things I've got are the pictures.'

'Whatever. We can't worry about that now, we've got to get you to the hospital. Your nose is broken.' He took hold of Evan's chin. Turned his head to look at his ear. 'Looks like just a scratch on your ear. You'll probably have to buy a new shirt though.'

'It doesn't feel like a scratch.'

'Don't be such a baby. I'd suggest another drink while we wait for the ambulance. Except I don't think they'd let you back inside looking like that. People would think the bouncers had done it.'

'I can drive.'

'No, you can't. Two small beers might be okay, but two beers plus shock isn't.'

Evan couldn't argue. He let him call the ambulance on his cell phone.

'Lucky for me you came out.'

'I changed my mind about having any more to drink. Suddenly I just didn't fancy it any more. Probably talking about Brenda. The noise was getting to me as well. I don't know why you suggested the place. I came out to see if you were still here to give me a ride.'

'The benefits of self-control are manifold.'

'I can have him picked up if you like.'

Evan shook his head, flicking little drops of blood at Faulkner.

'What's the point? There are no witnesses. You didn't see his face and you're loaded anyway.'

FAULKNER RODE WITH HIM in the ambulance. At the hospital his nose was cleaned up and realigned and they taped up his ear. Despite what Faulkner had said, it was more than a scratch as he'd suspected. The doctor said a large bite had been taken out of it.

'You could probably match the biter's teeth to the shape of it.'

'Don't worry, if I get the chance, I'll knock them out and bring them in.'

Once they'd dealt with the visible injuries, he asked the nurse whether she had any soothing lotion she could massage into his aching balls. She declined politely and professionally with a tired, heard-it-all-before smile, although Evan could see she was tempted. At least she didn't report him for sexual harassment.

Faulkner asked him where he was going to spend the night. 'Does this guy know where you live?'

'I'm not sure. He knows where my office is, so probably yes.'

'You think he'll come back to finish what he started?'

'Those were his parting words. He's certainly wired enough.'

Faulkner laughed when Evan told him about McIntyre chasing his car down the road.

'Sounds like he's got anger management issues.'

'That's what Stanton said. But I'll be ready for him if he comes back.'

Faulkner wasn't impressed by the show of bravado.

'Not if you're comatose from all the painkillers you're going to need tonight. You can stay at my place if you like.'

Evan considered the offer.

'You know, when I see cowboy boots like that I start thinking *Brokeback Mountain*. And I don't usually go back to a guy's place on a first date.'

Faulkner punched him on the shoulder. Evan winced.

'Sorry. Forgot about that.'

'You're right about the painkillers. Do I get the bed?'

DESPITE THE PAINKILLERS, EVAN didn't sleep well that night. The couch was uncomfortable and he could hear Faulkner snoring like a warthog with bad sinuses through the thin wall. His nose hurt like hell. And he kept rolling onto his half-eaten ear.

He also had too many things running through his mind. He was going to have to do something about the situation with McIntyre. He wasn't going to let it drop, whatever it was. The more he thought about it, the more convinced he became that it must be something to do with the photos he'd taken. There just wasn't anything else it could be. Perhaps there was something in them more damaging than just being caught in bed with your partner's wife. He'd take a better look at them as soon as he could, even though he had no idea what he might be looking for.

About five in the morning he gave up on trying to sleep. He got up, went and sat in the kitchen. After he'd made himself coffee, he sat looking at the photographs on the wall. His gaze kept coming back to the one of Faulkner's wife and her folks. He got up to take a closer look at it. There was something about it that he couldn't put his finger on. It was taken a long time ago—forty years at least—and he didn't recognize any of them. She had been a beautiful young woman in her youth, that was for sure. She reminded him vaguely of someone. The old folks must have been dead for years. And now Faulkner's wife was dead too. But there was something that niggled him. And it was going to bug the hell out of him until he worked it out, even though he had more important things to think about.

After Faulkner made them eggs and bacon for breakfast, he dropped Evan off at the bar to pick up his car. He was relieved to see that McIntyre hadn't come back to vent his spleen by trashing it. There was no doubt he knew which one it was because he must have been following him around for days. He was dismayed to think that he hadn't noticed. Some private eye he was.

CHAPTER 18

EVAN HADN'T WORKED OUT what to do next to move forward with the Clayton case, so he went to the office to take a good look at the McIntyre photographs. He ran into Tom Jacobson in the parking lot, getting out of his Volvo.

'What the hell happened to you?'

'Our friend, Hugh McIntyre, caught up with me.'

'I hope he looks worse.'

'Afraid not. He blind-sided me with a baseball bat and I never got another chance. Luckily he was interrupted or I don't know what would have happened.'

'He's definitely got it in for you. Persistent, too. You need to be careful.'

'Don't worry, I'm about to get onto it now.'

'Just let me know if you need any stronger painkillers. How's the 'Clayton Case' coming along?'

Evan shrugged.

'I'm not sure. The more I dig, the more complicated it becomes. Nobody knows a thing. Despite that, they all manage to point the finger at each other. They're like a bunch of kids.'

Jacobson smiled knowingly at him.

'So, the police aren't complete idiots then?'

'Not complete, no,' Evan conceded. 'It was actually one of the detectives who came to the office who put her onto me—the woman.'

'Really? That was good of her. She must have some faith in you.'

'I'm not sure if I'm grateful or not.'

'At least you haven't got your face busted up because of it. Anything in particular that's holding you back?'

'A couple of things. Did you ever hear anything about Robbie Clayton running off with another woman?'

'I heard the rumors,' Jacobson said carefully, 'and some of them were a lot nastier than him just running off with her.'

'I know, Linda told me.' Jacobson raised his eyebrows. 'She's very forthright. You didn't mention them.'

He didn't mean it to come out as an accusation. Jacobson took it that way, nonetheless.

'I'm not a gossip, Evan, and that's all it was.' His tone of voice implied there was no room for disagreement. 'Insensitive bastards spreading tittle-tattle, not giving a damn what harm it might cause. I'm sure some of them actually enjoyed the hurt they caused.'

'There's a chance there could be some truth in it.'

Jacobson looked surprised. Evan told him about Barbara Schneider and how she'd disappeared at about the same time. He saw recognition at the name in Jacobson's eyes.

'The Schneiders were patients of mine. The husband was very odd. I'm not sure I ever believed a word he said. He wasn't who you'd call Mr Oral Hygiene, either.'

'You said they *were* patients—what happened?'

'They just stopped coming. I thought they'd moved away or found someone cheaper, that's all.'

'Were they married?'

Jacobson frowned. 'Yes, why?'

'Because Max Schneider says that Barbara was his sister, not his wife.'

Jacobson's eyes widened. 'That's ridiculous. I know people who were at the wedding.'

'He says she was playing around with other men before she disappeared. It's probably a story he's made up to make himself feel better. He's not quite all there.'

'As I said, he never was. I can definitely understand her running away from him, but Barbara and Robbie . . . no, I can't see it.'

He shook his head emphatically.

'Apparently some of the rumors say Robbie and the woman he ran off with—whoever she was—killed the boy.'

Jacobson's face darkened. 'I know, I heard it all at the time. It's amazing what you hear when you've got someone in the chair. Sometimes I feel like going just a bit too deep with the drill to teach them a lesson.'

Evan winced, a shiver running down his back, at the thought of it. They were outside Jacobson's office now.

'Don't waste your time on that one, Evan. It just didn't happen. What was the other thing that's bugging you?'

'It's nothing to do with the case, just me being nosy really. The bus driver, Carl Hendricks, lives in this beautiful old farmhouse with acres of land and barns and who knows what else. How the hell did he do that on a bus driver's wages?'

'Nosy or jealous?'

'Both, probably.'

'Either way, I couldn't say off the top of my head. But I know someone who might know. I'll look into it and get back to you.'

CHAPTER 19

EVAN'S OFFICE HADN'T BEEN trashed either which was a relief. His computer was still on his desk. He fired it up and found the photographs from the Stanton file. He was just about to go through them when Tom Jacobson walked into his office.

'That was quick. I might offer you a job full time.'

'No, I haven't had a chance to ask about Hendricks yet, but I think I might have found out why friend McIntyre is so jumpy.'

'Jumpy isn't the word I'd choose. More like homicidal.'

Jacobson dropped a copy of the local paper onto Evan's desk. 'Read that.'

Evan picked it up. It was folded open at the business section. It didn't take long for him to spot the news item Jacobson was talking about. There was a picture of Stanton and McIntyre standing smiling with an older man Evan didn't recognize. The headline read 'Suicide Jeopardizes Bailout Deal'. He started reading.

> The recent suicide of Kevin Stanton has potentially jeopardized critical funding for local software development company, McIntyre Stanton

Associates Inc. Kevin Stanton and Hugh McIntyre started the business five years ago and, through a combination of cutting-edge products and innovative marketing solutions, have built it up to the point where it now employs almost fifty staff. However, the recent downturn in the economy has put the company under increasing financial strain and the business now requires an urgent injection of capital. A potentially life-saving deal has been brokered, but not yet signed off, between the company and local entrepreneur, Frank Hanna, for a rumored seven-figure sum. Hanna, a self-made multi-millionaire is the father-in-law of Mr Stanton, who tragically committed suicide last week. Stanton's suicide has been attributed to severe stress caused by the company's financial situation. In an interview yesterday, Hanna, who is said to be very close to his son-in-law, said: 'I just can't understand why Kevin did it. I know it's been a really stressful time, but the deal was almost there. If the lawyers had just got their fingers out it would have been a done deal weeks ago.' Asked whether the deal would still go ahead without Stanton, Hanna said: 'I have every confidence in Hugh McIntyre. I just need a little time to think it all through now Kevin is out of the equation.' Mr McIntyre was not available for comment and the company's bankers refused to comment on whether they would continue to support the company if the deal falls through.

Evan dropped the paper onto his desk, leaned back in his chair and stretched his arms. 'Ha! That would explain it.'

'It certainly would. Reading between the lines, it sounds like Hanna is having doubts about the future of the company without Stanton.'

'And if he found out McIntyre was playing hide the salami with his daughter—'

'Which was the *real* reason his favorite son-in-law topped himself—'

'He'd pull out of the deal in a flash.'

They grinned at each other. Evan swivelled back and forth in his chair.

'Then the good-time bankers would pull the plug and McIntyre would lose everything. He's probably given personal guarantees, might even have put his house up as security,' Jacobson said.

'That's why he's desperate the photographs don't come to light. He wants to make sure all the copies are destroyed.'

Evan got up to get a glass of water and pop some more painkillers. Apart from a little residual tenderness, he was feeling okay below the belt but his head still felt like it had been used as a football.

'I just can't understand why he would be so stupid,' Jacobson said. 'With your whole future in the balance, why risk pissing off the one person who can save you for the sake of a quick screw in some seedy motel.'

'People like that can't help themselves. It's like the politicians. They're arrogant. They think they're smarter than everyone else and won't ever get caught.'

'I bet he's asking himself if it was worth it at the moment.'

Evan was tempted to show him the photographs so that he could make his own mind up, but professional integrity prevailed.

'It's not just a case of getting the photos back either,' Jacobson went on. 'You made a fool of him in front of her, so his machismo demands revenge.'

Evan touched his nose gingerly.

'He's had that already. You know, after last night, I feel like calling this guy Hanna and putting him in the picture. That'd serve him right.'

'I can't say I blame you. Unfortunately, if you did and the company goes down the drain, fifty other innocent people would lose their jobs too. It's not just McIntyre.'

'I'd forgotten about that. Not that I'd really do it.'

Jacobson picked up the paper, waved it in front of Evan.

'Now you know what's going on, you need to decide what you're going to do about it. You need to convince McIntyre you're not a threat. And you'd better hope Hanna signs the deal or McIntyre is going to be looking for someone to take it out on.'

'It'd be easier to blackmail him and leave copies in a safe deposit box with instructions to send them to Hanna if anything ever happened to me.'

Jacobson gave him a disappointed look, like his favorite son had just been caught playing with himself in public.

'I don't mean for money. Just to keep him off my back.'

'Even so, blackmail is blackmail. Or is that whitemail? Anyway, it's not your style.'

'You're right. Thanks for your help Tom,' Evan said as Jacobson turned to go. 'See if you can be as quick with the Hendricks assignment I gave you.'

He ducked just in time as the newspaper whistled past his damaged ear.

CHAPTER 20

EVAN COULDN'T JUST SIT around and wait to see if Jacobson's network of neighborhood busy bodies would throw up any information. The question of how Hendricks was living where he was had really gotten under his skin. He was going to have to do some digging himself.

His best bet was to take a drive over to the county recorder's office and dig out the property deeds to see if he could get any information. They would show who transferred the property to Hendricks. If it was his parents that would explain it. If not, he had a lot more digging to do. He wasn't sure why he was so keen to find out. Even if he discovered Hendricks had bought the farm out of the proceeds of doing something illegal, it wouldn't move him forward with his investigation, unless Hendricks had kidnapped Daniel and sold him to a pedophile ring.

The clerk at the recorder's office who showed Evan how to use the system was a real old battle axe. She had all the enthusiasm of a government employee a week away from retirement. He hoped he wouldn't have to ask her for help. He started out searching for

Hendricks' name in the grantee index but came up with nothing for the property called *Beau Terre.*

That wasn't a good start. Next, he searched the grantor index. There were plenty of Hendricks's but none for the right property. Presumably that just meant Hendricks' folks hadn't passed the farm to him, so he'd gotten hold of it some other way. Unfortunately, that meant he was going to have to enlist the help of the battle axe. She was at her desk, her teeth sunk into a ham and cheese sandwich. He explained his problem to her. She took the sandwich out of her mouth, the bite marks still visible.

'That sounds like a real nice place.'

'It is,' he agreed.

'I bet it's got a big barn and one of those post and rail fences too. Maybe some horses.'

'Two barns actually. And a big porch with a rocker. Not sure if there are any horses. But I think there could be chickens.'

He couldn't help himself.

She'd been sitting there nodding her head absently, her eyes glazing over as she contemplated the idyllic scene he described. Until he mentioned the chickens.

'I hate chickens. Lizards with feathers, if you ask me. Little bastards shit in your flower beds and eat all your plants. Never eat the damn weeds, mind.'

Looking at her, Evan was mighty glad he wasn't a chicken right then. He shrugged, as if sorry that he was unable to offer an answer to her problem.

'Chickens will be chickens.'

'Used to chase poor old Billy Bob all around the garden and peck him half to death.'

'Billy Bob?'

She picked up a framed photo and handed it to Evan. He expected to see some poor hen-pecked husband being mobbed by a gang of angry chickens but instead it was a scruffy pooch.

'He's in the big kennel in the sky now, God bless him.'

'Sorry to hear that.'

He replaced the photo, wished he'd never mentioned chickens.

'Funny name,' she said. 'Is it Italian?'

'What? Billy Bob?'

'No. Beau Terre, stupid.'

'Probably French.'

'I've never been to France. Been to Paris, Texas.'

It was time to take control of the situation before she launched into a detailed account of her visit.

'Are there any reasons why I can't find the property deeds?'

'Well, there's a couple of reasons that could be,' she started, in a painfully slow delivery. 'First of all, it could be that nobody by the name of Hendricks ever bought or sold a property called Beau Terre.'

That much he could have worked out for himself. He bit back any kind of a wisecrack response.

'Uh-huh.'

Satisfied that she had effectively gotten her first point across, she continued. 'It could also be that the purchaser—what was his name again?'

'Hendricks.'

'It could be that Mr Henderson never recorded the deeds.'

Evan didn't bother correcting her. 'Is that usual?'

'No. Most folks notarize and record them. But you don't have to.'

Evan realized that she was waiting for some response from him.

'Any other reasons?'

'Could be the records haven't been updated yet. How long ago did you say?'

'Ten years at least.'

'Should be done by now.'

She said it like she was just about to check on the cookies in the oven. It was completely matter-of-fact, without a hint of irony. Despite that, Evan suspected she might be wrong if her colleagues worked at the same pace as she did. Maybe he'd come back in another fifteen years or so.

'There must be some records relating to the property. Any other way to find them?'

'Depends if you've got the PIN.'

Did that mean *Pain In Neck* Evan wondered. I've certainly got one of those.

'Sorry, I don't even know what that is.'

Now she looked at him like *he* was the idiot. He was sure she was about to ask what they taught kids in school these days. Now that they'd dropped manners from the curriculum.

'That stands for Property... Identification... Number.' She beamed at him at the opportunity he'd given her to display her superior knowledge.

'Ah.' He put on his best *I have seen the light* face and asked, 'where can I get hold of one of those?'

'I can get that for you if you like.'

She smiled almost sweetly.

Ask and you shall receive! Couldn't we have got here a bit faster?

She put the property address into her system, came up with the number in two seconds flat. Armed with this vital new piece of information Evan left her at her desk looking down at her sandwich, as if trying to decide whether she wanted to bite into the same tooth marks again. He headed back to his terminal, fully expecting to have the answers he needed in the next few minutes.

Once again, he was disappointed. He found the property easily enough but the only property deed listed for anything like the right time frame was a transfer listing George and Mary Saunders as the grantors and L. J. Saunders as the grantee, which had taken place twelve years previously. There was no mention of Carl Hendricks at all.

He made a note of the details and, with a heart as heavy as lead, he made his way back to the clerk's desk and explained his latest problem to her. She looked at him with something akin to pity, clearly wondering how this poor boy managed to dress himself in the mornings. For one heart-stopping moment he thought she was about to embark on the same rigmarole all over again, but she seemed a bit sharper now.

'It's more than likely this Saunders sold the property to your friend Hendricks who hasn't bothered to record it, for reasons best known to himself.'

Probably so that the tax man doesn't get to see his ill-gotten gains, Evan thought. The clerk looked as if she was keen to take up their conversation about Hendricks' farm from where it left off before. He thanked her for her help and beat a hasty retreat.

CHAPTER 21

HE'D HAD NO SIGNAL on his cell phone inside the recorder's office. When he came out, he saw he had a missed call from Guillory.

'I've been doing a bit of digging into the Schneider case after what you told me,' she said. 'I don't think the old man did her in.'

'Why's that?'

'I've been talking to an old friend of hers who says she's heard from her since the disappearance.'

'But never thought to tell anyone.'

'Barbara Schneider asked her not to. She just got in touch because they'd been such good friends and didn't want her to worry.'

'Do you believe her?'

'I think so. From what she says about the husband, it's a miracle she didn't bury him in the backyard. Running away was the least she could do.'

A picture of Schneider concentrating hard as he made broken washing machine noises flashed into Evan's mind and made him smile.

'I can vouch for that. In fact, I think she might have buried him years ago but some dog dug him up again.'

'That's the trouble with those do-it-yourself graves.'

'Getting back to the friend—do you think she'd talk to me?'

'Well, she didn't want to—'

'Damn.'

'—until I told her what a great guy you are and what you're looking into. It's amazing the doors that open for you when you're doing something *worthwhile*, isn't it?'

Evan stifled a mock yawn.

'How will I ever repay you?'

'Don't worry, I'm working on that. Her name's Virginia Doyle. Take this number down.'

EVAN RANG HER AS soon as he got off the phone from Guillory. After he'd introduced himself, she invited him over to the house rather than discuss it over the phone. She didn't live far from the Schneider place and was waiting for him as he drove up.

'Detective Guillory told me about the case you're investigating. I vaguely remember it happening, but I didn't know any of the people involved.' She sounded disappointed, a missed opportunity. 'I can't imagine what it must be like to lose your only child.'

She looked across to a number of framed photographs sitting on top of a baby grand piano. A boy and a girl, the usual collection of graduation photographs and other family mementos. Lots of perfect dentistry on show. It would have made Jacobson swell with pride.

'That's why I agreed to talk to you. I wouldn't normally talk to a private detective. I thought they only did sleazy divorce work and that sort of thing.'

Her nose turned up, the words almost catching in her throat. She made *private detective* sound like the lowest type of life form she was likely to come across in her happy little suburban life. Her husband was probably a junior under-manager, acting vice president at some savings and loan association. Doubtless he turned people like Evan down every day of the week. Evan felt grateful he'd been allowed to sit on the couch without some sort of protective cover being put down first.

'There's a top and a bottom end in most jobs,' Evan said, wondering if Guillory had fully explained his role of repentant sinner atoning for past misdeeds. 'Can you give me a bit of background information on Barbara?'

'She used to come over here when she couldn't stand it at home any longer. She stayed over all the time.'

'What was going on at home?'

She gave him her *you wouldn't believe it if I told you* look and leaned in closer. He did the same. Her voice dropped to a whisper.

'Have you met her husband Max?'

Evan said that he had. He chomped down hard on the smile as the mental picture reappeared.

'Well, there you go. Do I need to say any more? He's a horrible man. He used to beat her all the time. I think it's because he's German. They never got over losing the war.'

'I noticed an accent.'

And I think I detect a whiff of xenophobia in this very room.

'When they got married, they lived with his parents in that house he still lives in.'

She made *that house* sound almost as bad as *private detective.*

Clearly it was dragging the whole neighborhood down, perhaps by as much as ten to fifteen per cent.

'His parents were German refugees. They were very strict with him. When she moved in they were equally strict with her too.'

'How so?'

'They treated them like they were children. Didn't like them to stay out late, that sort of thing. He was already indoctrinated and Barbara felt it wasn't her place to say anything because it was their house after all.'

'It doesn't sound like an ideal start to married life.'

The mention of it took him immediately back to the start of his own and Sarah's married life. They'd 'christened' every room in the house within the first day or two. He couldn't have imagined moving in with either his or her parents. He swallowed hard. When would these memories stop ambushing him?

'It got worse when the parents died. He laid down the law as if he owned her.'

It was clear from her tone of voice who wore the pants in the Doyle household. And it wasn't the junior under-manager, acting vice president.

'He isn't a sociable man. He had no interest in going out and he didn't want Barbara to either. But she was so full of life, she went anyway. Then when she came home he would accuse her of all kinds of horrible things and hit her.'

She looked down at her hands clasped together in her lap, as if the answer to domestic violence was hiding in the folds of her floral skirt.

'Did you ever think that was why she disappeared? That he'd gotten carried away and killed her?'

'When she first disappeared, it crossed my mind.'

'Did you say anything to the police?'

'I don't remember. I think I might have done. They obviously didn't take any notice.'

A slight flush had spread across her cheeks. She wouldn't meet his eyes. It was likely he'd be thrown out on his ear if he asked if it was *Fukner* that she'd talked to. And it didn't really matter who it was who didn't do anything.

'That seems odd.'

She looked up at him now.

'There was no history. She'd never had to go to the hospital or anything like that. She was too proud.'

'When I spoke to her husband, he said she was seeing other men. The trouble is, he's not the most rational man I've ever met. I don't know if I believe a word he says. Do you know if there's any truth in it?'

Virginia Doyle opened her mouth to say something and closed it again. She looked down at her lap again. There were still no answers there. She was obviously happy to chat until the cows came home about the faults of Max Schneider. Saying anything against her friend was a different kettle of fish.

'It's crucial to my investigation,' he said to get her back on track. 'My client really needs to find out what happened to her little boy.'

He put a lot of emphasis on the *little boy*.

Even though she would have liked to continue with her diatribe about Max Schneider, she could see that Evan wasn't about to let that happen.

'She was seeing someone else just before she disappeared,' Virginia said, nodding to herself as if it was only just coming back to her now. Then she added a little too quickly, 'But I don't know who it was.'

He was well aware he was only going to get carefully filtered facts. Anything was a help.

'Didn't she tell you who it was? You were such good friends after all.'

'She was terrified of Max. She thought the less people who knew, the better. Me included.'

The fact that her friend hadn't seen fit to trust her completely didn't sit well with her, that was for sure.

'Do you think she might have run away with him?'

'I don't think so. But you couldn't blame her if she did.'

'Detective Guillory told me that you heard from Barbara after she disappeared.'

She brightened visibly.

'Yes, she rang me about six months later. I couldn't believe it when I heard her voice. She sounded so happy.'

'What did she say?'

'She said she couldn't take it any more so one day she just walked out. Took one small bag with a few clothes, got on the bus and never looked back. Good luck to her.'

'She didn't mention anyone else.'

'She said she'd met someone else and was very happy.'

'But it wasn't clear whether she met them before or after running away?'

'No. But I got the impression she ran away on her own and then met someone else later.'

'Why's that?'

'Oh, I don't know. Just a feeling. Call it a woman's intuition.'

He would have liked something a little more concrete than that, knew he wasn't going to get it.

'Do you still speak to her on a regular basis?'

The brightness faded from her face as quickly as it had appeared.

'Not really. We don't have that much in common now. I'm sorry to say that most of our friendship seems to have been based on the support I gave her dealing with Max. Once that went away, there didn't seem to be much left.'

Her friend's rejection and lack of confidence in her had hurt her deeply, the pain still just under the surface after all these years.

'Do you have her number?'

'I do. But I couldn't possibly give it to you.'

He thought the amount of emphasis on the *you* was uncalled for. She looked at him as if he'd just asked her to open her knees a bit wider so that he could have a quick grope under her skirt.

'She specifically asked me not to let anyone know where she is or give them her number.'

'That's okay. If I give you my number, would you pass it on to her and ask her to call me if she wants to.'

He stood up and walked over to the piano. He picked up one of the photographs and admired it.

'It might help if you tell her why I want to speak to her.'

That pushed the right button as he'd hoped. She took his number and he left with confident promises that she would persuade Barbara Schneider to call him. He didn't share her confidence, particularly if it turned out that it was Robbie Clayton that Barbara had been seeing before she disappeared.

Would she have any interest in helping the wife of the man she'd been seeing and might have run away with? He doubted it.

CHAPTER 22

BACK AT HIS OFFICE Evan went down to see if Tom Jacobson had any more information for him.

'I've been so busy I haven't had a chance,' he admitted. 'How about you? What have you dug up?'

Evan told him about his visit to the County Recorder's office and the dead end he'd run into with the last recorded owner listed as L. J. Saunders.

'That's it? No first names?'

'No. That's why I was hoping you'd have something from the local grapevine.'

'I'm sure the person I have in mind will be able to clear it up for you.' He was pensive a moment. 'You know, there is another possible explanation you haven't mentioned.'

'What, like Carl Hendricks killed Saunders, buried him, and is living in his house.'

Jacobson nodded.

'In a manner of speaking, yes. What if Carl Hendricks is Saunders?'

It was so obvious. Evan couldn't believe he hadn't thought of it. He slapped the heel of his hand on his forehead.

'You mean he changed his name. I can't believe I didn't think of that.'

'And he didn't get around to notifying the recorder's office of the change.'

'That makes sense. You'd have to change your driving license and bank accounts and all the things you use every day. But maybe you'd forget the property deeds.'

'Or choose to deliberately not change them.'

'What makes you say that?'

'Maybe you've got something to hide. Why do people change their name in the first place? It's not just because you're born Dick Assman. That's a real name, by the way. He's a gas station owner in Saskatchewan. I saw it on the *Late Show* years ago.'

Evan wasn't sure he believed him, moved on anyway.

'Apart from that, I suppose it's to leave behind something you'd like to forget.'

'That's what I was thinking. And this just muddies the waters a bit more. A lot of people wouldn't be bothered to look any further. Blame it on inefficient local bureaucracy.'

'But not a super sleuth like me, eh.'

'Exactly. There is just one thing though.'

'What's that?'

'You've got to find out if it's true.'

Evan realized that it made such perfect sense, he'd already taken it as the truth.

'Right. I sort of got carried away there. Shouldn't be too difficult to find out.'

The questions and possibilities were already starting to multiply in Evan's mind. Certainly, none of them pointed to an innocent explanation.

'I would still like some local info, Tom. The official records might tell you what happened, but I need some insight into why.'

'Uh-huh. You realize insight can be spelled g-o-s-s-i-p.'

'I know, but it's still useful to have. A skilled investigator like me can separate the wheat from the chaff.'

He was almost out the door when Jacobson called him back.

'Hey Evan, before you go, can you do this next root canal for me?'

Evan laughed. He could see what was coming next.

'It's just that since I'm doing your job, I thought maybe you'd like to do mine.'

CHAPTER 23

HE WENT BACK UPSTAIRS and sat at his desk. The last thing he wanted was another trip to some local government offices to wade through more official records. It was four p.m. on Friday. He wouldn't be able to get to the District Court before it closed. That meant he was going to have to wait until Monday morning. That wasn't a massive problem in itself apart from the fact that it gave him a bit of a dilemma.

If Hendricks really was Saunders, then he would want to do a whole lot more digging to try to find out if he had anything in his past that he was hiding. In which case, the quicker he got started, the better. On the other hand, if Hendricks wasn't Saunders, he didn't want to waste a lot of time and effort chasing something that ultimately led nowhere.

But the real problem was, how was he going to pass the weekend if he didn't? Because his conversation with Jacobson had shaken loose a lot of doubts and worries that he didn't want to have to deal with.

He went back down to Jacobson's office. Jacobson was getting ready to go.

'Uh-oh, I see someone in need of a beer.'

'What are you, a mind reader?'

'No, I read faces. In my job you need to be able to see the level of fear in a patient's eyes. And I see fear in yours.'

'Fear of what?'

'Of being alone. Of not trusting what you might do left to your own devices. Come on, let's go.'

They went to the same bar as before. It was still early so they got settled into the best seats at the end of the bar. On the short side in the corner, not the long, front side where everyone buying drinks leans over you and drips beer on your pants. Jacobson got the first round in.

'What's on your mind?'

'Talking about people changing their names makes me think things I don't want to think. About Sarah.'

Jacobson nodded and sipped his beer.

'I've always thought something must have happened to her. Killed or abducted or whatever.'

He sat there with the terrible thoughts that plagued him pushing their way to the forefront of his mind. He didn't think he'd ever voiced them aloud. He didn't know if he'd be able to. He swallowed thickly. Took a long pull on his beer to give himself a few more seconds. Jacobson waited for him to continue.

'Or is it that I've always *wanted* to think that something happened to her? Because the alternative is too awful for me to deal with.'

It was easier to say than he had thought it would be. He didn't want to think about what that might imply. Christ, you could drive yourself mad.

'Because the alternative is that she *chose* to go.'

It was all pouring out now, there'd be no stopping it.

'Because she couldn't stand to be with me any longer. Just like the Schneiders. She made a conscious effort to disappear because I'm as bad as Max Schneider. Then changed her name so that I couldn't ever find her.'

Jacobson put his hand on Evan's shoulder.

'Don't do this to yourself, Evan.'

'I can't help it. Most of the time I'm okay. Then suddenly something will set it all off.'

'Okay. So what stops it again?'

Evan turned his head to look at Jacobson.

'A hangover usually.'

Jacobson slapped him hard on the back as he downed his beer, then ordered the next round.

'Coming up.'

But Evan couldn't let it go.

'I don't want to be too boring and practical, but I do need to know. If I knew she chose to walk out then I'd stop trying to find out what happened and try to move on.'

He met Jacobson's steady gaze, wondered if his life was as complicated.

'But if something happened to her then I can't ever give up. She could have been abducted and she's still alive in some shitty basement, hoping I'll find her. If there's a one in a billion chance of that being true, I've got to keep looking.'

Jacobson took a deep breath, let it out again.

'You certainly know how to torture yourself.'

'As I said, I'm okay most of the time. The possibility of finding her alive keeps me going. It's just that every now and then something happens to make me start thinking all this shit.'

'I'm guessing that's when you lock your door and hit the whisky bottle.'

'You know, Tom, you've really got to stop auditing the trash cans.' He grinned, but then it slipped off his face just as fast. 'Seriously, though, Stanton brought that bottle with him. Even if the cops didn't believe me, I want you to. I don't keep booze in the office. And I don't drink alone.'

Jacobson smiled. 'Glad to hear it. You get maudlin enough on a couple of beers. Talking of which . . .'

Evan ordered them two more. At this rate the hangover-induced catharsis was practically guaranteed.

'It gets even worse you know.'

'Is that possible?'

'Oh yes. It makes me question whether I ever really loved her.'

Jacobson swivelled in his chair. He clamped a huge hand on each of Evan's shoulders and shook him violently.

'Enough, already!'

Evan started to speak again. So Jacobson shook him even harder. After Evan didn't say anything for a few seconds Jacobson took his hands away. Evan leaned away from him and lifted his hands up in appeasement.

'Just let me just say this, okay?'

Jacobson shook his head sadly but didn't say anything else.

'If I really loved her then I'd want her to be alive and happy whether it's with me or someone else. But if it's not with me then I'll feel a whole lot better if she's dead. That way I can go on living with my memories and not have to look at myself too hard. I'm putting my feelings over her life. Does that sound like the dictionary definition of love to you?'

'There's no hope for you Evan. You're determined to give yourself a hard time. I suggest we try the hangover method first and if that doesn't work, I'm prescribing a lethal dose of novocaine.'

CHAPTER 24

EVAN FELT A LITTLE off-color the next morning. Something unpleasant had crawled into his mouth during the night and died. Jacobson was a big guy and had drunk him under the table. But despite his physical symptoms Evan felt a lot better for having gotten it all off his chest. He felt like he had a chance of making it through the weekend at least.

In his drunken state the previous evening it had occurred to him that it might be worth checking with Faulkner to see if he knew anything about the possibility of Hendricks having changed his name. He was in his car on his way to Faulkner's trailer park when his cell phone rang. He didn't recognize the number, answered it anyway.

'Mr Buckley, this is Barbara Schneider.'

In his surprise he swerved and almost hit a car coming in the other direction, its horn blaring and then receding into the distance.

'I can call back if you're driving.'

She had a lovely voice. Probably the sort of voice you heard if you called a phone sex line, not that Evan had ever done that.

'No, no, it's okay.' He came off the gas and pulled onto the shoulder.

'Ginny Doyle said you wanted to talk to me. She said it was very important.'

He couldn't think of any gentle way to ease into the questions he wanted to ask. He didn't know how much Doyle had told her. He needn't have worried. She carried on without waiting for him to say anything.

'She said you wanted to ask me about when I left my husband.'

'I realize this might be difficult—'

'It's ancient history. Don't worry about me. Just ask me what you want to know.'

'I wanted to ask if you . . .'

He couldn't think of a nice way to put it.

'Ran away with another man when I left my husband?'

'Yes.'

'The answer's no. I ran away on my own. Does that help you?'

He was finding the conversation very unsettling. The strange combination of her directness coupled with her lovely voice made it difficult to think clearly. He got the impression you could ask her anything.

'I think so.'

'You don't sound very sure.'

He heard the amusement in her voice, wondered if she was used to having that effect on people. On men in particular.

'I'm not.'

'Would it be easier if you came over to see me?'

'I thought you didn't want anyone to know where you are.'

She laughed. It was a lovely laugh too. It made him wonder about the mouth that these lovely sounds came out of.

'I think Ginny is being a little melodramatic.'

She gave him an address which was only about a hundred miles away.

'You didn't go far.'

'Why would I? That idiot Max never leaves the house. And there wasn't anyone else to worry about. Can you come straight over? I have to go out later.'

He decided to visit Faulkner later. He didn't want to risk her changing her mind, told her he'd be there in a couple of hours. Then he turned his phone off so that she couldn't ring back and cancel.

BARBARA SCHNEIDER WAS EVERYTHING her laugh and phone sex voice promised and then some. She was attractive in a slightly risqué sort of way, with a little too much makeup for this early in the day. The lips that let slip the wonderful sounds were full and coated with dark red lipstick. She was shapely too, broad across the beam—in a good way—but cinched in at the waist and with a generous bust to top it all off. The bust was very much on show. You don't get half a dozen of those in an egg box, Evan thought, as he admired the magnificent display.

He almost felt sorry for Max Schneider and his doomed attempts to keep this much woman in check. And what had she ever seen in him?

He looked around, not exactly nervously, as he entered, to see if there was any evidence of a man living there. He felt a lot like an unsuspecting fly that had just been tricked into entering a big, fat spider's web.

Barbara wore a crisp white blouse that was totally inadequate for the job it was expected to do, tucked tightly into a plaid skirt a little too short for her age and the size of her backside, but a great testimonial for the strength of the seams nonetheless. It also slid up easily and alarmingly over her powerful thighs when she sat down. Evan wouldn't have wanted to get his head stuck between those, especially not with his damaged ear. He wondered if she liked being called *Babs*.

'What happened to your face?' She looked as if she wanted to reach out and touch it, see if it was real.

'A dissatisfied client,' he said, and grinned.

She smiled back, revealing perfect teeth. Was that the tip of her tongue poking through?

'I don't believe that for a minute. You look like Mr. Satisfaction Guaranteed to me. Anyway, what do you want to know?'

He was having difficulty stopping himself staring at her chest. His eyes just kept slipping downwards. As a result, he was making himself stare at the point where her eyebrows met. It was a trick he used when talking to people with crossed eyes. He never knew which one to look at and this trick made it look like you were looking at both of them and not favoring one or the other.

He was doing it now because if he stared too fixedly into her eyes she would think he was hitting on her, but every time he averted his eyes they immediately dropped to her breasts. The problem was it made him look like he was holding his head stiffly.

'Have you got something wrong with your neck as well?' She made no attempt to hide the hint of a smile on her lips as she said it.

She knows exactly what she's doing.

'I slept badly. Anyway, let me start from the beginning.'

He told her the basic outline of the case, about Daniel and then Robbie disappearing and the rumors about Robbie running away.

He missed out the nastier rumors. And he didn't mention any names.

'So you want to know if I ran away with the father.'

She shifted in her chair and her skirt rode up some more to reveal the lacy tops of her pantyhose—*at this time in the morning?*—and a small slice of smooth, pale flesh. He was aware of faint stirrings in his own underwear. He'd noticed before how frisky he felt when he had a bad hangover.

It was nothing obvious at this stage. But he didn't want it to go any further. Unfortunately, it seemed like Babs—he had to admit it was the only thing to call her—had exactly the opposite idea. He was convinced she kept glancing down at his crotch. He crossed his legs primly, which made her smile again.

'You'd have to tell me his name first,' she said.

He opened his mouth to tell her when she beat him to it.

'No need, you're talking about Robbie Clayton, aren't you?'

'Yes. So you knew him.'

'I knew him before I ran away. You've talked to Ginny, she probably told you what my husband was like.'

He nodded. 'I've met him too.'

'Lucky you! You've seen the amusing side of him, no doubt. Amusing if you can laugh at his stupid antics and then leave. Not so amusing if you live with it day in day out. And it's not all harmless fun.'

'I know. I saw the temper as well.'

'Well, it was a lot worse than you saw or Ginny said, I can tell you. I didn't tell her, or anyone else, the half of it.'

Again, he nodded and made encouraging please-continue noises.

'I was a very attractive woman back then.' She put all the

emphasis on the *very*, and then paused. And paused. It was a fishing expedition, but Evan wasn't biting. She didn't seem to mind.

'I had all the young men flirting with me. It drove Max wild. He used to beat the shit out of me. Try to make me less appealing.'

He made the appropriate sympathetic sounds, knew how totally inadequate they were.

'It was very flattering. And that's all it was to begin with. I was married and I took that seriously. We went to Church regularly.'

Good God, I hope you didn't go dressed like that.

'But Max was a real shit.' Her whole body crumpled in on itself as the memories came flooding back. 'Then I met Robbie and everything was different from then on.'

'But he didn't run away with you?'

She shook her head sadly. 'No. I begged him to and I think he would have come with me—'

'But then Daniel disappeared.'

'Yes. He changed then. It brought his family life back into focus. I was just a bit of fun on the side. He was obsessed with finding out what happened to his boy.' Her gaze passed straight through Evan, back in time to what might have been. 'Compared to that I wasn't important any more. Not important enough, anyway.'

Suddenly it was a very different woman sitting in front of him. The clothes were the same but now they were just inappropriate, not provocative. Or had that all been in his mind—and underwear. The body inside the clothes didn't look quite so full and bursting with life. More like someone had pulled the stopper out of an inflatable mattress. Bumps and hollows in all the right places but not very exciting.

'I'm really sorry I had to bring all this up again.'

'It's not your fault. And in a way, it's made me feel better too.'

'How's that?'

'I never knew Robbie had disappeared as well as Daniel. I thought he just went back to his happy family life, with or without the boy, and forgot all about me.'

'I don't think he'd ever have forgotten about you.'

He hoped he hadn't overdone it, wasn't sure if he wanted to bring back too much of the original Babs.

'What do you think happened to him?' she asked, as if she hadn't heard.

'I think something bad happened to him as well. He's not with his wife, and he's not with you. The police think he ran off because he killed Daniel. I don't believe for a minute he did anything to Daniel and I think if he'd run off, he'd have taken you with him.'

She smiled at the compliment. It was as if a light had been turned back on inside her.

'I think you're right. He couldn't have hurt that boy in a million years. And he might have chosen family over me, but if he was going to turn his back on his family, he'd be with me now.'

Her spirits seemed to be fully recovered already.

'Did he have any suspicions about what might have happened to Daniel?'

'Not really. I know he didn't agree with the police. They thought it was the boy's teacher, but Robbie didn't buy that. I can't remember what it was now but he thought their "evidence"'—she did the quotes thing with her fingers—'was pretty thin. He thought the teacher was a good guy.'

He knew she was talking about Hendricks' evidence, didn't say anything.

'Did he try to find out what happened?'

'I don't really know. I know he felt really guilty, as if it was his fault. As if it wouldn't have happened if he hadn't . . .'

Been with me?

She couldn't finish the sentence. Just sat looking down at her hands in her lap. Then she looked up at Evan.

'I think he also blamed me in a way because he was with me that afternoon. There, I've said it.' She took a deep breath and bit down on her bottom lip. He hoped she wasn't about to cry.

'I don't think it would have made any difference if he was with you or getting drunk in a bar, which is what he said he was doing.'

She smiled at him again.

'Thank you for saying that. You know, you're the first person I've talked to about all this. You don't exactly go up to people and say, *Hi, I'm Babs. I was in bed with a married man when his boy got abducted*. It tends to limit the number of dinner party invites you get. Turns you into something of a pariah.'

She shifted in her chair, revealing another inch of thigh. Her knee brushed his. He jumped slightly, a shiver rippling through him.

'He didn't say anything about trying to find out what happened himself?' he said in an attempt to stop her descending into a pit of remorse and self-pity again.

And to take his mind off the effect she was having on him.

'No, we never saw each other again. What with all the interest in the disappearance and everything else, he couldn't have risked it even if he wanted to. The one thing I can tell you for sure is that he didn't run off with me.'

He was pleased to hear what she said. He truly believed something bad had happened to Robbie. It meant he wouldn't have to go back to Linda and tell her that *her Robbie* had run off with another woman like all the old gossips said.

That was a huge relief, but he immediately felt guilty. Once again, the price of his peace of mind was another person being dead.

She laid her hand lightly on his knee.

'None of this helps you, does it?'

In any other situation it would have been a gesture of comfort or support. But not today. His voice when he found it was suddenly gravelly.

'I'm afraid not. I feel like I've gone backwards.'

'A bit of a wasted journey. All that way for nothing.' She traced a pattern on his thigh with a bright cerise fingernail. 'We wouldn't want that, would we? Can't have you going away empty handed.'

There was something in her tone of voice. Something primeval and predatory. Something hungry. The hairs on the back of his neck bristled. Empty handed wasn't going to happen, not in this room, not today. From where he was sitting, he could see exactly what he'd like to fill those empty hands with. They rose and fell steadily as her breath quickened, her nipples hard, clearly visible through the thin material. His fingers ached to reach out and touch them.

She leaned forwards to give him a better view down her blouse to the lacy bra underneath.

'I hope you don't mind me saying, but I couldn't help noticing how you can't take your eyes off my breasts.'

She looked down at them herself as if seeing them for the first time, pleased with what she saw.

'I know you've tried so hard, given yourself a stiff'—she licked her lips and paused before the next word—'neck trying, but you still need to work on it. Some people might not like it.'

From the way her lips parted and her tongue darted out and ran along her teeth, it was clear she didn't count herself in that number. *Some people* liked it a lot, in fact. Lived for it. He could feel the heat coming off her body, smell her perfume.

He couldn't deny it. The evidence against him was growing by the minute. Now it was her who couldn't take her eyes off him. He swallowed thickly as she took hold of his hand, put it where she wanted it.

'It's got me slicker than deer guts on a doorknob, if you know what I mean.'

He had a pretty good idea. He also couldn't see any good reason why he shouldn't get over there next to her before it was too late.

CHAPTER 25

DRIVING BACK FROM BARBARA'S house, Evan felt more relaxed than he had since he couldn't remember when. Bryan Adams' *Thought I'd Died and Gone to Heaven* was playing on the radio. It was maybe a bit strong for how he was feeling, but he was still feeling pretty good.

He would have liked to have come away with some ground-breaking insights into the case but he was happy enough with his consolation prize. He marveled, as he had many times before, at the way people reacted to bad news by reaffirming their own life in the most basic way—although basic wasn't the right word for some of what they'd gotten up to.

Now he had to decide whether to go around to see Faulkner and ask him whether he knew anything about the possibility of Hendricks changing his name. Surely that would have come up in their investigation.

More importantly he wanted to see Faulkner's reaction to the fact that it was looking highly unlikely that Robbie Clayton had killed his son and run away. It wasn't conclusive proof by any means, but he believed Barbara's story. Robbie Clayton sure as hell wasn't living there now and he doubted he ever had been. Although it was still possible that he'd run away on his own, he didn't think it was likely.

The afternoon's extracurricular activities had taken a large bite out of his day, but he decided to go anyway. One thing was for sure—he wouldn't be going for another beer with him after what happened last time.

Despite his best efforts he'd somehow managed to get his damaged ear caught up in the elastic of Barbara's pantyhose when she clamped his head tight between her thighs and refused to let go. Now it was hurting like hell. At the time, the sight of her heavy breasts swinging wildly as she laughed uncontrollably while he clutched his ear had made it worthwhile, but now he wasn't so sure.

It was still light when he got to Faulkner's trailer park. There was an old Dodge Ram pickup truck parked next to Faulkner's car in the driveway. He parked behind it and got out, walked up to the trailer. Inside he heard two men's voices. They weren't shouting but it was a very heated conversation. He knocked on the door and waited. The voices stopped abruptly. After a few moments' silence Faulkner opened the door.

Seeing who it was, he stepped outside and closed the door behind him. 'What the hell do you want?'

Evan caught a quick glimpse of the back of the other man inside before the door closed.

'It's nice to see you again too. I thought you'd be interested to hear how I'm doing after you took me to that bar the other night.'

'You're right, I haven't been able to sleep at night with the worry. Anyway, I'm in the middle of something right now. Can this wait?'

'Sure. I just wanted to let you know I went to see the woman Robbie Clayton was seeing before he disappeared. I think it's pretty certain he didn't run off voluntarily.'

He watched Faulkner carefully to see how he took the news. As far as he could see, he might as well have been telling him what he'd eaten for breakfast for all the reaction he got. Maybe his eyes narrowed a fraction but that might have been the late afternoon sun slanting through the trees.

Faulkner snorted.

'I'd be interested to hear what kind of proof you think you've got, but I'm busy right now. What are you doing tomorrow?'

Evan was momentarily distracted by a movement at the window behind Faulkner. It was too quick for him to get a look at Faulkner's visitor. Faulkner waved a hand in front of Evan's face.

'Sorry. What have you got in mind?'

'If you can haul your lazy ass out of bed in the morning, why don't you come back about seven tomorrow morning and I'll take you fishing?'

'Fishing?'

'Yes, you know, you go out in a boat with a rod and a reel and catch fish. Millions of people do it every day. It's called a hobby.'

'Well—'

'I'm going anyway. If you're here by seven, you can tag along. I've got enough gear for both of us. There's an added attraction for you, too.'

Evan didn't really want to give Faulkner an easy shot at him, but he asked anyway.

'What's that?'

'Even you should be able to see McIntyre coming if you're half a mile from the shore in the middle of a lake.'

HE'D ALMOST FORGOTTEN ABOUT McIntyre, despite the throbbing pain in his ear. Driving away from Faulkner's place he knew he had to think of a way to deal with him. He didn't want to risk meeting him even if it was somewhere public. The man was clearly a maniac.

An idea took form in his mind. It wasn't perfect but it was the best he could come up with. He still had Kevin Stanton's numbers in his phone. Although he'd never called the home number, he'd taken it down just in case he couldn't get him on his cell.

No time like the present. He pulled onto the shoulder, found the number and hit the dial button. She picked up straight away.

'Mrs Stanton, my name's Evan Buckley.'

There was a long silence, made him wonder if she was still there.

'Hello?'

'You're the bastard who took the photos and gave them to Kevin.'

'Yes. I'm very sorry about the way things turned out.'

'Sorry? You're sorry! Your pictures killed my husband.'

It wasn't an appropriate moment to point out that if she hadn't been screwing Hugh McIntyre, there wouldn't have *been* any pictures. Or that, as far as he could see, she hadn't given a shit about her husband in the first place.

She was still talking, if that was the right word to describe the venom coming down the phone line.

'You sick bastard. I can't believe you're calling me.'

Thirty seconds in and he was already wondering if this was such a good idea. But she hadn't hung up on him, he might as well plow on.

'I need to talk to you.'

'Is this how you get off, you pervert? You got bored jerking off to the pictures already? Now you want phone sex. Is that it, you filthy pervert? Got your credit card ready?'

She was screaming at him now, anything and everything she could think of to call him. He didn't say anything, let her rant on for a while longer. She needed to get it off her chest. Finally, she quietened down enough for him to get a word in.

'Did you know Hugh McIntyre attacked me a few nights ago?'

'Yes, he told me. If he'd brought you back here, I'd have bitten off a lot more than your ear, you sick bastard. I hope your balls never come back down.'

He smiled to himself—he'd already had the opportunity to road test the aforementioned equipment. And it had all passed with flying colors. But it wasn't a thought he wanted to share with her right now.

She'd gone quiet for a moment, which was a relief. He wasn't sure, but he had a suspicion she'd covered the mouthpiece with her hand. When she spoke again it was in a much calmer, more reasonable tone of voice.

'I don't want to talk on the phone. Why don't you come over? Sorry I was so rude.'

Nice try, but no coconut. Do I look like I was born yesterday?

'Don't worry about it. But I don't think that's a good idea in the circumstances.' He decided to pretend that he hadn't seen the newspaper report. 'I wanted to ask you what this is all about.'

That set her off again.

'What do you mean what's it all about? What do you think it's all about? Are you stupid as well as sick? Is that why you spend your life ruining other people's, because you're too stupid to get a proper job—'

'I understand why he wants to hurt me. I don't understand what else he wants. The police have the photographs. There isn't anything else.'

'You must have copies.'

'I delete them as soon as the case is over.'

He felt a little bit guilty thinking about the copies he'd mailed to himself at home. But that was just insurance. He'd delete them as soon as this was all sorted out.

'Why would I keep them?'

Incredibly, she passed on the opportunity to accuse him of jerking off again. He figured he would continue playing dumb.

'I don't see why the photographs are so important. Your husband is dead. As far as I know, McIntyre isn't married. The damage is already done.'

'You don't understand.'

'Then tell me.'

'What, so you can blackmail us. Do you think I'm stupid?'

This wasn't going anywhere.

Added to which, yes, he did think she was stupid. If he had been looking to blackmail them, she'd as good as told him there was something to blackmail them about. All he had to do was look in the paper.

'I don't want to blackmail anyone, but that's irrelevant because there aren't any more pictures anyway. The reason I'm calling you is because I would like you to pass the message to McIntyre.'

'What message?'

God, give me strength.

'That there aren't any more copies. So there's no point in McIntyre stalking me, trying to abduct me and then torturing the truth out of me, or whatever else he had in mind.'

'I can tell him. I don't think it will make any difference. He never listens to me.'

At least he's got some sense, Evan thought. At that moment, his car was rocked violently as the pickup truck he'd seen outside Faulkner's trailer blew past, doing eighty at least. He hadn't been paying attention to the road, didn't get a chance to see the driver.

He pulled back onto the road to follow it, too good an opportunity to miss.

'I've got to go now. I'd be grateful if you'd pass on the message. There's not a lot else I can say. Except you can also tell him that if he wants a crack at me without creeping up on me first, all he has to do is call this number.'

She started to say something. He ended the call, cut her off, sick of the righteous indignation in her cheating voice. He hoped McIntyre called. He'd welcome the chance to settle the score—not just for himself, for Kevin Stanton too.

THE PICKUP TRUCK WAS a quarter mile up ahead, still burning up the road. Evan put his foot down, got up to eighty himself, then kept his distance. It didn't particularly matter because he didn't think the man in the trailer had seen his car. But it didn't hurt to be on the safe side.

After a couple of miles, the pickup slowed and took a left, then came off the gas, slowed right down on the smaller road. He recognized the road as he turned left, couldn't immediately place it. It suddenly came back to him. A mile further on it was confirmed when the pickup turned into the driveway of a nice-looking property on the right.

He kept on straight, glanced at the sign at the entrance to the driveway as he passed. *Beau Terre* looked as picture perfect as it had last time he'd been there. Carl Hendricks was climbing down from the pickup's cab. He looked up as Evan drove past.

It was a quiet road and didn't get much traffic, probably the neighbors and not a lot else. Evan looked away quickly, not sure whether Hendricks recognized him or not. It wasn't often he wished he'd gone for the drug-dealer style tinted windows that everyone had these days, but this was one of those times. At least his window was up. There was a chance the reflection on the glass would have obscured his face.

Not wanting to turn around and drive past Hendricks' place a second time, he drove on for a couple of miles until he found another left turn which eventually looped back and took him to the main road back into town. He took it easy through the back streets to his apartment block, driving on auto pilot, his mind spinning with the implications. He stayed sitting and thinking in his car for a long while.

Two things were glaringly obvious. Faulkner and Hendricks knew each other. And Faulkner hadn't mentioned that particular to Evan. It also looked like they'd just had an argument, what with the raised voices coming from inside the trailer and then Hendricks taking off like a bat out of hell.

What wasn't so clear was what did it all mean, if anything? There were a million questions flying around in his mind. Did they know each other before the disappearances? Or had they got to know each other subsequently? Was that why Faulkner hadn't looked very hard at Hendricks?

But most importantly, could he trust Faulkner? The man had been good to him after McIntyre attacked him. Now they were about to become fishing buddies. Should he even go on the fishing trip tomorrow? Maybe McIntyre wasn't who he should be worrying about when he was stuck half a mile out in the middle of a lonely lake.

CHAPTER 26

HE HADN'T BEEN BACK to his apartment since the day before McIntyre attacked him and he'd stayed with Faulkner. On that occasion he'd been surprised that the thumb drive he'd mailed to himself hadn't arrived. It was there when he collected his mail that evening. Perhaps the postal service had siphoned it off thinking it was suspicious, or maybe the postal workers union had held a day of action, but whatever it was, it had arrived now.

It might have been the thumb drive in his hand or even the acrimonious phone call with Stanton's wife, but he got the first twinge of apprehension riding up in the elevator. A vague, nameless unease. It intensified as he walked down the corridor to his apartment, his pace quickening. It was obvious before he got there that something was wrong. The door to the apartment was standing ajar. He carefully pushed it open all the way, peered in. From where he was standing outside, he could already see the chaos inside. He stopped. Cocked his head, listened carefully. He didn't hear anything. Stepping cautiously into the hallway, he crept forward, made his way towards the living room at the end.

Suddenly there was a fast blur of movement, a started yowl. Something black exploded into movement, shot between his legs and out into the corridor. He jumped, almost lost his balance, let out an involuntary yelp as his heart slammed in his chest. It was just his neighbor's cat. He could be confident there was nobody in the apartment now. The stupid creature would never have ventured in if there was. The whole place reeked of cat spray. The pesky animal had been enjoying its new-found territory for at least a couple of days—since the evening Evan had been attacked.

The whole apartment had been turned upside down, more for effect than anything else. Surely McIntyre—it couldn't be anyone else—didn't believe he'd hidden the pictures inside the books on the bookshelves. He'd thrown them all over the floor just the same. Evan had some nice first editions. They'd be ruined now. He bent down and picked up a Robert B. Parker, put it back on the shelf. What would Spenser do now, he wondered? Go around and kick McIntyre's ass, that's what. Unfortunately, he didn't think he was up to it, not for a couple more days.

He'd had the lyrics to Bob Dylan's *Sara* framed for his Sarah. Now they were lying on the floor, the glass smashed. He'd always teased her, said that Dylan got the words the wrong way around. And she would say she was Sarah, not Sara, so it didn't count. He picked the frame up, tapped the broken glass out into the trash can, hung it back on the wall.

The only consolation was that McIntyre hadn't ripped open all the upholstery as well. Probably allergic to feathers.

There wasn't any point in calling the police. McIntyre might be acting like a maniac, but he wasn't a stupid idiot. He wouldn't have left any evidence. Not that the police would have been interested anyway, not if they sent someone like Ryder around.

What he did do, was call Stanton's wife again.

When she heard who it was, she started ranting again as if the call had never been interrupted. He talked straight over her.

'Since we last spoke, I've found out McIntyre ransacked my apartment. You probably knew that last time we talked. I don't give a shit either way, but will you please try to get it into his thick skull that I haven't got any copies'. He didn't even feel any guilt this time. 'Also point out to him that if I was a blackmailer, I wouldn't just leave all my valuable evidence lying around for some amateur sneak thief to break in and find. If it existed, *which it doesn't,* it'd be in a safe deposit box.'

He paused to catch his breath. She'd gone quiet, shocked by the force of his outburst.

'One last thing. I haven't been to the police about the attack and I'm going to let this ride as well. But that's all. Any more of this shit and I'll tell them everything I know. Then maybe they'll start poking *their* noses into the things you're so worried about. I hope we're clear on this. The only time I want to hear from or about him again is when he's ready to call this number.'

He ended the call before he said anything he regretted. He'd been a hair's breadth away from saying he'd tell her father about the affair. Then they'd have to deal with that shitstorm, photos or no photos. He really didn't want to have to do that. It would turn him into the blackmailer they were so certain he was.

He spent the rest of the evening putting his apartment back together. It didn't do his mental state any good at all. There were a lot of memories of his life with Sarah spread around the apartment, except now they were spread around the floor. On a day-to-day basis they tended to merge into the background. He didn't really see them. But an evening spent picking up the pictures that McIntyre had thrown across the room, and all the other mementos of their life together plunged him into a trough of despondency. What was even worse was that he started feeling guilty about his afternoon romp with Barbara. It was ridiculous, but there it was.

Once he'd gotten the place back into some kind of order, he had a quick nightcap and took himself off to bed. He fell asleep immediately and his subconscious mind ran riot. He dreamed of a fishing trip with Faulkner and Kevin Stanton, catching one Largemouth Bass after another, all of them with Sarah's sad face and Barbara's perfectly-formed breasts, then laughing wildly as they gutted the furiously flapping fish, while Hugh McIntyre stood naked on the shore and shot at them with a high-powered rifle.

CHAPTER 27

HE WAS UP EARLY the next morning like a small boy excited about his long-awaited fishing trip with a favorite uncle. In reality, he wasn't looking forward to it at all. There were too many awkward questions to be asked. Perhaps he should ask them in the car before they got out onto the lake, where he had a chance to get away. It was a ridiculous thought. If he was thinking along those lines, he shouldn't be going at all. Apart from being a bit gruff at times, Faulkner had treated him well.

What niggled was that Faulkner was holding something back. Not only that, the more he looked into the case, the more it seemed Faulkner was hiding. The only way he was going to find out the whole truth was by talking to him.

So here he was, driving the now familiar route to Faulkner's trailer park at this unearthly time of day. He hadn't been fishing since he was eight years old when his old man used to take him before his health gave way. It looked like it was going to be a beautiful day. If it hadn't been for the doubts he had about Faulkner, he couldn't have imagined a better way to spend it. Well, thinking back to yesterday's unexpected delights, he could—he'd swap Faulkner for Barbara—but this wasn't such a bad alternative.

He couldn't see any signs of life when he got to Faulkner's trailer. He'd expected to see a pile of fishing gear ready and loaded into his car, hopefully a jumbo icebox full of cold beer too. Perhaps Faulkner had overslept. He smiled to himself. It would be just perfect. He was looking forward to waking him up with a few choice words to get him back for his comments the previous evening. They'd see who couldn't haul their lazy ass out of bed.

He knocked on the door a lot louder than was necessary. Then did it again without giving Faulkner a chance to get to the door. Despite all the noise, there was no sound or movement coming from inside the trailer. Nobody could have slept through all that. Maybe he was on the can. He gave it another couple of minutes and knocked again. Still nothing. Something wasn't right.

Looking around, he saw an old packing crate lying behind Faulkner's car. He carried it over, put it under the window next to the door, then climbed up onto it and looked through the window.

'Hey, you. What the hell do you think you're doing?' a voice shouted from behind him.

He jerked around at the sound and slipped off the crate, raking his shin on the edge as he went. He hadn't heard the guy coming. He was big and aggressive and didn't smell too good, a grubby T-shirt stretched over his belly.

'What do you think you're doing?' he said again, still advancing on Evan, fists like mallets hanging at his side.

Evan held up his hands. 'Looking for Matt Faulkner. We're supposed to be going fishing.'

'Fishing?'

Evan decided against trying out Faulkner's wiseass comments

on the guy. He didn't look as if he was in a laughing mood.

'Yes, fishing. We agreed I'd meet him here at seven, and we'd go fishing together.'

Grubby-T grunted, calming down a bit. 'Maybe he overslept. No need to go waking the whole trailer park. Why don't you try ringing his phone, instead of trying to break his door down?'

Evan felt stupid that he hadn't thought of that before this meathead. He got out his phone and dialled Faulkner's number. They heard it ringing inside the trailer.

'It's ringing out.' He closed the connection. 'I was about to see if I could see anything through the window.'

Grubby-T shrugged. 'Give it a go, why not.'

Evan was pleased to get the official go-ahead from the park's unofficial security force. He climbed back up onto the crate and peered through the window, shielding his eyes with his hands against the glass. He couldn't see anything.

'Can you see anything?'

'Nothing.'

'Try knocking again. But not so loud this time.' He made a keep-it-down gesture with his hands. 'I don't want you waking up the wife. Only damn time of day I get to myself.'

Evan had a bad feeling about the whole situation. He didn't think there was much point in knocking, but he was anxious to keep the guy happy. He climbed down and knocked again. They stood and waited together in the early morning light.

'What happened to your ear.'

'Somebody bit it.'

Grubby-T gave him a look like he'd never heard of such a thing. Which was odd. Because, in Evan's opinion, if there was going to be any ear biting going on, this guy looked exactly like the sort of person who'd be doing it. He was shaking his head in amazement.

'You don't say.'

'I know, unbelievable, isn't it?'

'What did you do to him?'

Evan wasn't about to put himself down by admitting he'd done precisely squat. Besides, he wasn't here to pass the day shooting the breeze with Faulkner's neighbors. He was here to catch fish. He cocked his ear theatrically.

'I think I heard something inside.'

'I didn't hear anything and I've got two good ears,' Grubby-T said with a smirk.

Evan made a point of knocking on the door again even though it was obvious he wasn't going to get an answer.

'Is there a superintendent or somebody with another key?'

'I've got a key.'

'Really?'

'Yeah, really.' He couldn't fail to pick up on the surprise in Evan's voice. 'What, don't I look responsible enough to have one?'

Evan certainly didn't want to go down the road of insulting the man's trustworthiness.

'I think it would be a good idea if you went and got it. Then we can check to see if he's okay.'

'I suppose. He's an old guy and all.'

He lumbered back to his trailer, opened the door gingerly and tip-toed back inside. He was scared stiff of waking the slumbering wife inside. He'd learned to walk quietly. That was why Evan hadn't heard him coming. He reappeared a few seconds later carrying a big ring of keys. He caught Evan staring at them.

'Surprise, surprise, eh. Lots of folks trust me to keep a spare key.'

Evan had no idea where his defensive attitude was coming from. All he knew was that it was wasting time.

'I think you're the most trustworthy person I've seen all day. Shall we just open it up and see if he's okay?'

Grubby-T found the right key and unlocked the door, pushed it open. Then he stood back, gestured for Evan to go in first. Evan climbed the steps, an odor like meat going off in the sun flowing down to meet him. His stomach clenched at the smell.

'Faulkner. You in there?'

He went in, looked left and then to the right. Everything looked exactly like it had the last time he was there. Apart from the fact that Faulkner was lying face down on the floor, half in and half out of the bedroom. He looked as if somebody had taken an axe to his head, a vicious open gash behind his ear, a pool of congealing blood surrounding it, matting the steel-gray hair.

Evan leapt across the room in a single stride, felt for a pulse. It took him a while to find the right spot, it was so faint. Faulkner's chest rose and fell with each shallow breath.

Grubby-T had just entered the trailer. Evan yelled at him.

'Get an ambulance.'

'Oh shit. There's no way she's gonna sleep through all this.'

'I'm sure Faulkner will be touched by your concern for his welfare. Call an ambulance. Now!'

The guy's mouth was hanging open, his face ashen. Evan threw his cell phone to him.

'You don't have to live with her, buddy,' he said, catching the phone and fumbling with the keys.

Evan looked down at Faulkner helplessly while he gave the details to the 9-1-1 dispatcher. He had no idea what to do. Faulkner had lost a lot of blood. And it wasn't good that he was still unconscious after this length of time. A gaping laceration where the skin had been split wide open looked like an autopsy had been started early. Evan couldn't see any visible bone fragments, no exposed brain. The bleeding had already stopped. All he could do was sit tight, wait until the ambulance arrived.

It didn't take long for them to get there.

When they arrived, Grubby-T was back outside, sitting on the packing crate with his head in his hands. *Some tough guy you turned out to be*, Evan thought. He explained the situation to the paramedic in charge as his crew loaded Faulkner into the ambulance.

'Do you have any idea what time it might have happened?' the medic asked.

'Sometime after seven p.m. last night. That's when I last saw him.'

'That's a twelve-hour time frame. Did anyone else see him after that?'

'He had a visitor who was still here when I left. Apart from that I don't know. You should probably work on the basis that he's been out for twelve hours.'

Which in his opinion was exactly when it happened, down to the last quarter hour—between the time he left just after seven p.m. and precisely fifteen minutes later when Carl Hendricks blasted past him on the highway.

CHAPTER 28

HE GAVE GUILLORY a call to put her in the picture. With any luck she would get the case assigned to her. It took her a while to pick up.

'Have you any idea what time it is? Do you even know what day it is?'

'It might be the last day of Matt Faulkner's life.' Maybe it was a little melodramatic, but it sure got her attention.

'What the hell are you talking about?'

He took her through the morning's events, didn't say anything about his suspicions yet.

'Are you still at Faulkner's place?'

'Yeah, I'm still here with the guy that let me in.'

'Wait there. I'm on my way over. I'll call the department and let them know I've got it.'

She got there in under ten minutes. Evan was relieved to see that she didn't have her partner, Ryder, with her. Grubby-T was still sitting on the packing crate, busy excavating the contents of his nose with his finger. Evan called him over, introduced him to Guillory.

His name was Briggs. He'd got a bit of color back into his face and had stopped looking as if he was going to be sick any minute. She asked him to tell her what he knew. Briggs ran through the morning's events, didn't add anything to what Evan had already told her.

'What about last night?'

'I was out having a couple of quick beers with some of the guys.'

'Good for you. Did you see anything unusual is what I meant?'

Evan reckoned Briggs would have been lucky to be able to see his trailer after the *couple of quick beers* he'd consumed.

'No. Nothing. Sorry.'

'What time did you go out?'

He made a pretence of thinking about it. Evan would have bet dollars to donuts that he'd gone to the bar at the exact same time for the last twenty years.

'About six, I suppose.'

'When did you get back?'

'About eleven.'

'As you say, just a couple of quick beers,' she said, nodding like she'd heard it all before. 'Lots of people see you in the bar?'

'Yeah, everyone knows me.'

'I bet. How come you've got a key?'

'Because I'm his neighbor and that's what neighbors are for.' He was getting indignant again. 'You're as bad as him.' He jabbed a none-too-clean thumb in Evan's direction. At least it wasn't the finger most recently seen buried in his nose.

'I don't know if you've noticed, but there are a lot of other people live here. They're all neighbors too.'

'Probably because I've been here the longest, then.'

'Okay, Mr Briggs, I think we're done here. Someone will be around to take a statement later. I think your wife wants a word.' She nodded towards Briggs' trailer.

Briggs turned and looked at the diminutive woman standing in the open doorway to the trailer with her hands on her hips. His face dropped.

'Sure you don't want me to hang around? Something might come to me.'

'Well if it does, you be sure to let us know.'

She turned to face Evan. Behind her Briggs gave her the finger, then walked unhappily back to his trailer.

'Okay Mr. P, what have you got for me? I can see you're fit to burst with something.'

'I'm pretty sure I can tell you exactly when it happened and who did it.'

She made a show of looking at her watch.

'And it's not even eight o'clock yet. Not bad. How about motive? Or do I have to wait until eight thirty for that?'

He ignored the sarcasm. It would be gone in a minute when he got to the good stuff.

'I was here around seven last night. That's when I arranged to go fishing with Faulkner.'

'Fishing?'

Too good to pass.

'Yes, you know, you go out in a boat with a rod and a reel and catch fish. Millions of people do it every day. It's called a hobby.'

She gave him a look, didn't say anything. He was sure she wanted to laugh.

'Anyway, when I got here, Faulkner had a visitor. There was a Dodge Ram in the driveway.'

'A Dodge Ram.' She shook her head in mock amazement. 'You know, I don't think I've seen one of those for I don't know how long, must be two or three minutes at least. I don't suppose there can be more than two hundred thousand of them in this state.'

She held up a finger as if something had just come to her.

'That's okay though. If you took down the license number.' Her eyebrows lifted in anticipation of a positive response.

He shook his head. She nodded.

'Maybe next time. Did you see who the visitor was?'

He shook his head again.

'Faulkner shut the door. I couldn't see in.'

'Uh-huh. Does this get any better? I don't exactly feel like I'm drowning in a sea of hard facts.'

He ignored her, wait until you hear the next bit.

'When I was driving home, I had to stop on the shoulder to make an urgent phone call. While I was sitting there, the same Dodge Ram went past me, going like a bat out of hell.'

'You're sure it was the same one? Even though you didn't have the license number.'

'It was the same color. I'm pretty sure it was the same one.' He could hear how weak it sounded as he said it. 'I can't be one hundred percent certain.'

'Shame. That's what license plates are for I suppose. Okay, what happened next?'

He got the impression she wasn't taking him seriously. He'd soon change her tune.

'I followed it.'

'Any particular reason?'

'Nothing I can put my finger on, but that doesn't matter. What matters is who was driving it'

'For Christ's sake Buckley, just spit it out.'

'Carl Hendricks. I followed the pickup to his farm and saw him get out of it.'

He was disappointed with her reaction. He didn't get the *Hallelujah* he was hoping for. She didn't even whip off her hat and toss it in the air. Instead she folded her arms across her body, cradled her chin in her hand.

'Let me get this straight. Your theory is that Carl Hendricks was the man in Faulkner's trailer. Shortly after seven last night he brained him with some unidentified heavy object and then hightailed it back to his farmhouse. And this theory is based on the *possibility* that the two Dodge Rams you saw were one and the same.'

Despite her skeptical tone, he was sure that was exactly what had happened.

'Yes, that's exactly what I think.'

'Any ideas about why he might have done it?'

'No, but I heard Faulkner and the other man arguing.'

'You didn't mention that. Did you hear what it was about?'

Luckily, she didn't give him a chance to say no, he didn't know that either.

'Doesn't matter. I'll allow for the possibility that the man in the trailer was the one who attacked Faulkner. But you've still got a problem connecting the two pickup trucks.'

He felt completely deflated, like she just pricked him with a pin, all the excitement and enthusiasm escaping into the crisp morning air.

'Don't you even think it's worth looking into?'

'Did I say it's not worth looking into? Did I?' She gave him an exasperated look. 'I'm just not going to go jumping to conclusions before I've even started—unlike some people I could mention.'

She put a hand on his shoulder, steered him towards his car.

'If it was up to you, Hendricks would be in prison already. You ought to forget this detective stuff and get a job as a hanging judge.'

CHAPTER 29

EVAN WAS GENUINELY DISAPPOINTED he wasn't going to spend the day afloat, catching fish and drinking cold beers with Faulkner. Apart from anything else, he now had an empty day to fill. While most people spend Monday to Friday wishing their life away and don't want the weekend to end, he couldn't wait for the working week to start again. Sadly, he was going to have to. He gave Jacobson a call to see if he had any news.

'Didn't you get my text?'

Evan checked his phone.

'No, there's nothing.' It reminded him it was time he bought a new one.

'I spoke to the person I told you about,' Jacobson said.

'That's good.'

'I told her what a nice young man you are. She can't wait to meet you, and fill you in on five, ten, twenty years of local gossip, whatever you want.' Evan could feel Jacobson's smile on the other end of the line. 'I'd allow three to four hours if I were you. You didn't have any plans, did you?'

Evan told him about his aborted fishing trip.

'So what do you think's going on? Do you think Hendricks, or whoever it was, is trying to shut Faulkner up?'

It suddenly struck Evan that he didn't know what he thought. He'd told Guillory that he'd overheard an argument. Trouble was, he had no idea what it meant. Or even if it had any bearing on anything he was doing. They might have been arguing about football for all he knew.

'I'm not sure. I don't really know what I think.'

'You sound a bit despondent. Go and talk to Audrey Aubrey. Hell of a name, eh? Maybe some of the pieces will fall into place.'

Jacobson gave him the address and a phone number. As soon as he'd finished with Jacobson, Evan called her. She told him he could drop in any time.

IF HE WAS EXPECTING Audrey Aubrey to be a matronly old lady with a blue rinse, he couldn't have been more wrong. Her hair was cut short and it was gray, not blue. It would have been called distinguished in a man. He had no idea how old she was but he was sure she didn't look it.

She looked like she'd be in huge demand with the pension industry advertisers who targeted *active seniors* and put full page advertisements in the Sunday supplements—the ones with the seniors freewheeling downhill on their bicycles, their legs sticking out and huge grins plastered on their virtually wrinkle-free faces.

She invited him in and got him settled in the living room, then went off to make some coffee.

'I hope you don't want decaf,' she called from the kitchen. 'I wouldn't have that crap in the house. What a complete waste of time that is. I like a good dose of caffeine to keep me regular.'

That was a little more information than he felt was appropriate in the first two minutes of their acquaintance. But he liked his coffee strong too, said that would be just fine. She brought it in with a piece of cake the size of a shoebox.

'This is my maple-pecan danish coffee cake,' she said proudly as she put it down on the side table. He was sure the table dipped under the weight. 'You look like you need feeding up.'

He noticed she didn't take a piece for herself, dug right in just the same.

'I don't eat it myself.'

Looking at her still-trim figure, he could believe it.

'Tom Jacobson says it rots your teeth. Sugar, not just my cake, of course.'

He was sure that if he listened closely enough, he would actually hear the decay eating into the enamel of his teeth. Like it was a competition—could he get through the cake before the cake got through his teeth?

'I had a lot of dental work done,' she carried on. 'Look at this.'

The maple-pecan danish coffee cake was heavy going. He let her prattle on about her dental work for a while longer while he worked on it.

'Tom tells me you're the go-to person for local knowledge around here,' he said, feeling pleased with the adroit way he segued from Tom the dental maestro to Tom the flatterer-of-old-ladies.

She smiled indulgently. 'Tom's full of shit. But he's right, up to a point. I worked on the local paper for twenty-five years. There wasn't much went on I didn't hear about. But that was back then. Now I'm retired and I don't really get out so much.'

'That's not a problem. It's the background information that I'm interested in.'

She leaned forward, her elbows resting on her knees.

'What is it you need to know? Tom wouldn't tell me what this is about.'

'I'm sure it's nothing, really. Just something that's been bugging me. There's a farm a few miles out of town called *Beau Terre*—'

'The Saunders place.'

'That's it. So you know it?'

'I've been out to the house a few times. I knew Mary Saunders quite well. And her husband George. Before they moved away.'

'Did they have a son?'

The question threw her. She stood up, walked through to the kitchen.

'Do you want any more coffee?'

He was afraid it would come with another couple of pounds of cake, said no. She came back carrying a refill for herself. He wasn't sure whether she was buying time to marshal her thoughts, or whether she was just committed to her caffeine-keeps-you-regular routine.

'There were two sons,' she said carefully, 'Pierce and Jason.'

The look on her face suggested the memories of the Saunders boys weren't all good. Either that or the caffeine was kicking in ahead of time.

'Actually, the younger son was christened Leonard. He always went by his middle name, Jason. I suppose he thought Leonard was very old-fashioned.'

Evan nodded to himself. Leonard Jason Saunders. Or L. J. Saunders as it was listed on the property deeds.

'It's Jason I'm interested in.'

Once again, her face gave her away, told him she wasn't

surprised.

'Then you're in luck, because I couldn't tell you anything about the older boy, Pierce. He was quite a bit older, got caught in the Vietnam draft. I don't remember if he was killed or missing in action, but as far as I know he never came home again. There was never any what they'd call closure these days. Back then you were just expected to get on with your life.'

'Okay. What about Jason? What was he like?'

'He was a little shit when he was growing up,' she said with unexpected force, 'and made his parents' lives a complete misery. I don't think he was actually kicked out of school but it came pretty close. And he was no better when he grew up.'

She leaned back, crossed her legs. Evan was treated to a view of her still-shapely calves. He was thankful she was far too old for there to be any risk of a repeat of the previous day's events.

'What happened to him?'

'Luckily for everyone around here, he got a totally uncharacteristic attack of patriotic fervor and joined the army. He idolized his older brother, took it really hard when he didn't come back. He was at an impressionable age—not that I'm trying to make excuses for how he turned out—but he was most likely trying to follow in his footsteps. Unluckily, he didn't get blown to pieces in some godforsaken hell hole like his brother did. Or instead of him.'

She looked down and picked imaginary pieces of lint from her white blouse. Evan was shocked at the intensity of her dislike for him. He wondered if there was any personal animosity but didn't push it.

'So he came back?'

She looked back up at him. Shook her head.

'No, he didn't come back, not here. Not so far as I know. He left the army with a dishonorable discharge and drifted around.'

'What did he do to get a dishonorable discharge? That's got to be pretty serious.'

'I don't know for certain. All I heard were rumors. And I don't want to spread them around—despite what Tom Jacobson thinks.' She seemed keen to be able to claim some of the moral high ground from Jacobson. 'Do you know, he told me that if patients start gossiping in the chair, he drills a bit deeper?'

He smiled, made a mental note to look up the sort of offences that could result in a dishonorable discharge. He had no idea whether records of specific cases were in the public domain or not. Probably not, the U.S. Army wasn't known for washing its dirty laundry in public.

'What happened after he left the army?'

She let out a short, harsh laugh.

'It gets better and better. He really was a son to be proud of! I know he spent some time in prison down in Texas. That much is fact. Again, I only heard rumors about why he was in there.'

He would have loved to push her into disclosing the rumors she'd heard. It would have been interesting to find out if the crimes inside and outside the military were the same. Unfortunately, there was no way she was going to tell him. She desperately wanted him to go back to Jacobson, tell him that she wasn't an idle gossip.

'It completely destroyed George and Mary. First, they lost Pierce. And then all the trouble with Jason. One thing after another. There were all these awful rumors flying around.' Her face darkened and she fell silent as she thought back. 'It got so they couldn't bear to go out.'

'What happened to them?'

'They moved away. At their time of life, they had to leave that beautiful farm and move away.'

She shook her head sadly, her mind full of the cruel injustices that lie in wait around every corner.

'Do you know if they're still alive?'

'No, sorry. I might be able to find out.'

'Doesn't matter. Did you know they gave, or sold, the farm to Jason?'

She sat up straight faster than if he'd goosed her.

'Well I never knew that. Some source of local information I turned out to be.'

'I went to the County Recorder's office and looked it up. That's where I start to get confused.'

'I don't understand.'

'The records show the last transfer was from George and Mary to Jason. It's listed as L. J. Saunders, but it's obviously Jason. There's nothing after that.'

'So?'

'The man who lives there now is called Carl Hendricks.'

A slight frown creased her forehead. 'That name rings a bell.'

He explained briefly about the case he was working on and Hendricks' job as the school bus driver.

'I missed all that. I retired right around then and went on a six-month world cruise. I'd always wanted to go. I vaguely remember hearing things when I got back but it had all died down.'

'None of that is really why I wanted to talk to you. It's just that I went out to Hendricks' place and ended up thinking how come he was living there. The place must be worth millions. Tom thought you might know.'

'I can't help you I'm afraid. I didn't even know Saunders came back.'

'Tom suggested that Saunders might have changed his name to Hendricks. That makes sense after what you've just told me about his past.'

'But there's no way on earth he'd have gotten the job as a school bus driver with a criminal record like that.'

'You're right. It can't be the same person. I'm back where I started.'

A flashback of what happened after he found himself back at square one with Barbara crossed his mind. Time to go.

'Even so, it's worth checking to make sure. Have you got a picture of Hendricks?'

He said he didn't but he could get one.

'Don't bother. I know where I can get one of Saunders. I'll email a copy to you.'

He gave her his email address and got up to go, thanked her for her time.

'I feel so sorry for his parents,' she said again at the door. 'It's totally beyond me how, after losing one son, the other one could turn out so badly. And when you think how well their daughter did for herself.'

'Their daughter?'

'Yes. Didn't you know? They had a daughter called Brenda. A lovely girl.'

He didn't know how he was supposed to have known. And while it was nice to hear that Brenda was a lovely girl and had done so well for herself, it didn't have any bearing on anything he was interested in. She wasn't living at the farm now. But he ought to show some interest to be polite.

'What did she end up doing?'

'She married the future Chief of Police, Matt Faulkner.'

CHAPTER 30

'ARE YOU FEELING OKAY?' Audrey asked. 'You look like you've seen a ghost.'

'I'm fine, just surprised.' He was anything but fine. 'I've talked to Matt Faulkner quite a lot recently. He never mentioned that his wife grew up in the house Carl Hendricks lives in.'

'Is that so unusual?'

'I think so. I specifically remember asking him how come Hendricks ended up living in such a big place. He said he had no idea.'

His mind was racing with the possibilities that were now opening up.

'We'd talked briefly about his wife. You'd have thought he'd say *No idea, but that's the house my wife grew up in*. We actually stood together and looked at a photo of her standing in front of the barns. Why wouldn't you mention such a massive coincidence? The fact that he didn't is suspicious, as far as I'm concerned.'

'I'm sure there's a perfectly good reason. Matt's a good man.'

He wasn't interested in her platitudes.

'There must be a reason he didn't want to make the connection. If that house was in his wife's family all those years, it's just not possible he doesn't know what happened to it after they moved away.'

'His wife would have known for sure,' Audrey agreed. 'Her brother had just come back to town and was living in the family home. Even if they weren't close, she would know if he sold it to this Carl Hendricks.'

'Or if he was still living there but under a different name. And if she knew, Faulkner knew. She couldn't keep something like that from her husband.'

He couldn't believe Faulkner had deceived him so badly.

'What all this means is that Faulkner knows for sure whether Jason Saunders and Carl Hendricks are the same person.'

As he said it, something went off in his brain. Audrey saw it in his face.

'What is it?

He couldn't believe he hadn't made the connection before.

'Faulkner took me to a bar a few nights ago. That's when this happened.'

He pointed to his face.

'Nice places he takes you. I didn't like to ask what happened.'

Evan wasn't really listening to her.

'We were talking about Hendricks and he said *Jason*. I'm sure of it. He passed it off saying I misheard him because the music was too loud. I'd completely forgotten. Probably because of this.'

He pointed to his face again.

'What happened?'

She was peering closely at his face now that the topic was up for discussion.

'I was attacked in the parking lot. The guy broke my nose and bit off a piece of my ear as well as kicking me in the . . . you get the picture. I've been worrying about the guy ever since and obviously buried everything else.'

Audrey was warming to the theme now. 'All this suggests that they are the same person and he doesn't want you to know.'

'Exactly. If Saunders sold the house to Hendricks, what's to hide? But if Saunders *became* Hendricks that means Carl Hendricks is—'

'Matt Faulkner's brother-in-law.'

'And that's something he's hoping to keep quiet.'

They were both quiet for a long moment as their words sank in. As far as Evan could see, there were no innocent explanations for Faulkner wanting to keep it a secret.

'It might just be that Matt doesn't want any association with Hendricks,' Audrey said. 'After all, if he is Jason Saunders, he's a bit of a scumbag.'

Evan's jaw dropped. Old ladies didn't use language like that. He gave her a reproachful look. She poked him gently in the ribs.

'Don't be such a prude. Anyway, it makes sense that the ex-Chief of Police wouldn't want to be connected to a criminal. And now his wife's dead, there's no reason to be.'

He was far from convinced. In his mind the possible explanations were a lot more sinister.

'It might also be that he was protecting and covering up for Hendricks.'

She sighed, sorry for him that he couldn't see it her way, only saw the worst in people.

'I suppose it's your job to have a suspicious mind. Myself, I just can't believe it. He was the best police chief this town ever had.'

He was well aware he had a very uncomfortable conversation with Faulkner coming up. Thinking about it made him feel nauseous. If it was true, it would blow Faulkner's whole reputation out of the water.

'I'm going to have to ask him about it. Before I do, I'd like to have my facts straight. It's got to be one hundred percent. I need that photograph of Saunders as soon as possible.'

'I'll get right on it.' She gave him a playful shove. 'Cheer up. You've got a face like a smacked arse, as my dear old husband used to say. That was before he buggered off—another favorite phrase of his—back to England.'

At least her language brought a grin to his face. But it didn't change the ominous feeling that he'd bitten off a lot more than he could chew.

CHAPTER 31

THE ONE POSITIVE THING to come out of the day's revelations was that he didn't need to schlep half way across the county to the District Court and spend hours trawling through the change of name records. All the evidence pointed towards it being true. As soon as he got Audrey's email he would know for sure.

He wished he was a bit more tech savvy so that he could get his emails on his phone. But he'd only just gotten the hang of texting. He'd have to go to the office to get it. A thought suddenly crossed his mind. He stopped, turned the car around and headed back the other way towards Faulkner's trailer park.

He parked outside Faulkner's trailer and tried the door. It was locked. Walking across to the neighbor's trailer, he heard the blare of the TV was coming from inside before he got near it, a football game by the sound of it.

Briggs came to the door. He had a beer can in his hand, scowled when he saw who it was.

'You again.'

He looked back at the TV. Evan saw a stack of empty cans on

the floor next to his chair. There was a smell coming out of the trailer like the catbox had caught on fire.

'Yes, me again.'

'What do you want? I'm watching the game.'

'I'm heading over to visit Faulkner. I thought you might like to come along. Being such good neighbors and all.'

Briggs looked at him like he was deranged.

'I told you, I'm watching the game.'

Evan tried to peer round him into the trailer.

'Doesn't look like your wife is in.'

'She's gone to see a movie with her sister.' He belched softly, sharing the smell of second-hand beer with Evan. '*Terminator* two hundred and twenty-five or something. She loves all that shit.'

'You're more of a *Bridges of Madison County* man, are you? See yourself as a bit of a romantic Clint Eastwood type. *Brokeback Mountain* perhaps?'

Briggs looked at him like he was something unpleasant on the bottom of his shoe. For a second Evan thought he was going to take a swing at him.

'Give my regards to Matt. Wish him better.'

He started to close the door. Evan put his hand on it.

'I want to take him some of his things. Can you let me in?'

'Jesus Christ. All I want to do is watch the game in peace. Is that too much to ask for?'

He disappeared into the trailer, came back with the big bunch of keys.

'Here, let yourself in. Don't forget to lock up again when you're done.'

He threw the keys to Evan, then closed the door in his face.

Evan found the right key after a few tries and let himself in. He didn't feel guilty in the slightest about misleading Briggs. He certainly didn't feel guilty about nosing around in Faulkner's home behind his back. Not after the duplicitous way in which Faulkner had treated him.

He knew exactly what he was after. And where to find it. He went into the kitchen and over to where the photographs were tacked to the wall. It didn't take him long to find the one he wanted, the one of Faulkner's wife with her parents outside a barn—a barn he now knew was sitting on Carl Hendricks's property. He pulled off, studied it more closely

He didn't completely recognize it. Apart from the fact that the photograph was at least fifty years old, he hadn't paid too much attention to the barns when he was there. But it was definitely one of them.

He put it in his pocket, then carefully scrutinized all of the others for any tell-tale signs that might mean something to him now that he knew what he was looking for. There was nothing of any use.

Damn.

That would have been too easy. There was a gap where another photograph had recently sat. That didn't necessarily mean anything. It could mean that Hendricks had removed it the previous night. Or it could mean nothing at all. It was probably nothing. Faulkner was hardly likely to have a picture of Hendricks on his wall, after he'd done his best to hide their connection.

He sat down at the kitchen table, thought about what to do next. He didn't have any qualms about searching Faulkner's place if he thought it would produce anything. But he wasn't sure it was worth it. Faulkner wasn't stupid. And he didn't know what he was looking for anyway. Then, just as he was about to lock up, he suddenly thought of something. It only took him five minutes to find what he was after. Faulkner wouldn't need it for the next couple of days. He slipped it into his pocket, locked up and dropped the keys off with the still grumbling Briggs before driving away.

CHAPTER 32

WHAT EVAN REALLY WANTED to do was drive straight to the hospital and confront Faulkner. He'd always been impatient, had to force himself to take it slowly, wait until he had all his ducks in a row. He needed the picture of Saunders before he talked to Faulkner, so he drove back to his office to see if Audrey had sent him anything yet.

The light was on in Jacobson's office as he walked past. Tom would want to know the outcome of his meeting with Audrey. He knocked and went in.

'Hey, Evan. How'd it go with Audrey?'

Jacobson was sitting at his desk doing something with some unpleasant looking surgical instruments. Evan picked up a box of what looked like serrated toothpicks.

'What the hell are these?'

'Barbed broaches. They're for removing dental pulp and other rubbish from root canals. Might be using one on you if you eat too many of Audrey's cakes.'

He winked knowingly at Evan, who wished he hadn't asked.

'I don't know how you do this job.'

He put the box back down. It made him feel queasy just thinking about it. He was sure he could feel a sharp twinge of pain coming from one of his back teeth.

'At least I'm the one dishing the pain out. My nose hasn't been broken recently. Got two complete ears as well.'

'Do you want to hear what Audrey said, or not?'

'From the look on your face, it's something important.'

'It was you who first suggested Saunders might have changed his name to Carl Hendricks.'

Jacobson nodded.

'It turns out Saunders was a bit of a scumbag, to use Audrey's term.' Jacobson raised his eyebrows and smiled. 'He also had a sister, Brenda, who got married and became . . . '

He paused for effect.

'Come on Evan, don't make me use one of these to extract the information.'

He brandished something that Evan didn't want to look at.

'Mrs Matt Faulkner!'

'You're kidding.'

He dropped whatever he'd been brandishing onto the desk, leaned back and put his hands behind his head.

'That means if Hendricks is really Saunders, then he's Matt Faulkner's brother-in-law.'

'Which throws an entirely different light on your case. One that doesn't reflect well on our ex-police chief.'

'It puts me in a difficult spot.'

He sat down on the corner of Jacobson's desk, picked up one of the surgical instruments.

'I can see that,' Jacobson said, taking it out of Evan's hand and putting it back down. 'I don't suppose you're looking forward to your next chat with Mr Faulkner.'

'No. He's suddenly turned into an uncooperative witness. Or maybe even a suspect. An accessory at least.'

Jacobson drummed his fingers on the desk.

'How does this tie in with your theory that it was Hendricks who attacked him.'

'I'm not sure. One obvious scenario is that Hendricks is the culprit and Faulkner covered up for him—'

'And now Hendricks is trying to tie up the loose ends. Permanently.'

'It would explain why Faulkner was so keen to blame it all on Robbie Clayton. A convenient fall guy.'

Jacobson frowned.

'What are you suggesting? That they did away with him as well to provide a false trail?'

'I don't know. It all seems a bit far-fetched. Blood's thicker than water, but that would be taking it to extremes.'

'I think you need to get your facts together before getting carried away by all this. It's too easy to make the circumstances fit with your existing theory.'

'I know. That's why I need the email.'

'Email?'

'Surely you know what email is, Tom. Even Audrey uses it.'

He slid off the edge of the desk as Jacobson picked up a dental scalpel.

'Audrey said she'd dig out a photograph of Saunders and email it to me. Then I'll know for sure if that's who Hendricks really is. I was on my way to see if she'd done it yet.'

'Why don't you get your email on your phone, like everyone

else? I do.'

'Because I'm a luddite. I'll go and check now.'

'I'll come with you. Just in case your friend is lurking upstairs.'

'You might as well bring the scalpel just in case.'

CHAPTER 33

EVAN OPENED HIS OFFICE and fired up his computer. Jacobson prowled around impatiently.

'That thing looks like you need a handle to crank it. We could walk to Audrey's place and ask her quicker.'

Evan ignored him and checked his email. Spam, spam and more spam. But then, there it was. She'd sent it just after he left her. If he'd thought she'd be that quick he'd have waited and had another piece of cake. He called Jacobson over, opened the attachment.

Audrey had gotten hold of a photograph of Saunders at his army basic training graduation ceremony. It was old and grainy and looked like it had been scanned from a local paper.

They both looked at the picture of the proud young man in his Class A uniform. Little did he know that a few short years later he'd be out on his ear, a dishonorable discharge on his record.

'It's him,' Evan whispered, as if by saying it too loudly it would cease to be so. 'I'm sure it's him.'

Jacobson studied the image carefully, his head gently shaking.

'I don't know what Hendricks looks like.'

Evan jabbed his finger at the screen.

'He looks like that.'

'I don't know how you can tell. His cap covers half his face. Try zooming in a bit.'

Evan zoomed in on Saunders' face. It didn't help. What they gained in size, they lost in quality. He zoomed back out again.

'You need to get a photo of Hendricks to compare it to,' Jacobson said.

'I don't need one. I recognize his nose. It's been broken and badly set at some time in the past. He's also got a scar across the bridge of his nose. You can't see it because of the shadow from his cap.'

'You're the expert on broken noses. What are you going to do?'

'First of all, I'm going to call the hospital, see if Faulkner's awake yet.'

'And if he is?'

'I'm going to take that photo'—he pointed at the screen—'and this one'—he pulled the one he'd taken from Faulkner's trailer out of his pocket—'and see if I can shake something loose.'

'You don't take any prisoners, do you? The guy's in the hospital. He nearly died. He might be dead now.'

'In which case, I can't hurt him. But he didn't tell me the truth. So if he's still alive, I want to know why he lied.'

'You need to be careful, Evan. There are some serious stakes here. His whole reputation is at risk at the very least. If you're right, he doesn't come out of this looking good, whatever happens.'

'I'm aware of that. Does that mean I should drop it?'

Jacobson held up his hands.

'I'm not saying that. Just be careful. If you tell Faulkner what you know and then Hendricks finds out, you'll be on his list too.

How many people after you can you handle?'

'I'm a little more prepared now.'

He put his hand in his pocket, brought out the SIG-Sauer P226 pistol he had taken from Faulkner's trailer. He was disconcerted how good it felt in his hand. Almost natural.

'Jesus, Evan, where'd you get that from?'

Jacobson took it from him like a fascinated schoolboy. He hefted it a moment before putting it down on the desk.

'I borrowed it from Faulkner.'

'Uh-huh. I assume he doesn't know about this *loan* he's made you yet.'

'Not yet. With any luck I'll have it back in his trailer before he gets back from the hospital. Or perhaps I'll keep it and blame it on Hendricks.'

Jacobson gave him his best reproving look.

'Do you know how to use it?'

'My understanding is that you point this end'—he pointed to the barrel—'at someone you don't like and pull the trigger. That's this little curved bit here.'

'Okay, smartass. I just hope you know what you're getting into. If you do end up shooting anyone with it, you are going to be in some serious shit. My advice is you take it back right now.'

CHAPTER 34

EVAN PRINTED OUT THE photograph Audrey had sent him and then sent her a quick email. After that he called the hospital and was told that Faulkner was awake and doing well. They were keeping him in for observation for a few days. When he asked if he could have visitors they said that was okay too. So long as they didn't tire him out too much.

That'll be the least of his worries, he thought and headed down to his car. When he got to the hospital, they told him Faulkner already had a visitor but he could go in too. They reminded him again that Faulkner was still very weak, told him not to be too long.

He had a good idea who the other visitor was. Sure enough, there was Guillory sitting comfortably in the visitor's chair when he walked in. Faulkner was sitting up in bed with his head in a bandage and a saline drip in his arm. Apart from that he didn't look too bad.

'If it isn't the local hero himself,' Guillory said, then started humming the Springsteen song.

Evan held up his arms to accept the accolade, knowing it wasn't going to last long.

'I sure hope that's going to stick like the last name you gave me.'

'Peeper, you mean? I doubt it.'

She chuckled. He realized she did it a lot, in stark contrast to her sour-faced partner. Not only that, but the sound immediately reminded him of Barbara Schneider. It could have been her if he'd had his eyes shut. It was a disconcerting discovery.

'Heroes come and go, but you know what they say, once a peeper, always a peeper.'

'Looks like we're quits,' Faulkner said. 'Thank you. Although I got to you before you were unconscious, so I'm still ahead.'

'Thank Briggs, not me. I was all for leaving you there. He said, no, call it in.'

Faulkner smiled, then winced. Evan felt a pang of guilt at the prospect of what he had to do as soon as Guillory left. Why did there have to be such an easy bonhomie developing between the three of them? Faulkner had no idea of what was coming. He was probably feeling good about being alive. Now his world was about to go up in smoke. *What the hell am I feeling guilty about* he tried to tell himself. It didn't stop him from feeling sick.

Guillory got up out of her chair and stretched, eased the kinks out of her back.

'Looks like you were right about the perp, too.'

He tried to keep the told-you-so look off his face and failed.

'Don't look so smug. You wanted to lock him up first and ask questions later.'

He looked at Faulkner who nodded, which made him wince again.

'It was definitely Hendricks. I came back inside after talking to you. He hit me upside the head as soon as my back was turned. I don't know what it was he used. Luckily it wasn't quite up to the job.'

'Have you been around to see him yet?' Evan asked Guillory.

'We went 'round there but he wasn't in.'

'Done a bunk or just out buying groceries?'

'Can't say. There was no sign of him or his pickup. That doesn't prove anything. We're heading back out there later on to see if we can catch him.'

She looked down at Faulkner sitting propped up in his bed.

'Look after yourself, Matt. I'll be in touch.'

Evan sat down in the visitor's chair before his legs gave out. He couldn't believe how nervous he felt. He wished more than anything that Audrey's photograph had proved him wrong. A cold sweat broke out on his forehead, his stomach churning. Faulkner was eyeing him carefully.

'You look as bad as I feel.'

'I can't stand hospitals.'

'It's fine by me. Bed's more comfortable than the ones in the morgue.'

Evan didn't know how to start. They both sat there in a slightly less than comfortable silence. Faulkner broke it first.

'Sorry about the fishing trip. Maybe we'll do it another time.'

Evan swallowed a lump the size of his fist. *I sincerely doubt that after tonight.* He stood up again.

'I've got to go to the bathroom.'

He splashed cold water over his face. Tried to calm down. His heart was thumping in his chest, his mouth dry. In the corner of the room a huge cockroach scuttled across the floor. He turned and stomped on it, felt it crunch and pop under his shoe. He felt as loathsome as the bug he'd just crushed. It didn't help remembering that Faulkner had lied to him. He liked the guy. Now he was about to destroy him and grind him into the floor like he'd just done to the roach.

Faulkner took things out of his hands when he came back into the room.

'What's on your mind, son? I might have a bang on the head but I'm not stupid. I can see something's eating you. Fire away.'

Evan didn't say anything. He took the two photographs out of his pocket, set them down in Faulkner's lap. Faulkner looked down at them. Then back at Evan.

'Uh-huh. I won't ask how you got these. Particularly this one'—he held up the one from his trailer—'but I can see why you look so green around the gills.'

Evan let out a big rush of air, felt a little better now the real reason for his visit was out in the open. He'd felt like a fraud during the banter with the two of them. Faulkner pre-empted his next question.

'You want to know why I didn't tell you Carl Hendricks is my brother-in-law.'

'That would be as good a place as any to start.'

'Because he's a low-life sack of shit. I've spent my whole life putting as much distance between him and me as possible.'

'I can understand that. I've heard some stuff about him. I'd feel the same.'

'But you're offended because I didn't take you into my confidence. Especially now we're drinking and fishing buddies. Is that it?'

'Don't be ridiculous. I couldn't give a shit about that.'

'What then?'

Evan forced himself to look Faulkner directly in the eye.

'It makes me wonder what else you're hiding.'

'I get it. You think Hendricks abducted Daniel Clayton and I knew about it and covered it up because he's my wife's brother. Blood's thicker than water and all that crap.'

'Wouldn't you?'

'I might. If I was the sort of person who was prone to jumping to half-assed conclusions.'

'You think I'm jumping to conclusions? So give me an explanation I can believe.'

'I just did. I was the Chief of Police. He'd been thrown out of the army and been in prison. How do you think that was going to affect my career prospects if I went around saying, *Hey, have you met my brother-in-law?* to all those upstanding local citizens?'

Evan started to say something but Faulkner cut him off.

'What I want to know is how my concerns for my career and social standing—however selfish you might think they were—somehow translates in your mind into me covering up a major crime. Maybe you can explain that to me.'

'I didn't say that, you did.'

'It's what you think though.'

'I don't want to think it, but there are so many unanswered questions.'

'Try me.'

'Why was he thrown out of the army? What did he go to prison for?'

'None of that's relevant.'

'Any reason why I'm supposed to take your word for that? Seeing as the whole reason I'm here is because you already lied to me.'

Faulkner jerked forward, almost pulled the drip out of his arm.

'I never lied to you. I just didn't volunteer all the information you feel you're entitled to.'

Evan didn't believe it for a minute but he let it go for the moment.

'How did he end up living in the farm?'

'Guilt. It's what makes the world go around. His folks thought they'd let him down. They blamed themselves for the piece of shit he turned into. So they gave him the farm and moved away. Felt like they'd evened the score.' He shook his head, equal parts despair and exasperation. 'And they say crime doesn't pay.'

'Your wife couldn't have been very happy about that.'

'She didn't care about the farm. She missed having her folks around of course.'

'What did she think about her brother?'

Faulkner didn't answer immediately. Was he concocting a carefully crafted reply? Or had it given him genuine pause for thought?

'It was her one blind spot. She couldn't see him for what he was. She saw him as a victim just like her folks did.'

'I bet that caused a few arguments between you.'

'That's none of your damn business,' Faulkner snapped.

He was right.

'Why did he change his name?'

Faulkner looked at him like he must be the one who just got hit on the head.

'What sort of a stupid question is that? Why do you think? So that he could start out as a brand-new scumbag, why else?'

Evan managed not to laugh. He liked Faulkner's attitude.

'I can see you're an advocate of rehabilitation.'

'Rehabilitation my ass. You couldn't rehabilitate him any more than you could rehabilitate a cockroach.'

Evan was reminded of the horrible crunch when he'd squashed the roach in the bathroom. And the disgusting mess on the floor afterwards. He'd read that they used elephants to squash the heads of convicted criminals in India. He pulled his mind back on track.

'How did he get that job? Surely changing your name doesn't just wipe the slate clean. How did he provide references and that sort of thing?'

Faulkner looked away but not before Evan had seen something in his eyes. Suddenly it clicked.

'Don't tell me you got him the job.'

Faulkner didn't say anything which was admission enough.

'For Christ's sake, Faulkner. He's a convicted criminal and you got him the job as a school bus driver.'

'You don't understand.'

'You've just spent the last ten minutes running him down, telling me he was beyond rehabilitation. Then I find out you went and got him that job. I just can't believe it.'

He ran his hand through his hair and held it back, enjoying the pull on his scalp, then released it again.

'You don't understand,' Faulkner said again.

'Then enlighten me.'

All the fight had suddenly gone out of Faulkner. He looked like nothing more than an old man sitting in a hospital bed. Evan couldn't help but feel a bit sorry for him. It was about to get a lot worse.

'I did it because my wife asked me to. She thought he deserved a break.'

'A break?' It came out as a squeak. He shook his head in disbelief. 'He'd just been given a property worth I don't know how much. How much of a break did he need?'

'She thought getting him a worthwhile job would help. Stop him from sitting around the house drinking and calling up all his old lowlife buddies. She was worried he'd get led astray and end up back in prison.'

Evan started to say that from the sound of it Hendricks would be the one doing the leading, but Faulkner wasn't listening.

'It's not as if he came to me and said *Hey, I'd really like a job as the school bus driver, because I want the chance to get close to the kids* and then I went out and found him one. My wife saw the advertisement in the local paper and suggested it. The idea came from her, not him.'

'And you thought, anything for an easy life. Keep the wife happy.'

He regretted saying it as soon as it was out. Especially as he'd have done pretty much anything for Sarah.

'No, that wasn't it at all. This was right around the time Brenda got ill.'

He picked up the photograph of his wife with her folks, the one Evan had brought from his trailer. He was looking through it to a time long ago. Evan was ashamed of the fact that he'd brought the photograph along, not to give an old man in his hospital bed some reminder of better times, but to use it as a weapon against him.

'There was even some suggestion that all this trouble with her brother started it off.'

Evan groaned. Even though Faulkner hadn't said it in an accusatory way, he felt a lance of guilt pierce him to his core. Faulkner had risked his own career in an attempt to make his wife's life a little easier. Now, ten years later and with the benefit of hindsight, Evan was giving him a hard time. He swallowed a lump the size of his fist. This wasn't how he'd pictured it panning out.

'Her doctors said she shouldn't get stressed out over anything because it would just make her worse. And she was stressed as hell over her brother.' He snorted, the sound full of disgust. 'She even gave herself a hard time because she had a nice life and her brother didn't. No wonder you never see a hungry psychiatrist.'

'Why couldn't she see what he was really like?'

'Who knows? That's families for you. Did you ever read the poem *This Be The Verse* by Philip Larkin? He had a different take on families.'

Evan ignored the question, plowed on.

'What did you do?'

'I told the school I'd run all the background checks for them. Then I told them he'd come out purer than the driven snow. The perfect candidate to drive their kids around.'

'Did it help your wife get better?'

'Definitely. For a while. Whereas my stress levels went through the roof. And stayed there.'

'Did you regret doing it?'

'What is this, some kind of psychiatric assessment?'

'Sorry, none of my business.'

'Don't worry about it. You know, it's actually something of a relief to talk about it after all these years.'

Unfortunately, they both knew it wasn't about to end there, with Evan assuming the role of Father Confessor, absolving Faulkner of his sins. It was about to get a lot worse for Faulkner. And he could see it coming.

'I've really dropped myself in it haven't I? As far as you're concerned, I've now got a compelling motive for protecting Carl Hendricks. If he goes down, I go down.'

They were both quiet as the unavoidable truth of Faulkner's

words sank in. The only sound was a comforting, quiet hum coming from the equipment in the room.

'That's only true if Hendricks was guilty,' Evan said, surprising himself as he came to Faulkner's defence. 'Why did he go to prison?'

Faulkner leaned back on the pillows, looked up at the ceiling. He closed his eyes. Took a deep breath. Something bad was coming.

'Unlawful sexual intercourse,' he said quietly, without opening his eyes.

Evan was beyond reacting. He leaned back and closed his own eyes.

'Girl or boy?'

'Fifteen-year-old girl. Fifteen going on twenty-five. Three of them were convicted. Him and a couple of buddies from the army.'

His voice was completely flat, devoid of emotion. A bare facts voice, as if that was sufficient to distance himself from his own culpability.

Evan was lost for words. He didn't know what to say, wished more than anything that he was somewhere else. And he wondered if all this would have come out in a small boat in the middle of a lake, or whether it was just Faulkner's weakened state.

'He spent two years in prison,' Faulkner continued, 'before the conviction was overturned on appeal.'

Evan sat up and opened his eyes.

'That's something, at least. Why was it overturned?'

'Apparently the original jury was deadlocked. So it can't have been black and white anyway. Then the judge reminded them about the time and expense involved with the trial, and possibly a retrial if they didn't make up their minds, which he shouldn't have done.'

'You mean he basically said *Hurry up, I've got a dinner date to get to.* I suppose it's just a job to him.'

'Something like that.'

'That means Hendricks got off on a technicality.'

'I suppose so.'

'What about the other guys?'

'Them too.'

Evan stood up and paced the small room. Faulkner was still lying back with his eyes closed, probably wishing Hendricks had hit him a bit harder.

'What did your wife think about all this?'

'She thought he was set up. That it was all the other guys' fault. One of them was seriously unstable, that's for sure. Her brother never actually did anything. He was framed. Everybody had it in for him.'

It had the sound of a well-worn argument. Evan knew that he'd been right about it causing more than a few problems between Faulkner and his wife.

'Is that possible?'

'Anything's possible. If you mean, do the police routinely fit people up for crimes they didn't commit? No. Do they make mistakes? All the time.'

'What did you think? Could he have done it?'

'Of course he *could have*. For what it's worth I don't think he actually did. He might be the lowest form of pond life, but he's certainly not stupid.'

'That's handy for your conscience.'

Faulkner tried to give him a hard stare. He looked a bit too comical with his head bandaged to pull it off.

'Let me ask you something, Mr Holier-than-thou. What would you be prepared to do to bring back your wife?'

'We're not talking about me here.'

'That's *handy* for you too.'

He picked up the photograph of his wife again, waved it at Evan.

'I didn't want to lose my wife so I went against my better judgement. I did what she asked me to do. I put my career on the line because I didn't want to make her life more difficult than it already was.'

He dropped the photograph onto the bed again.

'Something tells me you might bend a few rules to get your own wife back.'

Evan didn't have an answer for him. Faulkner was right and they both knew it. Faulkner wasn't going to leave it there either.

'The only thing that differentiates us is I already had to find out if I had the balls to do it. You, I'm not so sure.'

Evan wasn't sure how he'd allowed Faulkner to get him on the back foot. On the subject of Sarah too. It was time he turned the tables again.

'Okay, okay, you did what you had to do. Your wife's getting better, you're learning to live with it. Hendricks is keeping his nose clean . . . and then Daniel Clayton happens. That can't have been a good day.'

Faulkner snorted.

'Not for anyone, it wasn't.'

'I don't suppose you want to share your initial thoughts when you took that call?'

'Sure I do.' He smiled the smile of a man who just spat in the eye of his tormentor. 'Probably something along the lines of *I better not do a Buckley here.*'

Evan's bewilderment amused Faulkner. The smile grew wider, even if it didn't make a dent in the hardness in his eyes.

'It means I better not go off half-cocked, jumping at the first half-assed conclusion that enters my preconceived mind.'

Evan felt his cheeks burning, couldn't deny the truth in Faulkner's words.

'You expect me to believe it never crossed your mind it could have been Hendricks—and you'd given him the perfect opportunity? You must have been scared shitless the chickens had finally come home to roost.'

Faulkner shook his head emphatically and grimaced.

'No. For one, it was a young boy who went missing. That's very different to Hendricks and his piece of jailbait. A man who goes after a girl because she looks twenty-five isn't interested in prepubescent schoolboys.'

It sounded to Evan like the kind of homegrown psychology that Ray Clements had complained about. He was surprised at Faulkner, who must have come across plenty of degenerates who crossed the lines during his time on the force.

'Okay, let me put it a different way—'

'You can put it where the sun don't shine for all I care.'

'Just hear me out. Let's say you were looking into all the other potential suspects and one of them just happened to have a criminal conviction for unlawful sexual intercourse. Would that have flagged him up, made you treat him any different to the others? Maybe concentrate your efforts on him.'

'I didn't need to concentrate on Hendricks any harder. I already knew everything about him.'

'And chose to ignore what you knew.'

'For Christ's sake, Buckley, you're impossible. I didn't *ignore* what I knew. I made a judgement call on the basis of that information. '

'And that was it?'

'No, of course that wasn't it. We interviewed him along with everyone else. But, like I told you before, he had a perfect alibi. When the boy disappeared, he was driving a bus full of fifty screaming kids. Then he went to a strip club. To look at women's tits, not little boys' wieners.'

Evan had to admit he had a point. Everything he knew about Hendricks suggested he was a low-life pussy hound. Perhaps he was jumping to conclusions after all.

'What did your wife think when it happened?'

'She thought it was going to go badly for him. She was scared his past would get dug up and then everyone would jump to conclusions. Just like you.' He jabbed his finger in Evan's direction. 'Not to mention the effect it would have on my career and our lives.'

'But still no doubts about her darling brother? It must have seemed like one thing after another and it's never his fault. She didn't see any kind of a pattern there?'

'No. Nor did she see things that weren't there in the first place.'

Evan was well aware that the comment was directed against him.

'Better than deliberately not looking at things that are staring you in the face.'

Faulkner would have thrown something at him then if he'd had anything to throw apart from the cheap plastic TV remote. Instead, he lay back on the pillows and closed his eyes again. His face relaxed.

'I really don't think we're getting anywhere here. I'd like to get some sleep now.'

Evan agreed. Whatever Faulkner really thought and felt, he wasn't about to share it with him. He started for the door. Then stopped.

'One more thing.'

Faulkner groaned.

'Why did Hendricks attack you?'

'I have no idea. You'll have to ask him.'

'What was the argument about?'

'Nothing that would make him want to try to kill me.'

'I suppose I just have to take your word on that as well?'

'How about I just make something up? Will that make you go away?'

Evan wasn't going to get anything else out of him. He headed for the door again. Faulkner called after him.

'What are you going to do? I hope you're not going to go over all this again with Hendricks.'

'What do you care?'

'I don't want to be the cause of any more trouble as a result of what I've told you.'

Evan was instantly alert.

'What do you mean any *more* trouble?'

'Okay, that's it. We're finished here. Send in the nurse on your way out, will you. For some reason my head hurts twice as bad as when you arrived. Forget I said we're quits.'

Evan took the hint and left. Damn, he thought as he walked down the corridor, I forgot to ask if it was okay to borrow his gun.

CHAPTER 35

EVAN HAD NO IDEA what to make of Faulkner's comment about causing *more* trouble. He couldn't decide if it had been an innocent slip of the tongue or if Faulkner secretly believed Hendricks was guilty and felt responsible for everything that had happened.

He certainly had enough to lose. Back when it happened, with thirty years on the job, he'd already made it to the top. That was a lot to throw away. He just didn't seem like the kind of guy who would let a serious crime go unpunished to save his own skin.

Those were Faulkner's problems. Evan didn't have any such conflicts of interest. He knew exactly what he wanted to do. Now seemed like the perfect opportunity. With Hendricks lying low, it was the perfect excuse to nose around his property. Whatever Faulkner might think, he reckoned it was worth a more thorough look. Any kind of look would be better than doing nothing like the police.

It was early evening with a couple of hours of daylight left as he drove out to Hendricks' farm. He drove straight past it, checking for Hendricks' pickup. The driveway was empty. It could have been hidden around the back of the barns. That was a chance he was going to have to take.

He drove on until he came to a disused farm track about a half mile beyond Hendricks' place. It led to a five-bar gate which didn't look like it had been opened in years. He backed his car in as far as he could go, happy enough that it wouldn't be visible from the road unless someone was specifically looking for it. There was hardly any traffic on the road anyway.

Stuffing a pair of thin cotton gloves into his pocket, he felt the reassuring presence of the SIG-Sauer. Then he headed back down the road towards *Beau Terre.*

Nothing passed him in the time it took him to get there. There was a small stand of Red Maple trees just before he got to Hendricks' driveway. He made his way towards it as the daylight drained slowly out of the sky. Standing amongst their trunks, he was almost invisible, with a good view of the house and barns, most of the yard as well. He settled in to wait.

Fifteen minutes crept slowly by. He hadn't seen any lights come on, no movement in the house. There were other rooms on the far side of the house that he couldn't see, but despite that he was getting a strong impression that the place was deserted.

Suddenly a light came on by the front door. He stiffened, his breath catching, even though he was invisible from the house. He strained, every sense heightened, tried to see if there was any movement inside the house. Then a flash of white. He relaxed, let out the breath he'd not realized he was holding. The large white cat he'd seen last time lightly descended the few steps down from the porch, ran off into the bushes. It had been asleep in the rocker and set off the security light as it headed off for the evening. After a couple of minutes, the light went off again.

He'd given it long enough. He darted quickly across the yard, pulling on the gloves as he went. He tried the front door first. Locked. He headed around to the back. To his amazement the back door was unlocked. Either Hendricks was especially trusting or he'd left in such a hurry he forgot to lock up. Or he was sitting inside in the dark with a shotgun across his knees waiting for unsuspecting intruders.

He opened the door carefully. Stepped into the kitchen. No Hendricks and no shotgun. The key was in the lock on the inside. He locked the door behind him, dropped the key into his pocket. No point risking anyone creeping up on him. He had an hour of daylight before it got too dark to see without turning on the lights.

First of all, he wanted to check the whole house to make sure it really was empty. Everything in the kitchen was neat and tidy. No dirty dishes in the sink, no trash can overflowing with beer cans. He crossed the room, made his way slowly down the hallway, checking each of the rooms as he passed. Two living rooms, a dining room, a study, all of them empty. If he hadn't seen Hendricks sitting on his porch three days earlier, he wouldn't have been able to say if anyone had lived there in the last six months.

There was a door under the stairs leading down to the basement. He'd have to turn the light on down there to see anything. There wasn't any point wasting the little remaining daylight doing it now.

He crept up the stairs, his mouth dry, an empty feeling in the pit of his stomach. It was as bad as kicking down motel doors. Luckily nothing creaked under his weight in the solid old house. He reached a large landing with four bedrooms and a bathroom leading off it. He checked the bathroom first, then the two smaller bedrooms. No sign of life.

That left the master bedroom and a guest room. He checked the guest room first, leaving Hendricks' room until last. Somebody was obviously living in it. The bed was neatly made with what he thought were called hospital corners. It had definitely been slept in. There were a couple of pairs of men's pants, a dark blue blazer and half a dozen shirts hanging in the closet, all of them clean and pressed. Two pairs of shoes poked out from under the bed. He pulled the nearest ones out, a pair of meticulously shined black Oxfords. Looking down at the gleaming toe caps and the orderly way the clothes were hanging in the closet, he guessed the visitor was one of Hendricks' army buddies, the ones he went to prison with. Perhaps he lived here. There was some underwear and T-shirts in the drawers—even the T-shirts were ironed and folded like they were still on the shelf in the store—and some other stuff that was of no interest. No porn in the nightstand drawer, no crucifix above the bed either.

There was a shoe box on the top shelf in the closet. He lifted in down, could tell from the weight it was empty. Something about it smelled familiar. He couldn't quite place it. Then it came to him. Gun oil. He took the SIG-Sauer out of his pocket, sniffed it to compare. It had the exact same smell. Whoever the gun belonged to was carrying it around with him.

He moved on to Hendricks' bedroom. It was the largest, at the front, overlooking the driveway and the road and then the fields beyond that. The low sun slanted across the crops as he stood at the window admiring the view, thinking how unfair it was that Hendricks lived in such a lovely house.

The peaceful silence of the evening was broken by the sound of a car coming down the road. He stepped back from the window slightly, not that anyone would have been able to see him in the fading light. The car kept coming. To his horror, it slowed and swung into Hendricks' driveway. A blue Crown Vic, unmistakably a police car, unless someone had bought a used one on ebay.

Damn, it had to be Guillory. Where the hell had she been all this time?

He watched it park, saw her climb out from the driver's side. Then the passenger door swung open and her partner, Ryder, got out. He stretched and hitched up his belt. His gut wobbled like something just turned out of a Jell-O mold. Evan would have loved to see his ugly head explode in a cloud of red mist as Hendricks or his buddy shot him from the rooftops. It didn't happen. *Maybe another day.*

Guillory walked up the steps onto the porch, disappeared from Evan's view. The security light came on again, reflecting off Ryder's face as he squinted up at the window. Evan froze, held his breath, even though there was no way Ryder could see anything with the light in his eyes. Suddenly Ryder looked back down at his feet. The white cat had come back. It was rubbing itself up against his leg leaving white fur all over his pants. He half kicked, half pushed it away with the side of his foot. It howled and hissed, shot off across the yard. He glanced briefly up at the window one last time, then headed around to the back.

Evan relaxed. He let out his breath slowly, his heartbeat subsiding. Without warning Guillory hammered on the front door like she was trying to break it down. His pulse leapt crazily, his heart in his mouth. Then Ryder tried the back door. When it didn't open, he shook it angrily a couple of times, kicked it in frustration, gave up. Evan felt like a cornered rat, two terriers coming at him from either side.

Thank God I locked it from the inside.

Guillory he could have talked around, but not Ryder. Most likely he'd have shot him first, asked questions later before she could stop him. It was lucky he'd parked out of sight half a mile away.

Guillory hammered on the door a while longer, then came back down the steps and walked around to join Ryder. Evan heard them talking, couldn't make out what they were saying. Seemed they didn't think the house was worth any more attention. They walked towards the barns, disappeared from sight again.

Evan ran towards the back of the house to get a better view. There was a faded Persian rug on the polished wood floor of the landing. Generally, it stayed put when a person walked over it in a normal, sedate manner. Not when Evan ran across it. It slipped under him, sent him crashing into the door frame of the back bedroom. His damaged ear smacked right into the sharp wooden edge, a sharp hiss slipping through his gritted teeth. He clamped a hand to his ear, stumbled forwards into the room. Lost his balance and fell flat on his face in front of the window, sounding like a herd of buffalo just invaded the house.

He lay on the floor, hardly daring to breathe, desperate to peek out the window, see if they'd heard anything. But all he could do was wait to see if they came back to the house again. He couldn't hear them at all. Did that mean they were at this very moment stealthily approaching the house, pistols drawn, all careful footsteps and watchful eyes? There were times when he wished he didn't have such a vivid imagination. And his ear hurt like hell.

Outside, one of them laughed and the other one joined in. You wouldn't do that if you suspected there was a fugitive hiding out inside the house, would you? Unless one of them had said they were going to shoot whoever was in the house in the butt, and the other one laughed and said no, shoot him in the balls. Police humor.

He risked taking a look, slowly got himself onto his knees. Backing away from the window, he straightened up until he could see over the sill. Guillory and Ryder were standing in front of the larger barn with their backs to him. They were fiddling with the padlock on the doors. He moved forward and across to the side of the window to get a better view. The light was fading fast. He didn't have to worry about being seen now.

Ryder pulled the padlock free, opened the barn doors. Hendricks' pickup was inside. He either owned another vehicle or his army buddy was driving. Or he was holed up somewhere nearby where he didn't need a car. Guillory found the light switch. Evan watched them go inside and look around. From inside the house he couldn't see anything else in there, although he couldn't see all the way to the back wall. It didn't seem like there was anything of any interest in there anyway because they came back out again in under two minutes. Guillory turned out the light, closed and padlocked the doors.

They walked over to the smaller barn, tried the padlock on that one too. It was more of a challenge than the other one. They gave up after a couple of minutes. Looked like a little gentle persuasion was okay, shooting the lock off wasn't. Besides, it's difficult to relock a padlock that you've just shot off. After a brief conversation, they started back towards their car, Ryder leading the way.

Now, Evan thought, now's the time for your fat head to explode, for bits of bone and brain matter and blood to fly everywhere as a high-caliber round turns it into a red mist. Sadly, it didn't happen this time either. But he enjoyed the mental picture he had.

He walked carefully back to the front of the house in time to see them get into their car and drive away. They didn't give the house another look as they passed it. As if they had no further interest.

If only.

CHAPTER 36

HE SLUMPED DOWN INTO a rocking chair in the corner of Hendricks' bedroom, wondering what to do next. It was now too dark to do anything useful without turning on the lights. After Guillory and Ryder's visit, he didn't feel comfortable doing that. Driving away could be a ploy. They might come back. Then he remembered the basement. The lights turned on down there wouldn't be visible from outside. It was likely to be his best bet anyway—wasn't that where the bodies were always buried?

He went back downstairs to the basement door. The house was eerily quiet. It seemed very different in the dark. He felt for the comforting presence of the SIG-Sauer. He patted his pocket—nothing. He patted the other one—again, nothing. A frisson of panic went through him. *It must have fallen out when I fell.* He turned around, started back up the stairs. A number of the treads creaked as he stepped on them, sending a shiver across his skin. They hadn't creaked before. At the top of the stairs he groped his way around the wall to the doorway he'd crashed into. His ear throbbed in sympathy. He got down on his hands and knees, explored the area immediately around the doorway. No gun. It must be in the bedroom. He did a methodical sweep across the floor, starting at the door and moving towards the window. Still he couldn't find it. Under the bed? He got down on his belly, slithered underneath. Sure enough, he felt it in the furthest corner. It had come to rest against a pile of other junk. If he'd had some light, he might have had a look to see what was under there. But not in the dark. From the smell he'd have said there was at least one successfully deployed mousetrap with its decomposing victim. It didn't make him want to feel around blindly.

He slid back out with the gun in his hand feeling much better. He didn't want to lose Faulkner's property, after all. Straightening up onto his knees, he glanced out the window, did a double take. There was a sliver of light showing under the doors to the smaller barn. Then it was gone. Had he imagined it? It hadn't been on before. Guillory and Ryder would have noticed. But how was it possible for someone to be in there, if the doors were padlocked from the outside? There must be another door. Guillory and her partner should have checked. He'd have a word with her about her sloppy work next time he saw her.

What should he do now? Phone her, pretend that he'd just got there and seen the light? Perhaps he should go down to check first, see if there really was another door. He might be able to lock it from the outside so that whoever was inside—Hendricks presumably—couldn't escape.

He pushed himself halfway to his feet. Then froze like a mouse under a cat's paw. A faint noise came from downstairs. He held his breath. Listened. The low rumble of two voices. Had Guillory and Ryder sneaked back on foot? But it was coming from somewhere inside the house. And he hadn't heard the door open. He'd checked all the rooms—except the basement. Had they been down there all the time? It wasn't possible. They'd have heard him, especially when he fell. He was trapped. Even if they stayed in the basement, they would hear him if he tried to sneak back downstairs. The stairs would creak for sure if he did.

Any kind of decision was abruptly taken out of his hands as he heard the unmistakable sound of the basement door opening. He fought to control the panic that rose up inside him, dropped back onto his knees by the side of the bed. As quietly as possible he lowered himself down onto his belly, slid carefully back underneath, like a creature pulling itself back into the familiar safety of its lair. He turned his head so that he could see out. From his hiding place, he could see the rug on the landing. It was still rucked up. *Shit. He couldn't do anything about it now.* He wormed his way in as far as he could go, brushed something soft with the back of his head. The smell of rotting rodent assaulted his nasal passages, made him want to retch.

The light over the stairwell suddenly came on. Someone heavy started up the stairs. Evan drew himself further back into the darkness under the bed. He touched something else with the back of his head, heard the sharp snap of an empty mousetrap going off. The unexpected noise made him jerk his head away, bang the wooden slats supporting the mattress. To his hyper-sensitive nerves, it sounded like a thunderclap.

A voice he didn't recognize called from halfway up the stairs.

'Hey Jason, I just need to get something from my room before we go.'

The voice didn't seem to have heard anything.

'For Christ's sake, I've told you it's Carl now,' he heard Hendricks reply with undisguised irritation in his voice. 'Do I have to wear a name badge?'

'Yeah, right. Sorry, I keep forgetting.'

The voice had reached the top of the stairs. Evan couldn't see his face from where he was lying, just his feet and the legs from the knees down. Then the voice again, calling back down the stairs.

'Jas . . . Carl, what's been going on with the rug up here?'

Evan closed his eyes, prayed silently to a God he didn't believe in.

'What the hell are you talking about? We haven't got time for housework. Just get what you need and get back down here. We need to go.'

The guy grumbled something under his breath. It sounded a lot like *dickhead.* He went into the room that Evan had searched earlier. The light went on. A drawer opened. Evan couldn't remember seeing anything more important than clean underwear in them, hoped he hadn't missed something. The light went off. The guy came back onto the landing. He stopped dead.

Evan stared at the feet facing towards him, held his breath. The dust under the bed was irritating his nose. Now was not a good time to sneeze. The guy must be able to hear his heart thumping wildly in his chest. Had he seen something else? Blood smeared on the door frame? Seconds passed. What on earth was he doing? His feet hadn't moved. Then the soft rustle of a hand pushed cautiously into a pocket. Had he pulled out his gun?

The tickle in Evan's nose was unbearable. He was about to sneeze any second. It was building inexorably towards its explosive climax. Carefully he turned his head to face the floor, pressed his nose into it. He forgot it was broken. A sharp stab of pain made him gasp.

'Did you say something?' the guy called down the stairs.

'No, I did *not* say anything,' Hendricks' taut voice came back. 'What the hell are you doing up there?'

Evan heard him step onto the bottom tread, imagined him peering upwards, trying to see what his friend was doing. He stepped up onto the second tread.

'I heard something,' the one on the landing said.

A heavy sigh from downstairs.

'It's just mice. The place is alive with them.'

Evan's throat was closed tight. His heart felt as if two cold hands had taken hold of it, squeezing hard.

'*No*. I know what a mouse sounds like. This was like someone sucking in air.'

The hands squeezed harder.

'It's just the wind, for Christ's sake. It's an old house. Or maybe it's a ghost.'

The guy didn't reply. Evan imagined him standing stock-still, head cocked to the side, not breathing.

'Maybe you're right. I'm coming.'

But then the guy's OCD kicked in. Despite Hendricks' increasing impatience, he couldn't just walk past the rug. He tried to straighten it with his foot, only made it worse. Still facing towards Evan, he dropped to one knee, his body now visible from the waist down. He leaned forwards, spread his hands out on the rumpled folds to smooth them.

Evan stared at the top of his head pointing directly at him. If the guy raised his head six inches they'd be staring into each other's eyes. Evan's left eye twitched, then his nose wrinkled.

No, not now.

'What the hell are you *doing* up there?'

There was the fast scamper of feet as Hendricks came halfway up the stairs until his head was above the landing floor level. He was staring straight at the other guy's butt. Evan stared straight at the top of his head. If he stood up now, it was all over.

'I don't fucking believe it,' Hendricks yelled.

'Okay, okay. I said I'm coming.'

His hands came off the rug. He straightened his back. Through the fabric of his pants, Evan watched his thigh muscles tense as he prepared to heave himself to his feet. His knee joint clicked, the sound as loud as if they'd all pulled their guns and fired at once. He stood.

Through the guy's legs, Evan looked directly into Hendricks' face. His jaw was clenched tight, not breathing, his eyes closed, working hard to control his anger.

'Give me strength,' he spat in disgust as he turned back down the stairs. 'Keep this up and you'll have all the time in the world to tidy the rug in your prison cell.'

The guy turned away from Evan and followed him downstairs, muttering under his breath.

'It wasn't the wind. And it wasn't no mice either.'

Evan heard Hendricks' voice from the hallway.

'Got everything you need? Want to do a quick bit of vacuuming before we go?'

'Up yours, *Jason*.'

Evan pictured the smirk on his face and smiled with him.

Hendricks ignored him. 'Come on, let's go.'

Evan didn't know whether they were popping out for Pizza or whether they were about to leave for good. Hendricks couldn't possibly think he could stay hiding in his basement forever. On the other hand, was he going to simply walk away from everything he had here? The most likely answer was that he would lie low until he found out if Faulkner died or not. That meant they were probably coming back.

He considered going down, confronting them. He had Faulkner's gun. He could hold them until Guillory got there. It was too risky. *He* knew Faulkner was making a good recovery and might not even press charges against his brother-in-law. But Hendricks might think he'd killed Faulkner. That would make him desperate to escape. Added to that, the other guy also had a gun. And if it was the army buddy, he knew how to use it a whole lot better than Evan did. Discretion was definitely the better part of valor on this occasion.

He heard them go into the kitchen.

'Where's the damn key?' This from Hendricks, sounding very pissed indeed. 'It was in the lock.'

The tightness in Evan's chest came back with a vengeance that took his breath away. He had the key in his pocket. Why had he done that? He should have left it where it was.

'Don't look at me,' the other guy said, his tone defensive. 'I didn't touch it.'

'That makes a change.'

It went very quiet in the kitchen. Were things falling into place in Hendricks' mind? The rug and now the missing key. Surely it was obvious there was an intruder in the house. Or was he blaming his friend?

'Haven't you got a spare?' the friend said.

'Of course I've got a spare. It's in this drawer. But I want to know what happened to the one that was in the lock.'

'What the hell for? Was it your favorite?'

Evan heard the smirk again.

'Don't be stupid.'

'You want to watch who you're calling stupid.'

'Is that so?'

'I'm not the one who brained Faulkner. Now *that's* stupid.'

'Really. What would you have done? You're not exactly the go-to person for useful suggestions.'

Their voices were raised now. Evan prayed it would turn into a full-scale fight. Then they'd forget about everything else.

'I don't know. I wouldn't have brained *him*, that's for damn sure. If I was going to brain anyone, it'd be that other interfering bastard.'

Upstairs, Evan's blood ran cold. A cold sweat broke out on his forehead, his legs suddenly weak. Jacobson had been right. He was in real danger from Hendricks and his partner. Thank God he hadn't gone down to confront them.

Then a sudden realization took hold in his mind. His whole body trembled. He didn't know if it was from fear or excitement. He'd been worrying about them finding him in the house while they were trying to make their escape—because, like Guillory, he was after them for attacking Faulkner. But the *interfering bastard* remark couldn't be about that. He'd only spoken to Hendricks once. And that had been before Faulkner was attacked. Meaning, if they saw him as a threat, it was because his interfering was getting close to something else. And that could only be one thing.

The disappearance of Daniel Clayton.

CHAPTER 37

'MAYBE I'LL DO THAT too,' Hendricks said downstairs.

'Well if you do, make sure you do a proper job this time.'

Hendricks laughed derisively.

'That's great coming from you. At least I've got the balls to do it.'

'Is that so? It was you who got us into all this shit in the first place.'

'Me? You—'

Evan didn't catch the end of the sentence. It was drowned out by the sound of someone crashing into the table. One of them had shoved the other one. There was the scrape of chair legs on the floor, a slap. One of them grunted. Then Hendricks yelled, the words riding out on a tide of venom.

'You better put that back down, you retard. Or I'm gonna shove it up your ass sideways.'

Then, before it escalated out of control, there was a sound that stopped them in their tracks. Evan pictured them standing staring into each other's faces. Panting, their mouths hanging open, all thought of their argument gone as they heard it. The sound of a car pulling into the driveway. Coming fast, as if they hoped to catch somebody unawares.

'Shit. It must be the police again,' Hendricks hissed. 'Come on. Before they see us.'

Evan heard the pair of them run across the kitchen into the hallway. He heard the basement door open, then slam shut. Everything went quiet. Outside, the car drove around the side of the house, skidded to a halt outside the back door. The light in the kitchen was still on, spilling out into the yard. The car doors sprung open. Two people jumped out, slamming the doors after them. Seconds later, impatient banging on the back door, Guillory's voice shouting over the top of it.

Evan slid out from under the bed. He was happy to let them in now. Hendricks and his accomplice were down in the basement. He'd be able to send them down there after them. With any luck Ryder would go first and get shot before Guillory saved the day. His only concern was Faulkner's gun. He didn't want to be caught with it. He turned the landing light on, called down the stairs that he was coming. Then he ran into Hendricks' room, pulled open the drawer to the nightstand, dropped the SIG-Sauer in. *You can explain that to them as well, you bastard.*

Guillory was still pounding on the door as Evan trotted down the stairs and along the hallway to the kitchen.

He didn't want to use the key he had in his pocket. He wanted to keep that one for now. In case he decided to come back again. Hendricks had said the spare was in the drawer. He put his hands on his head just to be on the safe side and stepped into the kitchen. The table had been knocked across the room. One of the chairs was upended. An eight-inch kitchen knife was sitting on the table.

Too late he realized he was still wearing the cotton gloves. Hopefully they wouldn't notice with the shock of finding him there. Guillory's face through the glass door panel was a picture. Evan scanned the room quickly, saw one of the drawers pulled halfway out. Hendricks had been in the middle of getting the spare before they started arguing. He dropped his hands, held up his finger—*wait just one minute.* Then he walked over to the drawer and opened it all the way. He was in luck. There was a bunch of spare keys on a ring. He took them out, crossed the kitchen to the back door.

Guillory was standing outside with her hands on her hips and a hurry-it-up look on her face. Ryder was eating something without closing his mouth properly. Evan looked at the keys in his hand. He hadn't paid a lot of attention to the key he used to lock the door. Guillory was banging on the door now. There was a key on the ring that looked like a probable match. Heart in his mouth, he slipped it into the lock. It turned first time. *Yes.* He pulled the door open, stood aside as Guillory stepped past him.

'What in God's name are you doing here?'

Ryder followed her in without saying anything.

Be thankful for small mercies.

Evan hadn't had enough time to get a story together. He decided to say as little as possible. People with a guilty conscience always give too much information.

'I wanted to have a look around.'

'You mean you fancied a bit of breaking and entering,' Guillory said. 'I see you came prepared.' She pointed at his gloved hands. 'Or do you just feel the cold more than most people?'

So much for not noticing, Evan thought. He pulled the gloves off and stuffed them in his pocket.

'No, the door was unlocked. I locked it behind me.'

She didn't look as if she believed him but there was no evidence of a break-in.

'What time did you get here?'

He had to tell them the truth. He couldn't pretend he hadn't been in the house the last time they came. He'd just told them the door was unlocked. If they'd got there first, they would have found it open, not locked.

'I got here just before you did.'

'You can't have. We've been sitting down the road waiting for the past fifteen minutes at least. Nobody passed us. You didn't walk across the fields, did you?'

'I meant just before you arrived the first time.'

'You were in the house the whole time?' Her voice had taken on a sharp edge.

He nodded.

'Why didn't you let us in?'

'Because I was hoping to avoid this conversation.'

'I bet. And stop us doing our job at the same time.'

He started to say something but she cut him off.

'If the door was unlocked like you say, we could have had a look around ourselves.'

'And not had to come back again,' Ryder added sourly.

Evan was sensible enough to hold his tongue. He wasn't in what anybody would call a position of strength. It was time to play his ace.

'You'll be glad it worked out that way.'

'Oh, really?' Ryder said with no attempt to disguise the scorn in his voice.

'Yes, really. Because I can tell you exactly where they are.'

'They?'

'It means more than one person.'

'Okay Buckley, drop the wisecracks,' Guillory said.

He was sure he'd seen a smile cross her face.

'Who are *they*?'

'Hendricks and a friend.'

He'd been about to say he thought it was an army friend that Hendricks went to prison with, before he caught himself. He didn't know how much she knew, didn't want to have to start explaining it all from the beginning.

'Okay. Where are they? And what's been going on in here?'

She walked over to the table. Picked up the knife.

'They were starting to have a fight just as you got here. They're in the basement now. This way.'

He led them to the door leading down into the basement.

'I heard them run down there when you arrived.'

'You heard them?'

'I was upstairs.'

They didn't need to know he'd been hiding under the bed. He wondered if he smelled of decaying rat.

'Upstairs doing what?' Ryder said. 'You weren't hiding under the bed, were you?'

Evan said nothing. He didn't need to. His face gave him away. A huge grin split Ryder's normally sour face.

'Ha! I don't believe it. The big, tough detective was hiding under the bed while the bad men were downstairs.'

He laughed like it was the best thing he'd heard in a month, a year, his whole life.

Evan felt his face grow hot.

'At least I can fit under the bed.'

Ryder was laughing so hard he didn't hear.

'Okay children,' Guillory said, 'that's enough.'

Ryder wiped a tear away from the corner of his eye.

'We'll have to try extra hard to keep that out of the papers.'

Evan wanted to punch him in the gut but wasn't sure he'd get his arm back. He turned to Guillory.

'I think Hendricks' friend has got a gun.' He told her about the empty shoe box in the closet. 'Why don't you send Ryder down first? He'll provide an impenetrable shield for the rest of us.'

They both ignored him. It was business all the way now at the mention of the gun. Guillory told him to move back out of the way. They both drew their own pistols. Guillory's was the same as the one he'd taken from Faulkner's trailer. She pressed herself flat against the wall, turned the door knob. Pushed the door open. On the other side of the doorway Ryder reached around and flicked the light switch on. She called down into the basement, told the men down there to come up with their hands on their heads. Nobody came forward. She repeated the order, her voice harder. There wasn't a sound coming up from the basement, no movement either. She looked over, nodded at Ryder. Then took a deep breath and started slowly down the stairs. Ryder followed her down. It wasn't more than fifteen seconds before she called up to Evan that it was okay to come down. He hadn't heard a thing.

CHAPTER 38

HE WENT DOWN THE steps into the best-kept basement workshop he'd ever seen. Two of the walls were lined with metal shelving full of every imaginable kind of tool, dozens of tins of paint, boxes of screws and nails, and just about every other kind of household item you could imagine. There were bays along the third wall with lumber neatly stacked in them. Workbenches ran the full length of the other side, peg boards fixed to the wall above, more tools hanging from the pegs. A number of large woodworking machines filled the space in the middle of the room—a table saw he recognized and some others he didn't. Ryder was sitting on one of the workbenches swinging his legs. Guillory was poking through the contents on the shelves. The only thing missing was Hendricks and his buddy.

Evan looked around in amazement.

'I heard them come down here.'

'Are you sure you weren't taking a nap on the bed instead of hiding under it?' Ryder said. 'And you dreamed the whole thing.'

'Of course I'm sure.'

He still had the smell of the decaying rodent in his nostrils, a dull ache in his nose from squashing it into the floor, to prove it.

'So where are they? Hiding under this bench?'

He looked down between his legs.

'I don't know.'

Then Ryder's tone lost all of its mocking quality.

'Are you sure you didn't make all this up to try to distract us away from the fact that we caught you breaking and entering?'

'Why would I do that if it could be disproved so easily?'

'Beats me. But you meet some pretty stupid people—'

'If we're talking of stupid, the only reason you *caught me* is because I let you in. If I hadn't, you'd have just gone away empty handed again. I assume you weren't going to break in yourselves.'

'No, we leave that to people like you.' He smiled unpleasantly. 'You don't keep a dog and bark yourself.'

'Tell us again exactly what happened,' Guillory said over her shoulder, in an attempt to stop the bickering and get back on track.

'They were in the kitchen fighting when you drove up. Hendricks' buddy was threatening him with the kitchen knife. I heard them stop and then run down the hallway and down here.' He jabbed his finger at the door at the top of the stairs. 'I heard that door slam.'

Ryder wasn't having any of it.

'All I know is they're not here now. And you've been wasting even more of our time.'

'This is where they came from.'

Ryder slid down from the workbench he was sitting on.

'What?'

'They were down here all the time I was here. Then they came up and were about to go out when you turned up.'

'What were they doing down here? A spot of woodworking.' He kicked the workbench. 'Perhaps they've got plans to remodel the house.'

'I know what I heard.'

'And I know what I'm hearing. I'm hearing a crock of shit.' Ryder's face was getting redder by the minute. 'I think I'm going to book you for B&E and wasting police time.'

Guillory turned away from the shelves to face them. She didn't know it, but if she'd carried on just a little further, things would have worked out very differently. Especially for Evan. The simple act of stopping where she did was responsible for everything that came after.

'Give him a break, Easy.'

'Easy?' Evan said, confused. Then it clicked. He smiled. 'Please, not Easy Ryder. More like Up-tight Ryder, if you ask me.'

'Actually, nobody did ask you. Although that doesn't normally stop you poking your nose in.'

'Actually, it's E-Z for Edward Zachary,' Guillory explained, also smiling. 'His parents weren't to know they were going to make that film.'

'That's got to win some kind of award for the most off base nickname ever.'

'I've had enough,' Ryder said. 'You two jokers can stay down here. I'm going to check out the rest of the house.'

'There's nothing there,' Evan said, immediately regretting it—he'd given Ryder an easy shot.

'Really? Given the accuracy of your most recent information'—he threw his arm wide to take in the whole of the Hendricks-free basement—'you'll forgive me if I check it out for myself. Maybe use my eyes, not my ears.'

He headed up the stairs, then stopped again.

'By the way, you seem to have lost part of one of yours. Maybe it's under the bed.'

He carried on up the stairs, laughing to himself as he went. Evan gave him the finger to help him on his way.

'THIS WASN'T A VERY clever idea,' Guillory said, after Ryder had gone.

They could hear him banging around upstairs even though Evan knew the house was empty.

'I suppose you're right.'

He was quiet for a moment. He didn't care what Ryder thought of him, but he needed her on his side.

'Do you believe me?'

'I'd like to. But I have to admit I'm struggling.'

'There's something else. You're probably not going to believe that either.'

'Try me.'

He told her about the light he'd seen under the doors to the smaller, locked barn.

'Maybe there's another door. We didn't look around the back. We can take a look now.'

They went back upstairs and out through the kitchen door to her car. She got a flashlight out of the trunk and they walked over to the smaller barn. There was no light showing now. She played the beam over the padlock. It was new and top of the line.

'I can see why Ryder couldn't get past that,' Evan said.

'You know, I had this funny feeling someone was watching us. Who'd have thought it was you.'

They walked all around the barn. It was bigger than it looked at first. It wasn't as wide as the other one, but it went back a long way. There were no other doors, not even any windows you could climb through. The front doors were the only way in.

'Maybe I was mistaken,' Evan admitted. 'I'd just got out from under the bed. It must have been a trick of the light.'

'Don't let Ryder hear you make an admission like that. He'll never believe another word you say.'

'Is he like that with everybody, or is it just me?'

He kicked at a small rock, bouncing it off the barn door.

'I think it's just you.'

He looked across at her, saw she was smiling.

'Seriously though, he just doesn't like P.I.'s. Especially if they make extra work for him. Extra chickenshit work.'

'Isn't most of what you do chickenshit?'

She gave him a hurt look as they made their way back to the house. Ryder had just come into the kitchen when they got there.

'The place is clean. I didn't find anything apart from this.' He held out Faulkner's gun. 'Pinocchio here must have missed it. Looks like our jobs are safe for a while.'

Guillory took it from him, inspected it.

'We'll get it checked out to see if it's what he hit Faulkner with. Check to see if he's got a permit too.'

Evan would have liked to explain that they didn't need to bother on either count because Hendricks had never been near the gun in his life. However, he certainly wasn't going to admit what he'd done to Ryder. Guillory wouldn't have been able to help him out of that one.

'Must be an idiot if it is what he used,' Ryder said, 'seeing as it was just sitting there in the nightstand drawer.'

If it hadn't been for the fact that Guillory was getting drawn into the charade as well, Evan would have enjoyed watching Ryder go barking up the wrong tree.

'I also found out who the other guy is,' Ryder continued. 'His name's Jack Adamson. There was some work ID in his blazer pocket. We can check him out, see what he's driving and maybe pick them up in his car.'

Evan made a mental note of the name even though it meant nothing to him.

'Okay Mr P, time we all got out of here,' Guillory said. 'Where's your car? We'll give you a ride back to it, then show you the way back to town. We wouldn't want you to get lost. You might go around in a circle and end up back here.'

Ryder took that as his cue, gave Evan a hard look.

'And next time we won't be so understanding.'

CHAPTER 39

EVAN WASN'T GOING TO get any sleep that night. He played through it all over and over in his mind. He could remember their argument word for word, particularly the part about braining him as well. He wasn't about to forget that in a hurry. He distinctly remembered the sound of them running along the hallway and down into the basement, the door slamming behind them. He knew he wasn't mistaken. And he knew he wouldn't be able to let it drop. It didn't matter how many times he went through it all, everything pointed to the same conclusion—he was going to have to go back again. He was pleased he'd kept the key. His subconscious must have known he'd need it. Guillory had taken the other one with her after locking the back door. He wished he'd been able to keep the gun. As it turned out he could have kept it in his pocket the whole time he was with Guillory and Ryder. At the time it had seemed like too big a risk. Hindsight's a wonderful thing.

He found a flashlight that actually had some working batteries. It was a good omen, divine support for his decision. Then he watched the hands on the clock crawl round until just after two in the morning before driving back to Hendricks' place.

Hendricks and Adamson had been about to go out when the police interrupted them. He had no idea whether they had or not, and if they had, whether they'd come back. There was a chance they were still hiding somewhere on the property. Knowing he might need to make a quick escape, he slowly backed his car up the driveway, left the key in the ignition. Then he let himself into the house. He didn't lock the door behind him this time. Every second might count. He stood still. Listened. The house seemed even quieter than before if that was possible. He crossed the kitchen in the dark and crept down the hallway to the door at the top of the basement stairs. He put his ear to it and listened some more. Absolutely nothing. Pushing the door open carefully, he stepped through, then closed it behind him before flicking on the light.

Everything looked exactly the same as it had the last time. He made his way cautiously down the stairs. Standing in the middle of the floor, he peered all around the room.

There was nowhere to hide, that was for sure. He did a slow lap of the room. It was just as he remembered it. Shelving on two sides, workbenches on another, bays filled with lumber on the fourth wall. There were no other doors apart from the one at the top of the stairs. No other *visible* doors. But he knew there had to be another one. It was just a question of finding it. He ruled out the wall with the lumber. Nobody would want to move all that every time. Similarly, the wall with the workbenches. They only came up to waist height, you'd see the top half of a door. That left the two walls of shelving as the most likely candidates, the ones Guillory had been poking through until she gave up to stop Evan and Ryder arguing.

It didn't take long to find, once you were looking for it. The middle section of shelves on one of the walls hinged outwards revealing a door behind it. The shelves themselves were stacked with tins of paint. He picked one up, then another, and another—they were all empty. The whole unit swung back and forth smoothly without any effort. The hinges were cleverly concealed at the back of the metal uprights although you could see them if you knew what you were looking for.

Why on earth hadn't he thought of this before, when he was with Guillory and Ryder? He knew perfectly well why not. For one, he'd been so shocked to find that they weren't there, his mind had gone blank. Secondly, he'd already been feeling foolish enough as a result of Ryder's skepticism and mocking. He wasn't about to make it worse by saying there must be a secret door, even if he'd thought of it in the first place. Ryder would have crucified him. But now he'd found it, he ought to call them, wait for them before going any further.

That's what he ought to do. Instead, he pulled the shelves all the way open. He tried the door. It was locked. *Damn.* Talk about belt and suspenders. Then he remembered the ring of spare keys in the kitchen drawer.

Back upstairs in the kitchen, he located the drawer where he'd found them earlier easily enough. They weren't in it. Guillory had taken the spare back door key with her. He was sure she hadn't taken the whole ring. Where the hell had she put it? There was virtually no light coming in from outside. He could barely see a thing. He'd have to take a chance, despite the risk. He didn't have any option, not unless he wanted to grope around blindly all night. He flicked on the flashlight, played the beam around the room. It was only for a few seconds, a quick burst of light in a darkened room. But sometimes a few seconds is all it takes. He saw the keys sitting on the kitchen table, snapped off the flashlight, never so thankful for the comforting dark.

Making his way back down into the basement, he felt vulnerable without the gun, needed to arm himself in some way. He examined the tools on the pegboard, selected a couple of razor-edged chisels and a heavy claw hammer. Strapping on a workman's tool belt with lots of loops and pouches, he dropped his new-found weapons into place. He was as ready as he was ever going to be.

He found the right key to the hidden door after a couple of attempts, unlocked it, dropped the key ring into one of the pouches. Pushed the door open. A narrow tunnel stretched away into the darkness. It was roughly three feet wide and six feet high with a bare earth floor, shored up by two-by-fours and plywood. He'd never been in one, but he guessed it was what a mining shaft would look like. Electrical cords ran along the side wall looping in and out of bare bulbs in metal cages. He saw the switch, decided against turning the lights on. Footprints in the dry dust on the floor disappeared out of sight. He went back to the stacks of lumber and found a small wedge-shaped piece which he tapped gently under the door, jamming it open.

He hesitated. His mouth was dry, that empty feeling in the pit of his stomach again. It was just like in all those films he'd watched. Some woman who's lost one of her shoes and half of her clothing is just about to go down into the creepy basement where the lights don't work, and you ask yourself *Why would you*? Now here he was, in real life, about to do the same thing, even if he hadn't lost his shoes yet. Why? Pride, more than anything. He didn't just want to tell Guillory and Ryder about the hidden escape route. He wanted to . . . to what, exactly? He couldn't say. But he'd be damned if he backed out now. It was too easy to imagine Ryder's taunts; *So, the big, bad detective had to call in the real detectives when the going got tough.*

He switched on the flashlight. Started down the tunnel, ears straining for any sounds ahead. It wasn't a long tunnel but it curved round to the left. He couldn't see what was at the far end. He had a good idea where he was going to end up, anyway. He crept forward, pressing himself into the side, shielding the flashlight as much as possible. He needn't have bothered. He rounded the curve, saw another door a few yards further on. It too was locked.

His stomach clenched at the discovery, a sense of foreboding gripping him. What was he about to find that made Hendricks and whoever else used the tunnel take such elaborate precautions?

He put his ear to the door to listen, couldn't hear anything on the other side. On a hunch, he tried the same key as he had for the door at the other end. It worked. You might be cautious, but it doesn't mean you want a pocket full of keys. He pushed open the door, stepped through into another basement room.

Stepped through into a whole new phase of his life too, although he didn't know it then.

He played the flashlight beam around the walls. The room was identical to the one at the other end, apart from the fact that this one was smaller and completely empty. There'd been no attempt to conceal the doors. As well as the one he'd just come through, there was a second one on his left. Next to that was a six-foot sheet of plywood nailed to the wall. He tried the door cautiously, the handle turning smoothly and soundlessly. It was locked. He didn't bother trying to find the right key—he was more interested in the staircase leading up to a third door. He'd bet dollars to donuts that on the other side of that door he would find himself inside the small barn. He'd travelled the right distance underground. It all made sense.

The stairs were rough, unfinished concrete, a metal railing on one side. He started up a couple of steps. Then stopped in the semi-darkness. Above him, a crack of light framed the door. *What was he doing here?* He'd found the answer he was looking for. He'd worked out how Hendricks and Adamson had disappeared. That was why he'd come back, nothing more, no heroics. What would he do if they were asleep on the other side of the door? More to the point, what would he do if they were wide awake waiting for him on the other side? He took another tentative step up, placed his foot gently down, his whole body tensed, every muscle straining, head forward and turned slightly to the side, alert for the smallest sound—

The ceiling light suddenly flooded the room with light. Then a voice behind him.

'Help you with something?'

CHAPTER 40

EVAN JERKED UPRIGHT, let out an involuntary yelp. He dropped the flashlight as he spun around, slipped off the step he was standing on. His left foot landed on the flashlight. It rolled under him, turned his ankle over. The agonizing stab of pain told him it was broken. He went down hard. His right hip landed on the claw hammer hanging from a loop on his utility belt, paralyzing his leg from the thigh down.

Standing in the doorway to the tunnel Hendricks grinned at the pitiful sight in front of him, a Remington Model 870 pump shotgun held comfortably in his hands. Evan hadn't heard a thing. Worse, he'd made it easy for him to creep up on him by jamming the far door open. The soft, dry dust of the tunnel floor had masked Hendricks' footsteps.

His breathing came in short gasps as the shock subsided, his pulse trying to return to a normal level. He felt pathetic sprawled at the bottom of the stairs. He started to get up, his ankle immediately giving way under him.

Hendricks racked the slide on the shotgun. That unmistakable sound that few people experience first-hand but everybody recognizes instantly stopped him in his tracks, as it was meant to.

'I think I like you right where you are.'

Evan lowered himself into a sitting position, his eyes fixed on the wrong end of the shotgun pointing at his face. Hendricks had every right to shoot him and claim he was defending himself against an intruder—a persistent intruder at that.

There was no sign of Adamson.

'Where's your friend?'

'He won't be joining us right now. Lucky for you. He's a lot more volatile than I am.'

'So you've killed him as well as Faulkner. Planning on making me number three?'

Hendricks smiled an unpleasant smile at him.

'Don't try to rile me. Faulkner's okay. I called the hospital.'

Evan noticed how he didn't say anything about Adamson being okay.

'Then you've got nothing to worry about. I might as well get out of here.'

His ankle hurt like hell so he put a hand on the stairs behind him to try to push himself up.

'If you don't sit still, I'll shoot you in the knees. I'll tell the police I caught an intruder.'

Evan sat still. Fast. He had no doubts Hendricks would do it.

'Go ahead, call them now. Turn me in.'

'We'll see. You've got some questions to answer first.'

He walked the couple of paces across the room to where Evan was sitting. Without warning he kicked him sharply on the broken ankle with the pointed toe of his boot. Evan gasped, bit down on the pain.

Hendricks pulled a pair of handcuffs out of his pocket, dropped them into Evan's lap then stepped back again. With the barrel of the shotgun he pointed at the metal pole supporting the handrail running up the side of the stairs.

'Put your arms around the pole and cuff them together. Before you do it, take off the tool belt, throw it over there.'

Evan did as he was told. Hendricks put the shotgun down against the wall, picked up the tool belt. He pulled the hammer out of its loop. Tested its weight, a smile on his lips.

'Good choice. How's your ankle?'

Evan swallowed, said nothing. Hendricks slapped the hammer into his palm a couple of times.

'Let's get some things clear first. If you try to kick me or anything, I'm going to do a lot worse than smash your ankle. Am I making myself clear enough?'

Evan nodded, clear as day.

'Good. What are you doing down here?'

Evan hesitated. He didn't know what to say.

'Not a good start.'

Hendricks kicked him again in the ankle, exact same spot. Evan drew his leg back sharply, twisted his body away helplessly. The pain was infinitely worse than the last time.

'If you think that hurts, wait until I get going with this.' He slapped the hammer into his palm again as if Evan needed reminding. 'Let's try again. What are you doing down here?'

'I wanted to find out where you and your friend disappeared to when the police arrived.'

'What?'

'I was in the house when the police arrived. I heard you run down into the basement.'

Recognition crossed Hendricks face. He nodded as things fell into place for him.

'That's why the key wasn't in the door.'

'We came down into the basement and you weren't there. I knew there must be another way out.'

Hendricks wasn't really listening to him.

'Why were you in the house in the first place?'

Again, Evan hesitated. He couldn't tell him the truth. It was the wrong decision. Hendricks crouched down, swung the hammer briskly into Evan's swollen ankle. An agonizingly sharp stab of pain shot up Evan's leg, down into his foot.

'That's just a little tap. Imagine what this would feel like.'

He raised his arm above his head, brought the hammer down with all his strength into the dirt floor inches away from Evan's leg. Evan flinched, an automatic response, let out another gasp through teeth gritted so hard they'd crack soon.

Hendricks stood up. Walked away.

'I'm getting bored with this.'

Without warning he threw the hammer hard into the stairs above Evan's head. It smashed into the steps, sharp splinters of concrete spitting into Evan's face, and ricocheted off again. Evan ducked instinctively. But if Hendricks had wanted to hit him, he'd have a caved-in skull by now.

'I thought this would be fun, but it's too easy. You're going to piss your pants any minute. I know why you're snooping around anyway.'

Evan waited for him to go on. This time he didn't think he was going to be punished for his silence.

'It's about the kid who disappeared, isn't it? That's what you were asking about when you came out here the other day.'

Hendricks walked back towards him, looking for confirmation. Evan swallowed, tried to speak but his mouth was too dry. The delay cost him dearly. Hendricks didn't care if Evan couldn't or wouldn't answer him. He stamped down hard on Evan's pulsating ankle, ground it into the floor. Evan thrashed and bucked, gasped out a *yes*.

'I knew it. I just knew it.'

Hendricks spun away on his heel. He kicked the sheet of ply nailed to the wall, muttering something inaudible under his breath. Then turned abruptly and looked down at Evan.

'Okay you interfering bastard, I'll show you something. A lot more than you bargained for, that's for sure. There's just one thing though—it'll be the last thing you ever see.'

CHAPTER 41

HE WALKED BACK TO the tunnel entrance, smiled his joyless smile at Evan.

'Don't you go anywhere, I'll be back in a minute.'

With that he disappeared back down the dark tunnel. The shotgun was still leaning against the wall. It might as well have been in the trunk of Evan's car for all the good it did him. Even if he slid down onto his back and stretched out along the floor with his hands over his head, he still wouldn't be able to get anywhere near it with his feet. He couldn't have held it and fired it with his hands cuffed together anyway. There would be more chance of shooting his own feet than hitting Hendricks.

He didn't have enough time to do anything anyway. Hendricks wasn't away for more than a couple of minutes. He only went as far as the basement workshop to get some tools. In his left hand he had a crowbar, but it was the sledgehammer in his right hand that made Evan go rigid with fear, muscles tensing and bowels loosening, the back of his shirt drenched with sweat. He closed his eyes and prayed. He'd seen the movie *Misery* and winced along with everyone else when Annie Wilkes smashed Paul Sheldon's ankles with a sledgehammer to stop him from escaping.

Hendricks saw his reaction and laughed. He lobbed the heavy sledgehammer into Evan's lap. Evan managed to twist away, stop it landing on his balls.

'You've seen that movie too, eh? Don't worry, I'm not going to use it on you. I've got something much better lined up. You'll wish I'd caved your head in with it before this is over.'

He took off his jacket, rolled up his sleeves and retrieved the sledgehammer from where it lay, still nestled between Evan's legs. Then he walked over to the sheet of plywood against the wall that Evan had seen earlier, rested the sledgehammer against the wall. He jammed the crow bar under the edge of the plywood, levered it back and forth, prying it away from whatever it was nailed to. Evan watched, hardly daring to breathe, as he worked his way methodically up and down one edge and then the other. Finally, he threw the crow bar aside, rested a moment, then pulled the ply away from the wall altogether with his hands. Behind it there was a bricked-up doorframe. He tapped the brickwork with the wooden handle of the sledgehammer, a hollow sound echoing around the room.

Evan was filled with a feeling of impending dread as Hendricks stepped back and squared up to the wall in front of him. Then he swung the hammer into the middle of the brickwork. It flexed but nothing broke loose. He took another swing with the same result. He leaned the sledgehammer against the wall, turned back to Evan.

'I must have done a better job than I thought.' He slapped his forehead with the heel of his hand as if a thought had only just occurred to him. 'I've got a much better idea.' Fishing the key to the handcuffs out of his pocket, he walked over to Evan.

'Roll over onto your belly.'

Evan rolled over, lay with his arms outstretched above his head and around the pole. Hendricks put his foot between his shoulder blades. Then grabbed hold of his right arm and unlocked the handcuff. He dropped the key onto the floor. Stepping back quickly, he picked up the shotgun, waved it at Evan.

'You do it. Take off the other handcuff first. And don't try anything stupid either.'

Evan unlocked the other cuff, tried to stand up. He couldn't put his full weight on his ankle.

'I can't put any weight on this leg. How do you expect me to do it?'

'I can even them up if you think that'll help.'

The suggestion galvanized Evan into action. Through the pain, he hobbled over and picked up the sledgehammer. Even if he could walk properly, he wouldn't be able to get across the room before Hendricks blew him into little pieces. Steadying himself as best he could, he started on the wall. His ankle screamed every time his weight shifted onto it, stopped him from getting into a rhythm. Despite that, it didn't take long before the first brick punched through.

A draft of warm, dry air escaped through the hole as the brick dropped into the room beyond. After that the rest of the brickwork gave way easily. Soon the top half of the doorway was clear. He could easily have climbed through. A constant flow of warm air blew across his face, almost as if he was looking into another tunnel.

'That's enough for now,' Hendricks barked. 'I don't want too much work to do when I have to brick that up again.' He snickered. 'Drop the sledgehammer. Take a look inside.'

Evan dropped the sledgehammer. He didn't look inside. He

was overwhelmed by a dreadful foreboding at what might be in the cavity. Instead he turned to face Hendricks.

'It's too dark. I can't see anything.'

Hendricks picked up the flashlight that Evan had dropped. He rolled it across the floor towards him. Evan looked down at it like it was a fizzing stick of dynamite.

'Pick it up,' Hendricks said, the irritation in his voice growing, 'and take a look.'

'No.'

If Hendricks was going to kill him anyway, it didn't matter if he did what he said or not.

But Hendricks was fast. Incredibly fast. He took a couple of swift paces across the room, kicked Evan's good leg out from under him. Evan landed on his butt with a thump, a cloud of dry dust and dirt settling around him. Hendricks reversed the shotgun in his hands, clubbed him viciously on the side of the head with the butt, knocking him sideways into a dazed jumble of pain on the floor.

He dropped the shotgun, grabbed Evan's right arm, twisted it hard up behind his back. With his other hand on Evan's collar, he straightened up and hauled him onto his feet. Clamped together, he spun the pair of them around so that Evan faced the gaping black hole.

'Time to meet your new roommates.'

Evan did his best to struggle, useless as it was. He couldn't focus properly, couldn't make his muscles respond. With his ankle broken and his arm up behind his back, he didn't stand a chance.

Hendricks jerked Evan's arm upwards savagely, forcing his head and upper body through the hole, bending him double over the edge until his feet were barely on the ground. Evan thrashed from side to side but it was no use, it only made the screaming pressure on his shoulder worse.

In one fluid movement Hendricks released his grip on Evan's arm, dropped onto one knee and clamped his arms around his lower legs. He stood up sharply, tipping him all the way through the opening. Evan tumbled down a short flight of steps on the other side, landed in a heap at the bottom, the pile of broken bricks underneath him. Hendricks picked up the flashlight, leaned into the opening and bounced it off Evan's head.

'It would have been much easier if you'd picked it up when I told you.'

Evan lay still with his eyes closed for a minute to catch his breath. His chest was heaving from struggling against Hendricks. Every part of his body ached. His head was still spinning. He heard Hendricks moving around on the other side of the wall. Then he heard a sound that made his stomach turn to ice.

Hendricks grunted as he picked up the big sheet of plywood. He shuffled towards the hole with it, slid it sideways along the floor and over the doorway. The wedge of light slowly shrank as he pushed until it disappeared altogether and the small room was plunged into impenetrable darkness. There was a moment's silence as he caught his breath, then hammered the nails back into the wooden frame, the banging impossibly loud in Evan's makeshift dungeon, reverberating around inside his head.

CHAPTER 42

HE PUSHED HIMSELF INTO a sitting position, brushed the floor with his hand until he found the flashlight. Taking a deep breath, he switched it on, made a slow, hesitant sweep. He was in a small room not more than eight feet square. The walls and the ceiling were crudely lined with rough timber. The floor was dry and dusty. In the top right-hand corner an ancient air vent fluttered, a steady flow of warm, dry air coming from it. There were no lights.

The beam of light settled, as if drawn by some malevolent unseen force beyond his control, on the leg of a metal single bed along the back wall, the only piece of furniture in the room. He snapped off the flashlight, embraced the comforting darkness. He didn't want to look at what was on the bed. He didn't need to. He knew what it was. It didn't mean he had to look at it. He leaned his head against the wall behind him. Tried to calm down. It was impossible. He would never be calm again, not here, not in this room where panic surged relentlessly inside him, fighting to own him. He bent at the waist, pushed his thumbs hard into his throbbing, swollen ankle. The hot sudden pain made him gasp. He dug in deeper, gouging with his fingernails, squeezing out every last ounce of catharsis until he couldn't bear it any longer. Then he switched the flashlight back on and shone the beam onto the grotesque tableau laid before him on the bed.

The mummified corpse of Robbie Clayton—who else could it be?—sat upright on the bed leaning against the wall. His skin was a mottled brown color, leathery and split in places where it stretched tightly across his cheekbones and chin. His nose was shrivelled, his lips shrunken over yellowing teeth. The eye sockets were empty and gazed silently at the small figure that lay across his lap. His son. Daniel Clayton. Evan choked, swallowed a ragged lump as big as his fist and made of broken glass, his eyelids hot and stinging.

The mummification of Daniel's smaller body was more advanced, the dried tissues of his body powdery and starting to disintegrate, parts of his skeleton now visible. There was no smell, the drying process long since complete.

They hadn't been merely imprisoned, they had been immured. Robbie had starved to death. His son had not. Evan blinked rapidly, rubbed the back of his hand across his eyes. From the obscene angle of the child's head it was obvious his small neck had been broken. Mercifully broken by the despairing hands of a grief-stricken father. Broken with love to save him from the horrors of a slow, lingering death.

He switched off the flashlight. It made no difference. How could it? The horrific scene would be burned into his memory forever. How could it possibly be dismissed by the simple flick of a switch? He was thankful that for him forever was unlikely to last very long.

He sat contemplating his future, or, to be more precise, lack of one. Hendricks planned to leave him here to die just like the others.

He couldn't let him go now. The easiest thing was to simply lock all the doors and come back in a couple of months or years and brick up the hole again. For all he knew he might have already done just that. He'd conveniently left the key in the ignition to his car. Hendricks could dump it somewhere at his leisure. He would join the ranks of all the other missing persons, if anyone even noticed he wasn't there anymore. Just like Robbie Clayton before him, he had found Daniel Clayton. And he too would pay the ultimate price for his perseverance.

The thought of what had happened to Robbie compared to the vile rumors that had been spread around town about him made Evan despair. If he could only have escaped, he could have set all of that straight—as well as giving Linda Clayton the closure that had eluded her all these years.

His thoughts were interrupted by the sound of the crowbar being jammed between the ply and the doorframe. Had Hendricks come back already with bricks and mortar to seal him permanently into his tomb? A brief glimmer of hope crossed his mind—perhaps Guillory had suspected that he would return and had come back herself? But if that was the case, surely she'd have called out.

No, it could only be Hendricks. And this would be his one and only chance to escape. He had scant seconds to prepare himself before the makeshift door was pulled away. The unholy screeching of the nails echoed round the room, setting his teeth on edge like fingernails raked down a chalkboard, as, one by one, they were pried from the wooden frame.

The floor around him was littered with broken bricks. He swept the beam of the flashlight across them, saw two broken bricks still joined together with mortar, their edges sharp and jagged. He picked them up, hefted them in his hand. Together they must have weighed a good ten pounds. Heavy enough to make a decent weapon that was for sure.

Ignoring the pain in his ankle, he pushed himself up onto his feet. There was nowhere to hide. That didn't mean he'd make it easy for Hendricks. He stood off to the side of the steps and flattened his back against the wall, his head level with the bottom edge of the hole. If Hendricks wanted to shoot him, he'd have to poke the shotgun in which would give him a chance. Not much of a chance, but better than nothing. Grasping the rudimentary weapon in his hand he waited.

The plywood sheet had been worked away from the frame a few inches. A faint light spilled in from the basement room behind it—more than enough for him to see the gut-wrenching scene on the bed just a few feet away. He closed his eyes, concentrated on what was going on outside.

With a final protesting screech the board was pulled away completely. Light flooded in. Then Hendrick's mocking voice, hard on its heels.

'You still in there? I thought you might like some company. And just so you know, if I see anything appear in that hole, I'll shoot it.'

Was he completely insane?

Had he come back again just to shoot the breeze with him, before sealing him in again? Had he come back to gloat? From the snicker coming from outside, it seemed he had.

'Introduced yourself to your roommates yet? Although I don't think they're very talkative.'

The snicker was replaced by a full-bodied laugh. More than anything he'd ever known, Evan wanted to smash the bricks in his hand into Hendricks' face to stop that obscene noise.

'You're a monster. A sick monster.'

Hendricks stopped laughing, pulled himself together.

'You won't believe me, but it wasn't me, it was Adamson.'

He sounded like a pathetic child in the playground.

'You would say that, wouldn't you? It's always someone else's fault with people like you. The way I hear it, it's the story of your life.'

'See, I said you wouldn't believe me. But I'm telling the truth. Doesn't matter what I say now, you're never going to repeat it to anyone.'

'Where is he now?'

'Don't worry, you'll be seeing him again soon.'

The words rode out of his mouth on the back of a sick giggle.

'So what happened?'

'Why do you care now? It won't do you any good.'

'Call it a last request.'

Hendricks gave the request some consideration. And in the end, his need to justify himself, to bolster his view of himself as a victim, wouldn't let him deny the request. That, and the fact that he was only human, despite the inhuman acts he'd committed, and liked to talk about himself as much as the next man.

'Okay. Just don't think you're going to get a last meal as well. I'm afraid the room service isn't great where you're staying. Ask the other guests.'

He laughed again at his own sick humor.

'What happened?'

'I was trying to get my life straight. I'd had some bad breaks and I wanted a new start.'

If it hadn't been so sickening, Evan would have been amused to hear him describe his stay in prison for statutory rape as a bad break.

'I'd done some time in prison—'

'What for?'

'Doesn't matter. It got overturned anyway.' His candor obviously had its limits, even if his cockiness didn't. 'When I got out, I came back here and tried to make a new life.'

'You changed your name.'

'How the hell do you know that?'

'I heard Adamson call you Jason.'

Hendricks seemed satisfied. Evan almost felt him relax again on the other side of the wall. It was so bizarre talking to him like this, sitting not six feet from his victims as if they were just two people having a normal conversation.

'Stupid bastard,' he hissed.

Evan assumed he meant Adamson, not himself.

'He's the cause of all this shit. He ruined everything.'

Evan inched sideways to try to see where Hendricks was. The angle was all wrong. He inched back again. Waited for him to continue.

'I came back, got a nice easy job as the school bus driver. Everything was going just fine. I had a new identity, regular money and this nice house to live in.'

'And you dug yourself a nice secret chamber—'

'That wasn't me. It was already here.'

Evan was fully aware he was getting a carefully edited version of events. The gospel according to Carl Hendricks.

'And then something happened to spoil your perfect world?'

'You got that right. Jack Adamson happened.'

There was real, heartfelt venom in his tone. Evan heard a thud that sounded like Hendricks kicking something solid on the floor.

Then it struck him. Hendricks had either killed or knocked out Adamson, then dragged him back to the basement room. That's what he meant when he said he thought Evan might like some company. He was going to dump him in the room with Evan before sealing it up for good.

'He just turned up one day. He'd gotten out of prison a few days before and had nowhere to go. Been sleeping rough.'

'I'm having trouble seeing you as the Good Samaritan.'

'I owed him.'

'It must have been a hell of a debt. What did he do, save you from all the other cons when you were inside?'

Hendricks didn't say anything and Evan knew he was right. It was time to push him harder, try to provoke a careless reaction.

'It makes me wonder what you were in for if you needed protecting from the other prisoners. It's not like you're so pretty they were after a piece of your ass.'

'You can wonder what the hell you like. You're going to have plenty of time for thinking.'

The mix of sick humor and gloating smugness made Evan's gut clench, an overwhelming urge to smash the bricks he was holding right into his grinning face, turn it into a mass of blood and broken teeth, consuming him.

'I think it's because you were in for interfering with little kids.'

'You shut your mouth or I'll shut it for good.'

'Was it little boys? I think it probably was. You seem the sort to me. You can't handle women, can you, not grown ones anyway. Can't you get it up, *Jason*?'

On the other side of the wall Hendricks racked the slide on his shotgun.

'Don't call me that—'

'Okay, okay,' Evan said, not at all happy with the reaction he'd provoked. 'Get on with your story. Adamson turned up and you gave him a room.'

Hendricks didn't say anything for a minute. Evan hoped the immediate danger of being shot had passed.

'I thought he'd learned his lesson,' Hendricks said after a while. 'He'd had a really rough time in prison. I thought that was the end of it.'

'But it wasn't?'

'No. I had a few beers after work that day and when I came home, I found him here with the kid. I couldn't believe it. Less than a week since he'd gotten out of prison. Stupid bastard.'

There was the sound of another kick.

'How did he do it?'

'I had an old campervan at the time, just sitting in the barn going rusty. He didn't have a car so I let him use it. He picked the kid up as he walked home from school. Bundled him into the back and that was it.'

'And you told the police you never saw the boy leave the school campus to throw them off the scent.'

'Something like that. I didn't see him leave that day, as it happens.'

'Convenient you remembered that. Helped ensure they spent the whole time chasing their tails.'

'The police don't need *any* help doing that.'

'Why did you protect him? Why didn't you turn him in?'

'Like I told you, I owed him. I couldn't do that to him.'

Evan could think of a more persuasive reason.

'Nobody would have believed you weren't involved, would they? Not with your record.'

'No, they wouldn't, the sanctimonious bastards.'

He was working himself up into a frenzy at the injustice of it all.

'I hate this shitty country sometimes. They all talk about rehabilitation. What a crock of shit. You only ever get one chance and then your card's marked forever. I fought for this country and look what I got in return. Bastards.'

'You'd have gotten another chance if you'd turned him in. Proof that you were a reformed man.'

'I wish I had now.'

'Now that you've killed him anyway, you mean.'

'He's not dead, not yet anyway.'

The casual matter-of-fact way he said it chilled Evan's blood. The guy was insane. On the one hand, he was deeply hurt by society's prejudices and the injustices he'd suffered at the hands of the penal system—and on the other, he'd buried two people alive. Now he was about to add two more.

'What happened after you found them here?'

'We couldn't let the boy go so we kept him down here. Fed him and looked after him properly.'

'And sexually assaulted him. Once, twice a day? Was that part of looking after him *properly*?'

'That was Adamson. I didn't have anything to do with that. The guy's got a problem. He'd stick his johnson in a bucket of worms if they were wriggling nicely.'

'But you didn't try to stop it.'

Hendricks snorted.

'You obviously don't know Jack Adamson. You don't get in his way when he's like that. Not if you've got any sense.'

'Right. So there you were, all living happily together, some more happily than others, until . . . what? Until his father turns up on your doorstep?'

'That was Adamson's fault as well.'

'It would be. You are so misunderstood.'

Hendricks ignored the jibe.

'He panicked. The boy's father was going around to everyone asking if they'd seen the boy. He didn't suspect us, we were just one of the houses on his list.'

'What did he do?'

'Beat him half to death. Adamson's answer to most of life's little problems. He's not the sharpest tool in the box.'

'He sure sounds like an all-round nice guy.'

'That's good, because the two of you are going to be spending a long time together.'

'Why this?'

Evan waved his arm to include the awful scene in front of him, even though Hendricks couldn't see him. Hendricks knew what he was talking about.

'It seemed like a good idea at the time. Easier than killing and burying them and risk some animal digging up the remains.'

Evan was appalled at the casual way he weighed up a welcome saving of effort on their part against the lingering deaths of Robbie and Daniel Clayton, and came out on the side of the labor-saving option. Not to mention the fact that he now proposed to bury two more people alive in the interests of tidying up the loose ends.

'Anyway, I can't sit here shooting the breeze with you all day. It's time to move your new best friend in.'

CHAPTER 43

HENDRICKS DRAGGED ADAMSON'S INERT body across the floor towards the hole. Evan tightened his grip on the bricks, the edges sharp in his palm. He heard a barely audible *shit* escape from Hendricks, followed closely by a low moan.

Adamson was coming around.

It was his one and only chance. If Hendricks was dragging Adamson it was likely he had his back to the opening. Ignoring the pain in his ankle, he hobbled quickly up the steps and looked out. Sure enough, Hendricks had his back to him, leaning over the supine form of Adamson. It was the first time Evan had seen Adamson. Tall and sinewy with a ginger buzz cut, the back of his head was caked with dried blood. It seemed to be Hendricks' trademark.

Adamson's legs twitched. He let out another low moan. Hendricks picked up the shotgun, prepared to send his so-called friend back into oblivion. He lifted it with both hands, brought the butt down with a wet, fleshy thud onto the back of Adamson's head.

Evan drew back his arm as Hendricks straightened up again.

He hurled the bricks at the back of Hendricks' head, put everything he had into it and more. Hendricks heard the movement behind him at the last moment. He turned his head sharply, met the flying bricks full-on with his face. They caught him solidly on the cheekbone, split his skin and flesh wide open, sent him staggering away.

Evan hadn't waited to admire his throw. Or even to see if it had connected. By the time Hendricks' shocked gasp of pain was out of his mouth, he'd vaulted onto the jagged bottom edge of the hole, steadied himself momentarily, then launched himself through the air. One hundred and ninety-eight pounds of enraged muscle and bone slammed into Hendricks' back like a human wrecking ball. The shotgun went flying from his hands, their bodies crashing to the floor in a wild tangle of thrashing limbs.

He grabbed a fistful of Hendricks' hair, pulled back his head, slammed his face into the floor. Clamping his other hand on the back of Hendrick's head, he ground his face two-handed into the dirt. Hendricks cried out, bucking and twisting under him, flipped them both over, Evan on his back, Hendricks on top of him.

He lost his grip on Hendricks' hair as Hendricks jerked his head forward sharply then powered it backwards, smashing into Evan's nose and mouth. With the back of his head planted firmly on the floor Evan's face absorbed the whole force of the impact. Pain exploded, filled his whole head with a searing white light as his nose shattered for the second time in under a week. His top lip burst open against his teeth, the metallic, coppery taste of blood in his mouth. He whipped his head to the side, chose the wrong direction. Hendricks' second butt caught him on his chewed ear as if it was laser-guided.

Evan reached around, jabbed his gritty thumb into Hendricks' eye. Hendricks howled with pain as Evan dug in deeper, the eyeball slipping under his thumb. He felt the skin in the corner of Hendricks' eye tear, hooked his thumb viciously to rip it open. Hendricks rammed his elbow backwards into Evan's ribs, over and over, a relentless onslaught. Something cracked, forced a grunt of pain through Evan's busted lips. His thumb slipped out of Hendricks' eye, his nail raking the torn flesh.

Hendricks rolled off him onto the floor. He lay on his belly, panting like a demented hound. Blood trickled from his eye, mixing with the dirt and grime that covered his face. Snot ran from his nose, thick drools of saliva dripping from his lips, running down his chin. He let out an inhuman scream as he pushed himself up, shaking his head violently. Drops of blood and snot and saliva flew everywhere. His good eye glared murderously at Evan.

Out of the corner of his eye Evan saw the bricks he'd thrown a few feet away. He rolled over, stretching to reach, lunged at them, his cracked ribs shrieking in protest. Hendricks saw what he was after, grabbed hold of his shirt, tried to pull him back. Evan's nails clawed uselessly at the bricks, at empty air, as Hendricks hauled on his shirt, pulled himself up onto him, then brought his elbow down into the middle of Evan's back. The air erupted out of his lungs with an explosive grunt as Hendricks climbed further onto him.

Adamson's leg was only a foot away. Evan grabbed it with both hands. Heaved. Pulled himself forward an inch. He threw his arm out, got his fingers around the bricks. Hendricks lunged, clamped his hand round Evan's wrist. Evan smelled the rancid odor coming from his armpit inches from his face. Twisting his head to the side, he sank his teeth into Hendricks' arm, bit down hard and deep. Hendricks screamed, let go of Evan's wrist. Evan bit down harder, shaking his head wildly like a demented dog worrying a juicy bone.

He couldn't breathe, not with his mouth full of Hendricks' flesh, his broken nose full of blood and mucus. He held on for as long as he could, lungs burning, then released his bite hold just as Hendricks jerked his arm savagely away. The sudden release sent him sprawling backwards off Evan onto his back. In one fluid motion Evan rolled over and brought his arm around in a wide arc. It should have smashed the heavy chunk of brickwork into the middle of Hendricks' face, would have done if Hendricks hadn't turned his head to the side at the last second, the bricks barely grazing his head as they pounded into the floor.

Hendricks rolled away. He scrambled onto his knees, dived for the discarded tool belt. Came up with a chisel as Evan slammed into him, knocked him flat onto his back, sent the chisel flying from his hand. Lying on top of him, Evan pushed himself up until he was sitting astride him. Hendricks scrabbled desperately to get a grip on the chisel. Evan raised the bricks to smash them into his face.

Hendricks got his fingers around the chisel, slashed wildly with it. The razor-sharp blade sliced through Evan's forearm, opened the flesh like a ripe melon splitting. The bricks spilled out of his hand as a stinging, red hot pain seared through his arm. He grabbed hold of Hendricks' wrist with one hand, seized the fingers gripping the chisel with the other. Hendricks tightened his grip. Evan worked his fingers under Hendricks' little finger, bent it back sharply, snapped it cleanly at the first knuckle.

Hendricks howled, dropped the chisel. The bricks were in Evan's hands now. He raised them above his head, shaking with the adrenalin coursing through his veins, ready to drive them through the middle of Hendricks' face.

A whispered plea slipped through Hendricks' lips, unmistakeable, absolute terror in the eye Evan hadn't ravaged.

'No, please.'

A desolate, strangled cry escaped Evan's bloody lips. He imagined Robbie Clayton's utter despair as he tried to comfort his son, to tell him that everything was going to be okay—they'd soon be out of here and home again, laughing together in the bright sunlight. Imagined him holding the boy's head against his chest, stroking his hair, running his hand down the back of his head, feeling the delicacy of his small neck in his hand, and thinking thoughts that no father should ever have to think. How long did he ignore the foul thing that now lived and grew in his mind? How long before he finally accepted what he'd known all along he'd have to do? How long before the boy's pitiful crying became too much to bear, and he told himself it was kinder this way, he'd do it for an old dog that couldn't walk any longer, for Christ's sake, so why not his son? Evan saw him sitting where he still sat now after all these years, hot, stinging tears streaming soundlessly down his face as he held the boy's neck for the last time and tensed. Did his son feel him tense, feel something change in the way his father's gentle fingers touched his skin? Did he perhaps try to look up into his face? Stretch out a hand and touch the rough stubble on his chin? Feel the wetness on his father's cheek? Thank God for the merciful darkness that meant he didn't have to see Daniel's eyes searching his own. And thank that same heartless God for sweet, ever-loving nothing as he closed his eyes, his jaw tightening, self-loathing washing down through his intestines and up through his throat as he gave a sudden, sharp twist of his hands and snapped his son's neck like a dry twig. Evan heard the howl of anguish that climbed out of his mouth, like it had waited his whole life to do so, as he felt his son's dying body twitch, his legs spasm and kick weakly against his own, felt an indecent wetness seep into his lap as he soiled himself. And Evan prayed with him to a merciless, nameless deity that had entered the world aeons before men's flawed notions of a loving God, to take him now and still his tortured mind. All this Evan saw and felt and heard in that single heart-sickening moment between the *ple—* and the *—ease* of Hendricks' shameful cry for mercy. He let out an inhuman shriek and drove the bricks down with all his might. Five long years of his own pain and anger and anguish melded with Linda Clayton's lifetime of despair and her dead husband's living hell, combining to power his fists all but clean through Carl Hendricks' toxic flesh and bone.

There was a dreadful, sickening, but oh-so-satisfying crunch as Hendricks' nose and cheekbone shattered. He felt teeth break under the impact, felt the jaw dislocate, twisting obscenely, breathed in the foul odor as Hendricks' body sought to expel its own viscera. He drew in a monstrous breath, his chest flooding with righteous rage, calling on reserves of strength that came from who knows where deep within his core, and brought his arms up, his blood dripping onto the remains of Hendricks' face, to deliver a second crushing blow—

But it was all over.

Hendricks lay still underneath him, his face an unspeakable bloody pulp, a dreadful keening sound escaping from between his broken teeth.

CHAPTER 44

EVAN THREW THE BRICKS at the wall. They hit the locked door he'd tried earlier and bounced off again, landing close to Hendricks. It wasn't a problem, Hendricks couldn't have picked them up if his life depended on it. He climbed shakily to his feet, his head spinning, legs barely able to hold him. His ankle gave way with a sharp stab of pain, He dropped onto his knees with a heavy thump. Bright red blood poured eagerly from the deep cut on his arm, staining the dirt floor. He crawled to where the shotgun lay, dragged it with him over to the wall, then sat with his back against the wall to recover, the gun across his lap.

It had taken less than a minute. But he couldn't have told you what happened. His mind was a blank. The last thing he recalled was being in the cell. He looked at Hendricks and was appalled at what he'd done. If Hendricks hadn't been such a murdering sack of shit, he might have thought he'd gone too far.

He rested his head against the wall, his mouth hanging open, his breathing heavy and labored. The adrenaline comedown hit him like a freight train on speed. His hands shook as a tide of nausea rapidly overcame him. His head ached terribly. He was acutely aware of his injuries as the adrenaline leached away. The deep gash on his arm refused to stop bleeding, his broken ankle equally demanding of his attention.

He closed his eyes, focussed on a quiet place outside of himself, let the pain filter through him unhindered. He forced his lungs to breathe slowly and deeply until he felt a little better, the nausea gradually subsiding, receding into the background. His legs still didn't feel as if they would support him so he sat a while longer, listening to Hendricks' wheezy breathing as it bubbled wetly through his bloody lips. Adamson hadn't made a sound. Evan wondered if Hendricks had killed him with his second savage blow.

He opened his eyes, stared straight ahead. He'd made quite a dent in the locked door on the opposite wall when he hurled the bricks away. And now that the lights were on, he saw the key hanging on a nail hammered into the door frame. He stared at that door for a very long time, tried to push away the uninvited thoughts that crowded into his mind, thoughts that made the events of the past minutes pale into insignificance.

He made another attempt at getting up. It was too easy this time, the horrors that gathered apace inside him lending a new-found, unwelcome strength to his limbs, pushing the blood through his veins at breakneck speed, the oxygen infusing his muscles, all aches and pains long since forgotten as the adrenalin claimed him for its own once more.

He stood over Hendricks, the shotgun a makeshift crutch, felt nothing apart from a detached loathing. Not even the grim satisfaction of minutes earlier.

'What's in that room?'

Hendricks rolled his head from side to side, his good eye wild with terror at Evan's words—words that might be the last he ever heard. A faint, sibilant *no, no, no, no, no* slipped between his lips in a sac of pink drool.

Evan couldn't wait a moment longer. He hobbled away to stand before the door. He tried to clear his mind, to drive away the toxic thoughts that whispered their filthy lies to him. He snatched the key off the nail. Jammed it in the lock. Turned it. There was a smooth well-oiled click. He dropped his hand, his head, his will to live.

Hendricks moaned behind him, the sound galvanizing him. He took hold of the smooth, dust-free handle of a door that was used on a regular basis. He turned it sharply. Threw the door wide open.

Sarah's face filled his tortured mind, a million jumbled images of what he so desperately wanted to see assaulting his battered sensibilities.

The room was empty.

His shoulders slumped, his breath started up again. He didn't know whether to laugh or scream or cry. Thank God there wasn't another vile vignette to match the one in the adjacent cell—one far more personal to him. And what else had he hoped he might find?

Unlike its neighbor, this one had no steps down. But it had a light, as if the unfortunate guests were at least offered a choice of different facilities. He flicked it on. Shuffled into the middle of the small room. There was nothing, not even a metal bed frame. He turned in a slow circle. No, that wasn't true—something in the far corner caught his eye. A flicker of silver, half buried in the loose dirt floor. He picked it up and dusted it off, turned it over in his hand, the metal smooth to the touch. He read the first line:

We the unwilling

With eyes closed, he dropped it in his pocket. Point blank refused to think about it now. He didn't trust himself to say anything to Hendricks. He couldn't say where that might lead if he did. He would come back.

He found the handcuffs where he'd dropped them at the bottom of the stairs, then cuffed Hendricks' wrist to the metal pole he'd been cuffed to earlier himself. He didn't need to worry about Adamson—he'd be lucky to come out of it with anything less than serious brain damage. That's if there was a brain to damage in the first place, of course. Even if he did come around, his first priority would be getting even with Hendricks. And good luck to him.

Evan collected up the sledgehammer and the crowbar and all the other tools and dumped them in the tunnel. Then he locked the door, left the key in the lock so that nobody could unlock it from the other side, before heading upstairs into the house and out of this God forsaken hell hole.

'YOU'RE REALLY TRYING MY patience,' Guillory said when she finally answered her cell phone. In the background, a man's voice complained. Evan couldn't stop himself from wondering if it was her husband or just a boyfriend.

'I hope I didn't interrupt anything.'

Guillory snorted rather than articulated *I should be so lucky*. A hand covered the phone on the other end, a muffled conversation behind it.

'This better be good,' she said coming back on the line.

'It's better than good. It's what careers are made of.'

'I doubt that very much. You sound strange. What do you want?'

'Guess where I am.'

There was a weary sigh. Four in the morning isn't the time for games.

'I have absolutely no idea. And if I sound like someone who actually gives a shit'—there was a pause as the penny dropped—'No. I don't believe it. You better not be . . .'

He stifled a yawn. It had been a long night.

'I am. And I suggest you get your ass over here too. You just wait until you see what's hidden in the basement downstairs—you know, the *empty* basement. Better tell your husband or boyfriend you won't be back tonight. See you in five. Don't bother bringing Donut.'

He cut the call before she had a chance to reply, went to see if he could find a cold beer. Even murderous psychopaths got thirsty sometimes.

CHAPTER 45

TRUSSED UP IN HIS best suit and a black tie, Evan looked almost presentable when he knocked on Linda Clayton's door a week later to accompany her to the funeral. His face looked a bit more human, and now it had more, what you'd call, *character*. His nose had been set again—it would never be quite the same as before—and his chewed ear was on the mend. Jacobson had done some excellent work on the front teeth that Hendricks' head butt had loosened. He would have a mean-looking scar on his forearm, which would impress the ladies, and he was still walking with a limp. However, it was a small price to pay for what he had achieved. He was more than happy to pay it.

Linda Clayton had finally gotten the answers and closure she craved. After the initial shock had worn off, the improvement in her was a joy to see. He couldn't believe how good he felt about himself for being the cause of the transformation. The gossip mongers had gotten their comeuppance, a figurative poke in the eye, when the awful truth about Robbie Clayton's fate had come to light. The gruesome aspects of the case had guaranteed it attracted national media coverage. As a result, the previously recalcitrant life insurance company had paid out with heart-warming alacrity. Linda had insisted on pressing a generous chunk of it onto him, despite his protestations. On top of that, the media interest had generated more enquiries than he could handle.

Hendricks had been patched up and was in a secure hospital wing, taking his meals through a straw and contemplating the rest of his life behind bars. His buddy, Adamson, was still in his Hendricks-induced coma. It was fair to say that it was of no concern to anybody whether he pulled through or not. Although plenty of people thought it would be best to pull the plug and save the tax dollars.

Guillory came out of it smelling of roses. He was happy to let her take most of the credit. The kudos she enjoyed was matched in equal measure by the decline in Faulkner's reputation. Scandal-hungry journalists quickly unearthed the Faulkner-Hendricks connection. He had a rough time of it, even though there was never any suggestion that he had been involved in any way.

The same couldn't be said about the unexplained fire that broke out and burned the two barns to the ground, destroying the secret chambers forever. Whoever did it probably experienced something similar to what the allied troops must have felt blowing up the Nazi gas chambers—a sense of putting the lid on one more example of man's limitless capacity for cruelty towards his fellow man. It seemed the emergency services encountered some unusually heavy traffic on the way over—apparently, they also had a problem with their siren—and by the time they got there, there was nothing left.

Then a neighbor said they saw a car that looked a lot like Faulkner's in the vicinity at about the time the fire must have started. The police department went through the motions of sending somebody over to talk to him. A lot of tongues wagged but, in the end, no one really gave a damn. It cut down on the number of enquiries from people looking to buy the place, now that the crazies would have to start afresh and build their own torture chamber from scratch. Most people just thought good riddance.

There'd been no sign of McIntyre. Evan liked to think he'd had second thoughts about taking him on without blindsiding him first—especially if he'd read the exaggerated accounts of Evan's bloody, hand-to-hand struggle with Hendricks.

He couldn't remember feeling as good for years. Life felt like there was something worth living for again. He hadn't realized how much the sleazy work he'd fallen into had been dragging him down. Still, he wasn't completely out of the woods.

AFTER THE SERVICE A few people went back to Linda's house. Kate Guillory was one of them, looking good in a dark pant suit and white blouse. Evan was relieved that the odious Ryder didn't feel the need to pay his respects. She cornered him after most people had left, a small, almost untouched glass of white wine in her hand, gentle amusement in her denim blue eyes.

'You're not so bad for a pee—sorry, *ex*-peeper. I honestly never thought it would turn out like this when I put Linda on to you. You surprised me.'

She sipped her drink, took hold of his chin and turned his head, cocked hers.

'Not sure about the ear, though.'

He shrugged—an *all part of the everyday rough and tumble* gesture—very aware of the time it took her to let go his chin.

'What are you looking at me like that for?' she said, her head still cocked.

'It's nothing. I haven't seen you wearing lipstick before, that's all.'

'That's because I was *working*. I'm not working now.'

Those were the words that came out of her mouth. But it seemed to him what was said was something very different: *I'm surprised you noticed.*

He nodded.

'Right. Nice color, by the way. I suppose I should thank you for the kick up the ass.'

'Long overdue kick up the ass, you mean.'

'You got it. Thank you. And if there's any more old cases you're having trouble with, you be sure to let me know.'

She laughed, that same deep, throaty sound he'd noticed in the hospital, a sound you don't expect to hear from a cop.

'Don't get carried away now. Anyway, I've got to run.' She pressed her glass into his hand, a perfectly-formed imprint of her lips on the rim. 'Put that in the kitchen for me, will you?'

Then it was just Evan and Linda.

'You're very thoughtful,' she said, laying a hand on his arm.

She considered him with her clear blue eyes, so different from when he first met her. It seemed like every woman in the room wanted to dissect him today—first Guillory and now Linda.

'I suppose. I've got a lot to think about.'

He dropped his eyes, didn't want to get into a conversation about himself. Not now, on an emotionally charged day like today. But it wasn't his call. Never was. She looked at him for a while longer. He wouldn't meet her gaze.

'You also look like a load's been lifted. It's called hope.'

He looked up sharply. She was smiling triumphantly at his

reaction.

'Ha! Not as green as I'm cabbage-looking, eh?'

'Is it really that obvious?'

'No, of course not. You're a man, you're tough. You don't wear your heart on your sleeve. You're a closed book. Shall I go on?'

He shook his head. 'No need. You're right.'

'Of course I'm right. What you've done for me makes you wonder if the same thing will ever happen for you. It gives you faith in yourself.'

She paused, took his silence as tacit agreement.

'You've never told me what happened, you don't have to. Kate hinted at it and I can put the rest of it together. And now you feel you can deal with it, whatever you find out. You've always known how you *wanted* things to turn out, but now you're not afraid of the other possibilities.'

She was right. It wasn't just what he'd achieved for her. Surviving the nightmare in Hendricks' do-it-yourself crypt, coming within a hair's breadth of a drawn-out, solitary death, made him realize he could now deal with whatever adversity and misfortune life threw at him.

Which was lucky, because he had a strong premonition life was at this very moment gathering up its ammunition.

The smile suddenly slipped from her face like he'd flicked off the light switch.

'That's not all though, is it?'

'No.'

He hesitated. He absolutely didn't want to talk about himself. But he needed to get it off his chest, needed to tell somebody, before he went crazy. So he showed her what he'd found in Hendricks' basement, told her what had been eating him up ever since.

She listened in silence, lips parted, eyes wide, as he took her through the whole story, all the way back to a place where it sometimes felt his life had come to an abrupt halt. She put her hand on his knee, very different emotions behind the gesture to when Barbara Schneider did it.

'What are you going to do?'

'I was going to go back there when everything dies down, have a better look around.'

'But then Matt Faulkner, sorry, somebody'—she gave him a mischievous grin—'burned down the barns.'

He shrugged like it was no big deal. It didn't fool anybody.

'Anyway, I don't want to talk or think about it anymore today. I'm exhausted.'

'Okay. Like you said, it's probably nothing. One of those spiteful coincidences fate loves to torment you with. Hendricks and his buddy were both in the military. Presumably it belongs to one of them.'

The mischievous grin popped back onto her face. For an uncomfortable second, he had another flashback to his afternoon with Barbara Schneider. Then it was gone.

'I've just had a great idea,' she said.

'Let's see how much of a dent we can put in that lot.' He flicked his eyes at the table.

'Are you some kind of mind reader now?'

'Not me. But I can see a heck of a lot of booze sitting over there. And we're the only ones left to drink it.' He tapped the side of his nose with his finger. 'I'm a detective, remember.'

He fetched himself a beer and she said she'd have the same, forget the glass. She insisted on a toast, wouldn't be put off. He knew what was coming, hoped he'd be up to it, because it seemed life had just become a whole lot more complicated.

'To the future, whatever travails it might hold.'

They clinked beer bottles, the sound clear and sharp in the small room, echoing the word *travails* as it rang out in his mind, a reminder that things were only just getting started. There'd be a lot of pain and heartache down the road. Because, at the end of the day, there's no escaping your destiny.

THE END

ENJOYED THIS BOOK? YOU CAN MAKE A REAL DIFFERENCE.

Reviews are critical to the success of an author's career. If you have enjoyed this novel, please do me a massive favor by leaving one on Amazon.

Reviews increase *visibility* which is the life blood of an author on Amazon's crowded platform. Your help in leaving a review for any of my books will make a *real* difference.

Thank you.

GET TWO EXCLUSIVE EVAN BUCKLEY MURDER MYSTERIES

Building a relationship with my readers is one of the best things about being an author. I occasionally send newsletters (I won't clutter up your inbox) with details and previews of new releases, special offers and other exclusive content.

As soon as you join my Readers' Group, I'll send you this free exclusive content:

1. A free copy of *Fallen Angel*, a page-turning Evan Buckley (mis)adventure.
2. A free copy of *A Rock And A Hard Place*, an exciting Evan Buckley murder mystery.

Both of these books are exclusive to my Readers' Group – you can't buy them or get them anywhere else. Not now, not ever.

You can get your free content by visiting my website, www.jamesharperbooks.com. I'll look forward to seeing you there.

BOOKS BY JAMES HARPER

The Evan Buckley Thrillers

BAD TO THE BONES

WHEN EVAN BUCKLEY'S latest client ends up swinging on a rope, he's ready to call it a day. But he's an awkward cuss with a soft spot for a sad story and he takes on one last job—a child and husband who disappeared ten years ago. It's a long-dead investigation that everybody wants to stay that way, but he vows to uncover the truth—and in the process, kick into touch the demons who come to torment him every night.

KENTUCKY VICE

MAVERICK PRIVATE INVESTIGATOR Evan Buckley is no stranger to self-induced mayhem—but even he's mystified by the jam college buddy Jesse Springer has gotten himself into. When Jesse shows up with a wad of explicit photographs that arrived in the mail, Evan finds himself caught up in the most bizarre case of blackmail he's ever encountered—Jesse swears blind he can't remember a thing about it.

SINS OF THE FATHER

FIFTY YEARS AGO, Frank Hanna made a mistake. He's never forgiven himself. Nor has anybody else for that matter. Now the time has come to atone for his sins, and he hires maverick PI Evan Buckley to peel back fifty years of lies and deceit to uncover the tragic story hidden underneath. Trouble is, not everybody likes a happy ending and some very nasty people are out to make sure he doesn't succeed.

NO REST FOR THE WICKED

WHEN AN ARMED GANG on the run from a botched robbery that left a man dead invade an exclusive luxury hotel buried in the mountains of upstate New York, maverick P.I. Evan Buckley has got his work cut out. He just won a trip for two and was hoping for a well-earned rest. But when the gang takes Evan's partner Gina hostage along with the other guests and their spirited seven-year-old daughter, he can forget any kind of rest.

RESURRECTION BLUES

AFTER LEVI STONE shows private-eye Evan Buckley a picture of his wife Lauren in the arms of another man, Evan quickly finds himself caught up in Lauren's shadowy past. The things he unearths force Levi to face the bitter truth—that he never knew his wife at all—or any of the dark secrets that surround her mother's death and the disappearance of her father, and soon Evan's caught in the middle of a lethal vendetta.

HUNTING DIXIE

HAUNTED BY THE unsolved disappearance of his wife Sarah, PI Evan Buckley loses himself in other people's problems. But when Sarah's scheming and treacherous friend Carly shows up promising new information, the past and present collide violently for Evan. He knows he can't trust her, but he hasn't got a choice when she confesses what she's done, leaving Sarah prey to a vicious gang with Old Testament ideas about crime and punishment.

THE ROAD TO DELIVERANCE

PI EVAN BUCKLEY'S wife Sarah went to work one day and didn't come home. He's been looking for her ever since. This is her story. As Evan digs deeper into the death of a man killed by the side of the road, the last known person to see Sarah alive, he unearths a dark secret in her past that only drove her further down the road to hell in a desperate attempt to make amends for the guilt she can never leave behind.

SACRIFICE

WHEN PI Evan Buckley's mentor asks him to check up on an old friend, neither of them are prepared for the litany of death and destruction that he unearths down in the Florida Keys. Meanwhile Kate Guillory battles with her own demons in her search for salvation and sanity. As their paths converge, each of them must make an impossible choice that stretches conscience and tests courage, and in the end demands sacrifice—what would you give to get what you want?

Exclusive books for members of my Readers' Group

FALLEN ANGEL

WHEN JESSICA HENDERSON falls to her death from the window of her fifteenth-floor apartment, the police are quick to write it off as an open and shut case of suicide. The room was locked from the inside, after all. But Jessica's sister doesn't buy it and hires Evan Buckley to investigate. The deeper Evan digs, the more he discovers the dead girl had fallen in more ways than one.

A ROCK AND A HARD PLACE

PI EVAN BUCKLEY isn't used to getting something for nothing. So when an unexpected windfall lands in his lap, he's intrigued. Not least because he can't think what he's done to deserve it. Written off by the police as one more sad example of mindless street crime, Evan feels honor-bound to investigate, driven by his need to give satisfaction to a murdered woman he never knew

Join my mailing list at www.jamesharperbooks.com and get your FREE copies of *Fallen Angel* and *A Rock And A Hard Place.*

Other Books

BAD CALL – A PSYCHOLOGICAL THRILLER

RALPH DA SILVA has screwed up. Big time. He's had four Tequilas too many for lunch and now he thinks he might have killed somebody—somebody important. Somebody with a lot of very unpleasant friends. The question is—can he get himself out of the country before they strap him to a chair and get the electrodes out. One thing is certain—he can't afford to make another bad call.

DEDICATION

To Rills Smills, without whom none of this would have been possible.

Made in the USA
Columbia, SC
03 April 2020